PREMEDITATED
PEPPERMINT

D0009240G

USA Today **Bestselling Author**

Amanda Flower

KENSINGTON
U.S. $7.99
CAN $8.99

DON'T MISS ANY OF THE
AMISH CANDY SHOP MYSTERIES!

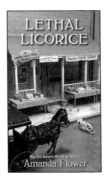

EAN

ISBN-13: 978-1-4967-0643-0
ISBN-10: 1-4967-0643-9

5 0 7 9 9

Praise for the Amish Candy Shop series and the Amish cozies of Amanda Flower

"A promising start to a new series."—*Suspense Magazine*

"Flower launches her new series by evoking the nightmare nuptials of The Final Vow (2017), throwing in a few Pennsylvania Dutch words to provide atmosphere in a cozy as light as the heroine's handmade mousse."—*Kirkus Reviews*

"Full of Amish atmosphere, a great heroine and fun characters, this is the start of a new series to be sweet on!"—*Parkersburg News*

"As it turns out, Amanda Flower may have just written the first Amish rom-com."—*USA Today*

"Flower has hit it out of the ballpark . . . and continues to amaze with her knowledge of the Amish way of life."—*RT Book Reviews*

"At turns playful and engaging as the well-intentioned Englisher strives to rescue her Ohioan Amish friends from a bad fate . . . a satisfyingly complex cozy. Alan is a pseudonym for librarian-author Amanda Flower."—*Library Journal*

"Reading the book is a visit to a town that feels like home."—*Kings River Life*

Also by Amanda Flower

Assaulted Caramel

Lethal Licorice

PREMEDITATED
PEPPERMINT

Amanda
Flower

KENSINGTON PUBLISHING CORP.

http://www.kensingtonbooks.com

KENSINGTON BOOKS are published by

Kensington Publishing Corp.
119 West 40th Street
New York, NY 10018

All Kensington Titles, Imprints, and Distributed Lines are available at special quantity discounts for bulk purchases for sales promotions, premiums, fund-raising, and educational or institutional use. Special book excerpts or customized printings can also be created to fit specific needs. For details, write or phone the office of the Kensington special sales manager: Kensington Publishing Corp., 119 West 40th Street, New York, NY 10018, attn: Special Sales Department, Phone: 1-800-221-2647.

Kensington and the K logo Reg. U.S. Pat & TM Off.

ISBN-13: 978-1-4967-0643-0
ISBN-10: 1-4967-0643-9
First Kensington Mass Market Edition: October 2018

eISBN-13: 978-1-4967-0644-7
eISBN-10: 1-4967-0644-7
First Kensington Electronic Edition: October 2018

10 9 8 7 6 5 4 3 2 1

Printed in the United States of America

For Alexandra Coley
Thanks for always looking out for Jethro!

Acknowledgments

Merry Christmas and thanks to my dear readers for their enthusiasm for my stories. Not a single book would be possible without you.

Thanks to my editor, Alicia Condon, and everyone at Kensington for giving Bailey, Swissmen Sweets, and everyone in Harvest a home. Special thanks, as always, to my champion in the book world, Nicole Resciniti, who never fails to find the right place for my stories and right direction for my career.

Thank you to Suzy Schroeder for her help with the recipe in the back of the book, and to Delia Haidautu for testing the recipe with me. Also thank you to my assistant, Molly Carroll, for all she does.

Hugs to my friends Mariellyn Grace and David Seymour for cheering me on while I wrote this book on a tight deadline. I'm grateful to have you both in my corner.

Love to my family Andy, Nicole, Isabella, and Andrew for their support of my career.

Finally to my Heavenly Father, thank you for Christmas.

Chapter 1

Peppermint is much more than a Christmastime treat. It has a thousand uses. It has been used to freshen breath, flavor beverages, calm nerves, and even grow hair. But as far as I could tell, it did not have the power to repel ex-boyfriends.

I wasn't considering this failing on peppermint's part when I awoke early that Thursday morning, two weeks before Christmas, and when I say early, I mean *very* early. It was before five AM, but there was much to do to prepare for the Harvest Christmas Market that would begin the next afternoon on the village square. I lived and worked just across the square at Swissmen Sweets, an Amish candy shop in Holmes County, Ohio, that I ran with my Amish grandmother Clara King. No, I wasn't Amish, but my father's family was. However, I did have peppermint on the mind.

Peppermint was the name of the game for our table at the Christmas Market. The organizer, Margot Rawlings, who typically was the instigator of all major events in the village, said that every table had to have a Christmas theme. Peppermint was the obvious choice for the candy shop. In addition to peppermint bark, we would have peppermint hard candy, fudge, hot chocolate mix, taffy, and thumbprint cookies.

It was midmorning now, and the shop smelled like the inside of a peppermint patty. My grandmother, her young Amish cousin Charlotte, and I worked in a companionable silence that had taken me some time to grow accustomed to. Up until a few months ago, I had spent most of my adult life in New York City working as an assistant chocolatier at JP Chocolates for world-renowned chocolate maker Jean Pierre Ruge. After my grandfather's death in September, I left city life behind to take over Swissmen Sweets. After working the busy, fully staffed chocolate shop in New York, where there was constant activity, it had taken me some time to get used to the quiet of Swissmen Sweets. Even when the shop was busy, it never felt as frenetic as JP Chocolates. I had grown to like the quiet and was looking forward to my first peaceful Christmas in Amish Country.

Down the counter from me, *Maami* cut her chocolate peppermint fudge into neat squares, and Charlotte packed them in small white boxes. She tied each box closed with narrow red ribbon. The pair softly murmured to each other in Pennsylvania Dutch while they worked. They looked much more like grandmother and granddaughter in their plain dresses and matching prayer caps than *Maami* and I ever would. I wasn't sure they even realized they were speaking a language I didn't understand at that moment, but I felt a stab of isolation at the other end of the counter as I worked on my own peppermint treats.

I tried to focus on the task at hand. I had hoped to make a few additional peppermint goodies before the market opened, but all my Christmas Market plans seemed to have flown out of my head a few hours earlier, when my ex-boyfriend crashed my candy shop. That was the moment when I realized peppermint's shortcomings.

The moment Eric Sharp walked into Swissmen Sweets, I was up to my elbows in a triple batch of peppermint and white chocolate, getting ready to spread the molten white chocolate mixture on a cookie sheet to cool. After the peppermint bark solidified, I would break it into pieces, place the pieces in cellophane bags, and tie the tops with bright red ribbons.

I was frozen by Eric's arrival. I had always wondered what I would feel if I ever saw him again. I expected hurt, sadness, anger, or maybe some of the old spark we'd once had, but I didn't feel any of those emotions. Instead, I was shocked and seriously annoyed. What on Earth did he think he was doing by waltzing into my peaceful shop at Christmas?

Eric smiled when he caught me staring gapemouthed at him. I had a strong urge to toss a piece of peppermint bark at him just to see if it would repel an ex-boyfriend, but wisdom prevailed. I didn't have superaccurate arm, and I could hit a paying customer. Besides, I didn't want to do anything to alarm my grandmother and Charlotte, who both stood behind the glass-domed counter in their solid-colored Amish dresses, black aprons, and white prayer caps over long hair that was tightly coiled in smooth buns at the napes of their necks.

Eric strode toward me, looking every bit the successful New Yorker dressed in designer clothes from his Burberry winter hat to his polished Gucci boots. My grandmother, who made most of her own clothes, would be aghast to know how much each article of clothing had cost.

My grandmother smiled brightly at him. "May I help you?"

I wanted to blurt out, "No, you may not help him. He's not staying!"

But, of course, I didn't say that. My sweet *maami* would be aghast if I shouted anything so rude.

Eric grinned that smug grin that once upon a time I thought was so confident and attractive. Now I saw it for what it was: condescending. "You're so kind, but I see what I need." He made a point of looking at me when he said this. "Hello, Bailey. It's nice to see you again."

"I can't say the same about you."

My grandmother and Charlotte stared at me, clearly shocked at my rudeness. I closed my eyes for a moment and recited in my head the six types of chocolate, as my mentor Jean Pierre had taught me. I hadn't even reach "white chocolate" when Eric chuckled. "I see you still say what you think. I'm glad living with the Amish hasn't robbed you of your spunk."

I ground my teeth. "What are you doing here, Eric?"

"I'm here to visit you."

My frown deepened. I wasn't buying it. "You flew to Ohio to visit me? A person you haven't spoken to in over three months?"

He nodded, doing his best to appear sincere. "I know how much you love Christmas."

It was true I loved Christmas. Christmas was my favorite time of the year. I loved the parties, the carols, the food, and more than anything, I loved the sweets, but I knew Eric hadn't flown all the way to Ohio because Christmas was just two weeks away and I was a big fan.

"I've taken a few days off from my bakeries, and I thought it would be a great idea to see what a real country Christmas is all about. It will be a nice change of pace from the hustle and bustle of New York."

My brow furrowed. "You took time from work? To see the country?" My voice rose an octave with each question. When he made that claim, I knew he was lying. Eric was the biggest workaholic I knew. He was a bigger workaholic than I was, which was saying something, since before moving to Ohio I easily worked one hundred hours a week at JP Chocolates. Eric didn't take time off from his bakeries. Ever. Something was most definitely up.

I was about to argue that point with him when the glass door to Swissmen Sweets opened again and two disheveled men walked into the shop. The older of the two was short and middle-aged. What hair he had left on his head was graying at the temples. He had a plaid scarf wrapped tightly around his neck and wore a heavy hoodie and jeans. He carried a large video camera on his right shoulder. The other man wore a similar outfit but no scarf, and that's where the likenesses in their appearances ended. He was Asian, half the other man's age, and at least a foot taller and a foot wider than the older, slighter man. He carried a boom microphone and wore the largest pair of headphones I had ever seen.

I dropped my spatula into the peppermint bark, most likely condemning the utensil to a white chocolatey death, but I didn't care. I had much bigger problems than a lost spatula. I scowled at Eric. "What's going on? Doesn't look to me like you took time off of work to see the country."

Charlotte and my grandmother stared at me openmouthed, then turned to look at Eric and his film crew. I was willing to bet they had never seen anyone like this group of men before.

Eric shuffled back with his hands raised. "There is no reason to make a scene."

My frown deepened. "What's going on, Eric?" But I knew. Just before we'd broken up, Eric had been given the chance to film a reality baking show. As he was a famously volatile and hot pastry chef of the NYC culinary world, he was just what a popular cooking network was looking for to boost its ratings and give it an edgier image.

Maami lifted the piece of wood that separated the front of the shop from the back counter and stepped through the opening. "Bailey, what is going on? Do you know these men?"

I winced. One advantage of my grandmother's being Amish was that she'd been shielded from most of my headline-making relationship back in

New York. She knew that I had been dating someone and I had broken up with him just before moving to Ohio. She didn't know who he was or what he did, and she most certainly didn't know he was standing in the middle of her shop with a film crew.

Before I could answer, Eric stepped forward. "You must be Bailey's grandmother. I've heard so much about you." He held out his hand to her.

Maami stared at his hand, and after a long pause she took it for the briefest of handshakes. I knew she didn't want to be rude, but typically Amish women didn't shake hands with people they didn't know, especially strange men, and to *Maami*, Eric must have looked very strange. He had perfectly styled blond hair and was wearing tight jeans, a leather jacket, bright blue scarf—because it matched his eyes, I knew—a Rolex watch, and the Gucci boots, both of which cost more than my car. It certainly wasn't the typical male uniform in Harvest, where plain trousers and a white button-down shirt was more the norm for men.

"I'm Eric Sharp," he went on to say. "I'm sure you have heard of me from Bailey."

Maami looked to me. "*Nee*, Bailey has never mentioned anyone by the name of Eric Sharp. Are you a friend?"

This only made Eric chuckle again. "Well, I will just tell you that Bailey and I were *very* good friends back in New York, and I have missed her."

It took all my strength not to roll my eyes.

"Since she hasn't told you much about me, I suppose that you don't know I am a pastry chef in New York, the best pastry chef, actually."

I stifled a snort.

Eric went on as if I hadn't made a noise. "I'm doing so well, in fact, that I have my own television show, and that's where you all come in. We're filming a holiday special set in Amish Country. We haven't settled on a title yet, but I know we will soon. As you can guess, the network is in love with the idea!" He smiled as if that was reason enough to let him keep filming. It wasn't. "This is my crew. Roden on camera, and Pike on sound."

Pike waved, and his face broke into a winning smile. "Hey." He peered over the counter. "Are you making peppermint candies? Peppermint is my very favorite!"

My sweet grandmother smiled at him. "We are preparing for the Harvest Christmas Market to begin tomorrow afternoon, and our table will be all peppermint. Charlotte"—she nodded at her cousin—"will be at the table selling our goods. You should stay for the market to see it."

"Wow!" Pike said. "A whole table of peppermint— count me in!"

Maami picked up a bag of peppermint meltaways, each candy individually wrapped in a small piece of cellophane, and handed the bag to Pike. "Here. Merry Christmas." She smiled, and her cheeks were rosy. She was the very picture of an Amish grandmother.

Pike took the bag. "These are my favorites! How much?"

Maami shook her head. "They are a gift to tide you over until tomorrow." She turned to Roden. "Would you like a bag too?"

"No." His voice was hoarse, perhaps from the cold. "I don't do sweets."

"Oh," *Maami* said as if she didn't know how to respond to that.

"Eric," I said, determined to move the conversation back to the issue at hand. "What are you doing here? Tell the truth this time."

"I do want to see what an old-fashioned Amish Christmas is like," he began, and leaned on the counter. "And it occurred to the network and to me that my viewers would too. My executive producer made a few calls and pulled a few strings, and here we are. Ready to film your little Amish town and little Amish candy shop."

My mouth went dry. It was what I had expected him to say, but that didn't mean it was any easier to hear.

He smiled his lopsided smile, which was so perfect I wondered if he had practiced it in the mirror until it was second nature. "The network was mad for the idea."

I forced a smile. "I'm sure the network loved the idea, and it is nice to meet you," I said, nodding at the two crew members, "but you just can't show up here unannounced and say you are going to film my family's shop. That's not how it works."

The men looked to Eric, and he nodded. They lowered their equipment and shuffled to the corner of the room beside the large display of jarred candies. Pike opened his candy bag.

Eric turned to me. "I don't know why you are making such a fuss, Bailey. Don't you realize what a show like this could do for your shop? Don't you want free advertising for Swissmen Sweets? It could really boost your Internet sales. Wouldn't that be something that you want for your business?"

I felt a twinge. He had a point. Of course, the free advertising was something that I wanted for the shop. The exposure could be unbelievable for business, but it wasn't that easy. I had to respect my grandmother's culture. Being on television wasn't very Amish, and I didn't know if her Amish district would approve. In fact, I suspected they would not.

He must have noticed my hesitation, because the smug grin was back on his face.

Before I could give him an answer, the shop door opened for a third time that afternoon, and the last person on the planet I would have wanted to see at that moment stepped inside.

Tall and loose-jointed, sheriff's deputy Aiden Brody stood just inside the doorway to Swissmen Sweets. His eyes were alert as if he could feel the tension in the room. As a seasoned law enforcement officer, Aiden was tuned in to the mood of his surroundings, and the current mood inside Swissmen Sweets was anything but welcoming.

He took in Roden and Pike in the corner of the room. Pike had his boom leaning over his shoulder like a baseball bat ready to be taken out onto the field as he tore through his bag of candy.

"Anyone want to tell me what's going on in here?" Aiden asked.

And that's when I knew my first Christmas in Amish Country would be anything but peaceful.

Chapter 2

Eric's sharp gaze swung to me. "You called the cops, Bailey? That's not much of a welcome for me to your little town."

I rolled my eyes. "I did no such thing."

Aiden looked from me to Eric and back again. When it was clear that neither one of us was going to answer his question, he turned to my grandmother. "Clara? Do you know what's going on?"

Maami shrugged her shoulders. "This is Eric and his friends, and they know Bailey from New York. They are here for Christmas."

My grandmother had sort of got it right, and I watched as a light dawned on the deputy's face. My grandmother might have been able to miss the media coverage of my relationship with Eric, but Aiden had not. He placed his hand lightly on the hilt of his gun. If I were Eric I would head toward the exit now. I knew that Eric worked out, but he'd never chased down a criminal or thrown one in jail as I knew Aiden had done countless times.

"Aiden, this is my old . . ." I searched for the right

word and then cleared my throat. "Aiden, this is Eric Sharp from New York."

Aiden's eyes narrowed as my words only confirmed what he had to be thinking.

"Eric is here to shoot a Christmas special for his reality baking show here in Harvest, and he was just telling us he would like Swissmen Sweets to be involved."

"I bet he would," Aiden muttered. He frowned. "Are you going to do it?"

"Well, I . . . I . . ." It was a difficult question to answer as the publicity opportunities danced in my head. Being part of Eric's show, which aired on Gourmet Television, a major cable cooking channel, would be a huge boon to the business. Our online orders could jump 300 percent. Even considering the possibility made me dizzy. I cleared my throat. "*Maami* will have to decide. It's her shop."

Eric grinned. "I knew you would come around, Bailey honey."

I ground my teeth. "I'm not your honey."

Eric held out his hand to Aiden. "I have always had the utmost respect for the police. What was your name?"

"Deputy Aiden Brody," Aiden said in a clipped voice.

I had a sinking feeling that this encounter was about to go from bad to worse.

"It's very nice to meet you, Aiden."

The door opened for fourth time, and I started to wonder if I should begin charging admission.

I hoped that it was an actual customer who was dropping by for a fudge sample, but I had a sinking feeling it was not as soon as a slender woman in a hip-length, wool trench coat stepped through the door. Her red hair was swept back from her narrow face by a pair of oversized sunglasses that rested on the top of her head. "Eric, where have you been? I have been looking for you for the last hour." She removed the sunglasses, and her silky hair fell like a curtain on either side of her face.

Eric went over to her and held out his hand. "What are you doing in here, Rocky? I thought you were waiting outside for the van."

She squeezed his hand for the briefest of moments and narrowed her eyes, which were an unusual color of smoky gray. "You expect me to wait for the van. Why can't the crew do that?" She nodded at the two men in the corner of the shop. Pike had a meltaway suspended in the air on the way to his mouth, and Roden just looked bored out of his skull.

"I needed them in here. In case we had a chance to start filming. I thought it was a good use of time to get some footage while we wait."

"I suppose it is," she relented. "Time is money, and the last thing I want to spend on this project is more money. We've already gone over budget, and on-location production hasn't even begun. This must be the shop you told me about. It's quaint. You're right—with a few tweaks, it would be a great platform." Rocky turned to me for the first time and looked me up and down. "You're Bailey. I recognize you from the papers."

My face grew hot. I knew the papers she was referring to, the weekly glossies that were sold on every corner of the city, the ones that had exposed Eric and me as a secret couple.

She held out her hand. "I'm Rocky Rivers. I'm the executive producer on this special. Eric tells me that we will be shooting segments of the show here." She glanced around. "This should work nicely. The lighting is great. We will have to put in a few more lights if we plan to shoot in the morning since your shop faces south, but we can make it work." She folded her arms when I didn't take her hand. "Is there any chance you can remove some of the clutter from the counter there? We love a clean prep place for our programs. Extra ingredients sitting around confuse the viewers, and when the viewers get confused, they stop watching. Remember that most television programming is geared toward a sixth-grade education. That goes for cooking shows as well. Although I have never met a sixth grader who liked to cook other than those adorable children we book for our kids' baking challenges, and we have to look far and wide for them. They can be difficult to come by." She took a breath.

Aiden, Charlotte, and my grandmother all stared at her. They were not accustomed to how fast a real New Yorker could speak, and everything about Rocky screamed that she was a real New Yorker: her look, her speech, her manners.

"It's nice to meet you," I said quickly because I wanted to get out what I wanted to say before Rocky could kick back into gear. "But I think there has been some sort of mix-up. Eric never got permission to film here. In fact, he just told us his plan a minute ago. My grandmother and I need to discuss it."

"*Guder mariye,*" *Maami* said.

"*Gud*—Good morning," Rocky said, seeming taken aback for a brief moment. She gave a quick smile. "Then you and your grandmother should discuss this."

I was about to ask her what was wrong when my words were interrupted by a honk that was so loud it shook the candies in the jars along the wall.

Honk! Honk! The blaring horn came again. It sounded as if someone was strangling a goose just outside the shop.

"What on earth is that?" *Maami* asked.

Charlotte's hazel eyes were the size of dinner plates.

Aiden strode to the front door of the shop and opened it. "What the—" was all he said before the door slammed behind him.

The rest of us, including Rocky, ran to the large picture window at the front of the shop and stared as a white van slowly rolled down Main Street with GOURMET TELEVISION emblazoned on the side. The van barely fit between the Amish buggies and cars parked on either side of the road.

Abel Esh, a large, red-haired Amish man, was tying his horse and buggy up to the hitching post across from Swissmen Sweets. He secured the reins around the hitching post and then shook his fist at the van driver.

The driver didn't so much as blink an eye, and when she was just past the front window of Swissmen Sweets, she took a sharp left turn off the road and onto the green. As the van rocked over the curb and onto the square, it sideswiped one of the gas-powered lampposts that lined the green, gouging its paint. Aiden stood off to the side with his arms folded until the van came to a stop.

On the square, Amish and English volunteers who were setting up for the Christmas Market stared gap-mouthed at the van as it barely missed running into the display of cut Christmas trees that were for sale.

"What is that?" *Maami* exclaimed, clearly never having seen anything like it.

"Van's here," Eric said happily while standing next to me at the window.

I glared at him. "That thing is yours?"

"Of course it is."

Rocky shook her head. "It belongs to the network, not you, Eric. You would do well to remember that."

Eric shrugged as if this distinction was a minor detail.

The driver slipped from the front seat of the van. She was a petite, dark-haired woman all in black. Aiden spoke to her, and from their body language I thought it was safe to say that the conversation wasn't going well.

"I had better play interference. Josie doesn't always have the best bedside manner," Rocky said, and strolled out the door. I caught a whiff of expensive perfume as she went. Eric and I were close on her heels.

I jogged across the street, passing Abel Esh, who patted his horse on its cheek and murmured to the animal as if trying to calm it after its close encounter with the van. Abel glared at me and said, "I should have known all of this had something to do with you, Bailey King. This was a quiet and respectable village until you came around."

I ignored him and hurried over to where Aiden stood. I'd given up making amends with Abel months ago. It seemed that he was determined to hold a grudge against me that dated back to when we were children.

"You can't park here," Aiden told the young female driver. "This is public land, not to mention the square is closed this week for the Christmas Market."

The small woman folded her arms over her chest. "All I do is my job and follow orders, and my orders told me very clearly to park in the middle of the Harvest village square, which is exactly what I've done. It's been a long trip from New York, and I'm done. I shouldn't even be stuck driving this thing in the first place. I'm hair and makeup."

"And," Aiden said, "I'm going to issue you a citation for scraping the side of that lamppost. There will be a fine."

"You can send it to the network," the young woman shot back.

"I hope everything is all right," Rocky said in a smooth voice.

Aiden spun around and faced us. "Does this have something to do with your arrival?"

"Yes," Rocky said. "This is our production van. We need it for film editing purposes. What seems to be the problem, Officer?"

"The problem is this van. You have to move it. It can't be in the middle of the square like this. There's no parking on the grass, not to mention the Christmas Market begins tomorrow afternoon. There isn't space for your van here when that happens." Aiden's voice left no room for argument.

"Officer, there is no reason to be upset," Rocky said. "We have permission to be here. Do you think we would be here if we didn't have permission? Would you like to see the paperwork?" She reached into the pocket of her expensive trench coat and pulled out a folded document. She handed it to Aiden. "That's our permit to park on the square and to film in the village."

I shivered on the sidewalk next to Eric. I wished I'd thought to grab a coat before I had run out the door. It was December in Ohio, after all, and even though there wasn't much snow on the ground, it was still bitterly cold and promised to get colder each day we drew closer to Christmas. The village volunteers went back to their business of setting up the booths and tables for the Christmas Market, but I could tell they had one eye on what was going on around the van. The Amish Christmas tree farmer seemed to be particularly interested. He had a long, dark beard and wore plain clothes. Instead of the black felt hat donned by most of the Amish, he wore a black stocking cap. The Amish man caught me staring and scowled. I looked away.

Aiden unfolded the piece of paper slowly as if he thought it might bite him. He scanned the document. "Margot Rawlings granted you permission to do this?"

Rocky nodded.

I should have known. Margot was on the village board of directors, and she was always looking for ways to bring new business and publicity to the village of Harvest. I should have expected her to be the one who would let a television crew park on the square. I hoped that the network and Eric would be paying her enough money to re-sod the square after the van tore it up. I wasn't sure that Margot had thought of that, not with a chance for publicity for the village and, I suspected, a good amount of money being waved in her face.

A fiftyish petite woman in a black and white polka-dotted peacoat came around the side of the van. The coat was a perfect match to her black and white polka-dotted potbellied pig, which walked at the end of a hot-pink leash.

"Is that woman walking a pig on a leash?" Eric asked from his place next to me.

"Yes," I said with resignation as I watched Juliet and Jethro make their way around the square in the direction of the church. I had little doubt that Juliet was on her way to pay a call to Reverend Brook, on whom she had a not-so-secret crush and who had a not-so-secret crush on her in return. There were bets running through the village that the pair would be engaged by the end of the year. Since it was December, time was running out on that bet.

Juliet waved to me, and I waved back, hoping that she would just continue on her way to the church. No such luck, as she made a beeline for me.

Eric gave me a side-eye. "You say that as if it is perfectly normal."

"In Harvest, it is. That's Juliet and Jethro."

"Jethro?" Eric asked.

"The pig."

"Ahh." He grinned, and his face lit up with that mischievous look that had once made me smile.

Juliet waved her hand at me. "Bailey, isn't this exciting? Our little Harvest is going to be on cable television! Margot was just telling me all about it."

"Where is Margot?" I asked. "If this TV thing was her idea, I would have thought she would be here for the crew's arrival."

"Oh!" Juliet clapped her hands. "She had to run an errand. She says she has a *big* surprise for the Christmas Market." She bounced on her toes as she spoke. "She said it will make a real difference in the number of tourists coming to the village this Christmas."

That sounded ominous.

Jethro stared up at his mistress in adoration.

"Who might you be?" Eric held out his hand. "I'm pleased to meet any friend of Bailey's."

Juliet took his hand in hers. "Well, how do you do? I'm Juliet Brody, an old family friend of the Kings." She nodded at her pig on the ground. "And this is Jethro, of course. You must be Eric Sharp." She blushed. "I have seen you on television. My, you are twice as handsome in real life."

Eric grinned. "Thank you. It's not often I get a compliment like that from such a beautiful woman."

I snorted. Yeah, right. I knew from personal experience that women tripped over one another to shower Eric with attention and compliments. I had never been like that with him. In fact, when I had first met him, I'd thought he was arrogant and self-absorbed. I should have stuck to that opinion. In this case, first impressions were dead-on.

Aiden stared at Juliet, who happened to be his mother, as we approached. "You knew about this?" He motioned to the van.

She scooped Jethro off the ground and held the pig to her chest. Jethro licked her nose with his pink tongue but made no other protest at being man-handled. "Of course, I knew. Reverend Brook was consulted about it, since he sits on the village council. Margot wouldn't have given the go-ahead for this if everyone wasn't on board. Margot will be here soon." She smiled at Eric and the two other women. "She will be thrilled to see you."

"We are equally thrilled to see her," Rocky said with a smile. She held out her hand to Juliet. "Rocky Rivers, I'm the executive producer on this show."

"Oh!" Juliet's mouth made a tiny O shape. "It's just so wonderful to meet you. You can leave your van here for the moment, but I'm sure there is a better place to park it. I don't think Margot would have wanted it here exactly. We do have the Christmas Market happening. As you can see, the entire village is in the process of setting up." She pointed at an elderly man who was stringing an impossibly long strand of twinkle lights around each pillar of the large, white gazebo in the middle of the square. "You came at the perfect time! The Christmas Market is the height of the holiday season in Harvest. We have so many wonderful things happening. There are Christmas trees, a bonfire with caroling, all the shops like Bailey's have stands, and we have a live nativity!"

Eric grinned at Juliet. "You make it sound quite thrilling."

Juliet squeezed Jethro just a little bit harder. "It is, trust me!"

"You still can't park on the square," Aiden said.

Juliet laughed. "Aiden can be such a worrier, but I think he might be right. The church parking lot might be the best place for your van. Right now, you are blocking the Christmas tree farm's access to the street. We don't want to have to ask people who are buying all those beautiful trees to walk around your van. And for the elderly, it would be better if they could drive their cars up to load their trees."

The Christmas tree farmer stood in front of his wares with his arms crossed. If he was going for the angry pilgrim look, he'd nailed it.

Rocky looked over her shoulder at the Christmas tree farmer, and her face went chalk white. She recovered quickly. "Right. I think you're right. Josie, can you move the van across the street to the church parking lot?"

Josie folded her arms. "You told me to park it on the square."

She pressed her lips together for a moment. "And now I'm telling you to move it."

Josie touched Eric's arm. "Want to ride with me?"

"You'll do just fine on your own, Josie," he said breezily.

"I was hired to do hair and makeup, not drive a van around Amish Country. I don't remember anything like that in my contract."

"Move the van, Josie," Rocky said, sounding as if she was losing her patience with the younger woman.

Josie climbed into the van and carefully backed it onto the street. At least, she knew enough not to drive it directly across the square. Truth be told, for someone who professed not to have been hired to drive, she sure did whip that vehicle around with the ease of someone driving a Prius. If she ever tired of fancying up faces, she could make a living driving semis.

"Why didn't you tell me?" Aiden whispered to his mother a second time.

"I thought you would have already known, Son, you are a sheriff's deputy, after all. You know almost everything before I do." Juliet didn't modulate her voice, speaking loud enough for everyone to hear.

"I didn't know," Aiden said.

"Son?" Eric asked me in a hushed voice.

"Juliet is Aiden's mother," I said.

"You call the deputy Aiden?" Eric whispered to me.

"It's his name," I said.

"Uh-huh. I've never known you to be on a first-name basis with a police officer before."

"This is Harvest, Eric, not New York."

He grinned. "Sure. If that's your excuse."

"I can't wait to hear more about the production," Juliet said. "But I must run. I have a meeting with the reverend about the live nativity. It will be spectacular." She wiggled her fingers at the entire group. Jethro snorted loudly, and the polka-dot pair hurried off.

After his mother had gone, Aiden shook his head.

"I'll need to talk to Margot about this," Aiden said, directing his comment to Rocky.

Rocky smiled as if she knew that she had won the argument. "You do that."

Aiden held up the permit. "Can I keep this?"

Rocky shrugged. "Go ahead. I have other copies."

Aiden pursed his lips. "I'm sure you do."

Chapter 3

Aiden folded the permit and tucked it into the inside pocket of his department jacket. "It says on the permit that you have permission for filming. What exactly will you be filming?"

Rocky clasped her gloved hands. "I'm so glad you asked. I'm sure you have heard of *Sharp's Sweet Kitchen.*"

Aiden's brow furrowed. "I'm afraid I haven't."

She threw up her hands. "How is that possible? It has only been on the air for a month and it is already the number-one-rated cooking reality show on cable television."

"I don't have a lot of time to watch television," Aiden said.

This made Rocky scowl. I think the last thing a television producer wants to hear is that someone doesn't like to watch TV. I guess I make the same face when people tell me they don't like chocolate.

She recovered quickly, and her television smile was firmly back in place. "The show is about Eric's life and work as the top pastry chef in New York. In the various segments he makes pastries and desserts for special events, his dates, and for parties. It shows the inner workings of his business. It shows the people who work with him and the people in his life."

There was an elevator pitch for you. It was clear that Rocky was well practiced at the craft of pitching. I supposed she had to be in her business.

"The show is going so well that the network saw an opportunity to produce a Christmas special. Since it is already December, we don't have a lot of time to throw it together to make our airdate of December twenty-third. There is a lot on the line as you can imagine, so everything must go seamlessly. Making our airtime is our number one priority."

"Okay," Aiden said. "But why here in Harvest? Wouldn't it have been easier to film the Christmas special in New York?"

"Perhaps, but the Sharp brand is bigger than the city. It's global."

I made a garbled sound, something between choking and a bark of laughter. Neither Rocky nor Aiden paid me any notice.

"Viewers need to see Eric outside of the celebrated city haunts," Rocky went on. "They need to see that he is at home in the country, that he's a man with a heart."

That was debatable.

"The Midwest is a major demographic and comprises a sizable part of TV viewership—our advertisers are particularly keen on connecting with *all* of America."

Right. So it was a matter of what they could sell. I knew that TV was driven by commercialism, but it was quite another matter to feel as if I was getting dragged into this exploitation, even if I had been wondering a wee bit about how we could capitalize on some of the free publicity for my *maami*'s business.

Rocky flung her arm in the direction of Swissmen Sweets. "We knew from the papers that Eric had this connection to Amish Country, and I thought it would be a gold mine. What better place could there be for *Sharp's Sweet Kitchen* Christmas special than in Amish Country? It was my idea, and the network went over the moon for it just like they did when I pitched Eric's show at the very beginning."

"I'm sure there are a lot of better places for your special," Aiden said.

Rocky shook her head. "Nonsense." She waved her hand around. In addition to talking fast, New Yorkers sure spoke with their hands. It was a habit I'd picked up too. "Look around us at this square, the shops, that big white church, and the gas lampposts. This place is like a Norman Rockwell postcard. Add in the live nativity and the Christmas Market and our viewers will be swooning to learn more about this adorable village and the people who live here. It's the perfect set for a cooking reality show. I couldn't have planned it better myself."

I glanced around the square. Although I had never noticed it because I had been coming to Harvest ever since I was a young child to visit my grandparents, I realized that Rocky was right. The apple trees and gazebo were wrapped in white and blue twinkle lights, greenery and red ribbons adorned each gas lamppost, and glittering glass ornaments hung from the fir trees. A giant wreath sat just below the church steeple. It *was* like a Norman Rockwell postcard or like the inside of a snow globe, I realized as giant snowflakes began to fall.

Rocky smiled at the snow as if the heavens had opened up to make her "set" even more perfect for Eric's show. "Amish is hot right now," she said. "It has been for a while, but the trend doesn't seem to be dying away. People in the big cities are craving a simpler country life even if they wouldn't last more than three seconds outside their area code. The grass is always greener somewhere else." Her voice caught for a moment.

"Are you okay?" I asked.

She smiled. "Of course. Why wouldn't I be?"

Because she sounded for a second there as if she was about to cry, but I didn't want to embarrass her by saying so.

"We plan to capitalize on that," Rocky said. "Plus, the story was already there because Bailey and Eric's breakup got so much media attention. People want to see them back together, and we need to capture their reunion on film."

And there it was . . . the catch.

The spidey sense that had been prickling along my arms since the moment Eric strutted through the sweetshop's door, it was all leading up to this.

I didn't dare glance at Aiden. I hated to think about what *he* must think of all this. Not that we had done anything other than toy with the idea of dating.

He worked long, unpredictable hours as a sheriff's deputy, and I had been focused on inching the candy shop into the twenty-first century. There hadn't been much time for either of us to even broach the topic, and it seemed whenever one of us was ready and willing to give it a go, the other was not.

"It's all here," Rocky continued. "The charming small town, the sense of community and family. Second chances at love. You know, the feel-good family stuff that TV watchers like to gobble up while ignoring their own families."

I was speechless. It was as if I'd eaten a peppermint gumdrop and it was lodged in the back of my throat.

Rocky made a slashing motion with her hand, causing her hair to swish over her shoulders. "If we are going to capitalize on that story, we have to do it *now,* before viewers forget. The American audience has the attention span of a gnat. We must hit them hard with something until they are ready to move on to the next thing, and we always have to be one step ahead with new ideas. It's the nature of the business." She stepped back and made a frame with her hands, putting Eric and me in it. "Celebrity Chef and World-Class Chocolatier drawn apart by work rekindle their romance over authentic sweets at Christmas, putting what really matters first this holiday." She smiled at the image she'd described. "Can you see it or what?"

"I'm sorry, Rocky," I said. "But to get that angle you would have to include me, and I have no interest in participating. If you have permission from Margot to do some kind of Amish Christmas special with Eric here in Harvest, go for it, but please count me out if Eric and I have to . . ." I trailed off. I was too embarrassed to say anything more because of Aiden's proximity. Could this situation get any more humiliating for me?

She opened and closed her mouth for a moment as if registering the shock of my words. "But . . . but Eric said that you were on board. He said he spoke to you." She scowled at Eric.

Eric held up his hands in surrender. "Rocky, I never said I talked to Bailey about this. I just told you that it wouldn't be a problem, and it won't. Bailey is always there when I need her." He grinned at me. "Right, Bai?"

My face felt impossibly hot. I should have stayed inside the candy shop when everyone else rushed outside, but no, my curiosity won out and now I had to listen to a TV pitch about Eric and me rekindling our romance.

"Surely there is something we can do to change your mind. The network has given me some money that I can offer you," Rocky said, seeming to have regained her composure.

"I don't want your money. Filming in Swissmen Sweets is one thing, although I still need to speak to my grandmother about that, but lying about my relationship with Eric is completely another."

She snorted. "Please, everyone wants money. Don't pretend that you are any different because you live some simple Amish life now. I know the

Amish aren't as good and wholesome as they claim to be."

Wow. That was a rather rude and sweeping statement. I turned. "I need to get back to work."

As I made my way across the frozen grass toward my candy shop, my phone buzzed in my pocket. I removed it and found a text from my best friend, Cass, in New York.

Incoming! Eric is headed to Harvest to film his reality show. Danger. Danger!

Too late, Cass, far too late.

I was just crossing the street back to the safety of my candy shop when I heard the click of high heels on the pavement behind me. I turned to see Rocky running toward me.

I stopped on the sidewalk and waited for her, only because my grandparents had drilled politeness into me as a very young girl again. Otherwise, I would have bolted.

Rocky's heels scraped on the sidewalk, and I pulled up short when she stopped next to me. "Listen, I can be flexible. Let us shoot in your shop, and you and Eric rekindling anything is off the table. We need you in this special. Without you, there is no logical reason for Eric to be here."

I bit the inside of my lip as I thought again about all the business Eric's show could bring to my shop. I had just launched an online store, but we had very little traffic on it as of yet. This could change everything for us.

"Eric needs this. The network needs this. I need this."

I frowned. "Why?"

She sighed. "Let me be completely candid with you. When we chose to have Eric do a show, the fact that he's a loud and critical perfectionist pastry chef was attractive, but things have changed in the television business, and we have to soften his image so that viewers like him again. The angry chef is all well and good for a few episodes, but soon viewers become fatigued by it. My theory is because they deal with too many people who behave that way in their real lives. That's where you come in. Who better to soften Eric's image than the beautiful and wholesome proprietress of an Amish candy shop?"

I opened my mouth, but for once I couldn't think of anything to say.

"If we don't turn this around, Eric's show may be canceled, and I'd hate to think I made a mistake turning down other opportunities to be his executive producer."

"And Eric and I could just be, what, friends on the show?"

She smiled. "Of course. We will leave it at that. Talk it over with your *grossmaami*." Her gray eyes were earnest and almost wistful. "And think on it overnight. I'll be by myself in the van tomorrow morning, close to seven. I like to be at work before everyone else just to make sure everything is in its place and we're ready to go. I know it's early, but that is the best time to come over in case you want to discuss this without anyone else around, including Eric."

She turned and hurried back across the street in the direction of the van before I could ask her why she had said *grossmaami* to find out how she knew the Pennsylvania Dutch word for grandma.

Chapter 4

I chewed on my lip and texted Cass back, telling her that Eric was already here, before I opened the door to Swissmen Sweets. The show would be a great opportunity for the shop, and if Rocky was telling the truth about taking my rekindled love with Eric off the table, it would be silly to turn it down. There was just one catch. Swissmen Sweets wasn't my shop. It was my grandmother's, so it wasn't my call to make.

I was about step inside when an orange blur shot out through the door of the candy shop. "Nutmeg," I cried, realizing immediately that it was my orange tabby, who'd recently decided that he wanted to be an escape artist. "Nutmeg!" I called again as the cat dashed down the narrow alley that separated Swissmen Sweets from the pretzel shop next door.

I let the front door close as I went after the cat down the alley. I knew where he was going. Nutmeg wouldn't be hard to find, but it was beginning to snow harder and I was afraid of his catching a chill.

As I came around the back of the pretzel shop, I

saw the figure of a man disappearing around the other side of the building. The figure was far too small to be sturdy Abel, whom I would expect to see behind his family's store.

Another person was behind the shop as well. Abel's youngest sister, Emily, stood there as the snow fell around her with Nutmeg cradled in her arms. This was where I had expected to find the little cat. Nutmeg had been her pet before he belonged to me. She had given me Nutmeg when Abel and her older sister, Esther, forbid her to keep a pet. Nutmeg still liked his visits with his first mistress, and he and I had always looked forward to Emily dropping by Swissmen Sweets each day. Lately though, Nutmeg had to go to the Eshes' shop to see her because she no longer came to mine.

Two months ago, Emily had been an invaluable help to me in a candy competition. I'd really needed her support throughout the competition, especially after I found a dead body. At the end of the competition, she had asked me for a job at Swissmen Sweets so that she could get out from under the thumb of her restrictive sister, Esther. I had seriously considered it because I could use more help around the shop, and I'd promised her that I would speak to my grandmother about it. Then my grandmother's cousin Charlotte ran away from her very conservative Amish community and needed a job and a place to stay. It made sense that *Maami* wanted Charlotte and not Emily to work at the shop. I would have loved to have Emily too, but we couldn't afford to hire two people.

When I told Emily our decision, she had been

heartbroken and started avoiding me. Although her family's pretzel shop was right next door to Swissmen Sweets, she hadn't come to the store in weeks to visit Nutmeg.

I wished there was a way I could make it up to her, but nothing could change the fact that we didn't need two candy shop assistants, and my grandmother seemed so much happier now that Charlotte was with us full time. Maybe if business increased as a result of my being a part of Eric's show, that would change. I pushed that thought to the back of my mind. It was *Maami*'s decision, not mine.

"Emily! It's nice to see you," I said as brightly as I could. Part of me wanted to ask about the Amish man I had seen leaving, but I knew that would be pressing my luck. It would be a breakthrough if Emily just said hello to me. As much as I wanted our friendship back to the place it had been when I'd first moved here, I wasn't hoping for much more than a "hello."

I realized I wasn't even going to get that much as she set Nutmeg down on the cold pavement and turned her back to me. Nutmeg stared up at her and meowed. Clearly, the little cat was confused by the way she was snubbing both of us.

"Emily, I think we should talk," I began.

My words spurred her into action, and she ran to the back door of her family's shop, threw it open, then disappeared inside.

Nutmeg meowed at me.

I bent to pick him up. "It's okay," I told the cat with a knot in my stomach. "She will come around eventually," I said, not knowing if that was true.

I carried Nutmeg around to the front of my shop and through the front door. When we went inside I brushed the snowflakes from his fur before setting him on the floor. Charlotte and my grandmother were behind the doomed candy counter again as if nothing out of the ordinary had happened that morning.

My grandmother smiled at me brightly. "Bailey dear, you are back. How are your friends?"

"I think they are all right. Aiden has his hands full, I'm afraid. I guess Margot has given the TV crew a permit to film on the square during the Christmas Market."

Charlotte's mouth made an O shape. "Does that mean I will be on television when I work at the market?"

"Maybe," I said. "*Maami*, can I talk to you a minute in the kitchen?"

My grandmother wiped the sugar and flour from her hands on a white linen towel. "Yes, my dear." To Charlotte she said, "Make sure that we have plenty of those peppermint meltaways for tomorrow. I think they will be quite popular. The young *Englischer* from New York certainly enjoyed them."

Charlotte nodded, and *Maami* and I went through the swinging kitchen door to the back of the shop.

My grandmother perched on one of the metal stools in the large industrial kitchen. "What is wrong, granddaughter? You seem distressed."

"I'm not distressed. Well, perhaps a little. I just saw Emily in the alley, and she wouldn't speak to me." I sat on the stool next to her.

Maami patted my hand. "She will come around."

I didn't tell her I had essentially said the same thing to Nutmeg. "*Maami*, I need to talk to you about Eric and what he and his producer would like to do here at the shop. It's really your decision, but I think it would be a wonderful boon to our business." I went on to describe the show and what Rocky proposed. I made no mention of the romance angle between Eric and me. Rocky had agreed it was off the table, so it was not worth even mentioning.

My grandmother listened in silence and only spoke when I was done. "You want to do this."

I nodded. "I do, but it's your decision. This is your shop. You've let me change so many things so far, it almost doesn't feel right to ask for anything more."

She squeezed my hand. "It is your shop too. I am just the caregiver for a time. Your grandfather always intended this to be yours. We expected you to run it your own way, so I have let you have your website shop. You will be the one to move us forward. I know the business will not thrive standing still. The Amish way is slow to change, but you are not. It is right for you to be the next at the helm of this shop. Your *grossdaadi* would never have asked you to leave New York, but it is what Jebidiah most wanted for you—to be here."

Tears sprang to my eyes as she mentioned my grandfather. I missed him so much, and I knew my grandmother had to miss him twice as much as I did. It was a miracle she could bear it.

"Being on television is not the Amish way. I will have to ask the bishop and the deacon," *Maami* said.

My heart sank. I knew that Deacon Yoder and his

outspoken wife, Ruth, would be against it. I should have known this would be my grandmother's decision.

"I will call the deacon's shed phone and ask for counsel," *Maami* said. "We must do what is right in the eyes of the church."

I tossed and turned all night in the small guest room that I shared with Charlotte over the candy shop. I was on the bed, and Charlotte slept on a cot in the corner of the room. The sleeping arrangements were far from ideal, but I had been working so hard to move the candy shop back into the black that I hadn't had time to search for an apartment. My goal was to find one before Christmas, but with Christmas just two weeks away, and with Eric in town, it was unlikely I'd have the time to look.

At some point I must have fallen asleep, because when I woke up, Charlotte's cot was empty. Since Charlotte had started working at Swissmen Sweets, she had been the one to rise early and help my grandmother make the candies for the day. That gave me more time to work on marketing and to experiment with new recipes. It also meant that I had time to meet Rocky at the production van, but I didn't know what to tell her. By the time I had gone to bed, my grandmother still hadn't heard from her district elders that it was all right to film in the shop. Part of me balked at the very idea of asking someone else's permission on how to run my own business. But I knew this was my grandmother's culture, and there was so much I respected about it. At the same time, this was something I could not wrap my head around as a non-Amish person.

I groaned and rolled over in the bed. I wrapped my pillow over the back of my head. I could hide all I wanted, but I knew that I would end up going to see Rocky even if I had no answer to give.

I rolled out of bed.

This late in the year, dawn was just breaking when I walked out the front door of Swissmen Sweets at seven to meet with Rocky. I was relieved when I walked down the stairs from the upstairs apartment and across the main part of the shop that neither my grandmother nor Charlotte saw me. I didn't want them to ask me where I was going.

I stopped by the gas lamppost that the van had grazed the day before and saw that the mark was much deeper than a mere scratch. It would take some doing to repair it. I wondered if Aiden had ended up ticketing the network or Josie.

A fresh blanket of snow covered the square. The frozen grass beneath the snow crunched and cracked under my steps. Each step was as loud as a gunshot in the sleepy village. Although I knew that all the Amish were likely awake at this hour because they were early risers, there was no one outside this early on such a cold day. No one except for me.

The booths were all set up for the Christmas Market, which was to run Friday and Saturday for the next two weeks leading up to Christmas. From what my grandmother had told me, the Christmas Market was a huge draw to English shoppers who visited Amish Country by the busloads and who were eager to find the perfect gifts for family and friends back home.

The only thing "off" about the market was the gazebo's blue and white twinkle lights—which drooped from the eaves. I wondered if maybe the wind had torn them down overnight, but when I looked around to see if anything else was disturbed on the square, I didn't see any evidence. I also thought I would have heard any high winds in the middle of the night, seeing as how I'd barely slept. I had tossed and turned and worried over Eric being in Harvest. Why was he in Amish Country *really*? Was it the television special, or was there another motive? I prayed the motive wasn't me.

I sighed. I was using my concern over the lights as an excuse to stall because I didn't have a straight answer to give Rocky until my grandmother heard from her bishop or deacon.

And maybe a tiny part of me didn't want to do the show. Obviously, it would be better for the candy shop. Really, any exposure on the prestigious Gourmet Television network would do wonders for business. But was it good for me? For my mental well-being? No. Certainly not. And, well, to be honest, I realized now that Eric wasn't someone I wanted to be tied to. I didn't like the reminder of the mistake I had made by staying with him for so long. I didn't trust him. And I certainly couldn't shake the niggling thought in the back of my mind that no good would come of his presence in Harvest.

As I drew closer to the gazebo, I made up my mind that I would fix the twinkle lights on the gazebo before I walked to the production van to give Rocky the bad news about my grandmother's decision to wait for a decision from the church elders. After that, I would go inside my candy shop and help my grandmother prepare our peppermint treats for the Christmas Market. I was happy that we had Charlotte working for us now. She had volunteered to mind the booth during the market days. *Maami* and I would help as time allowed. If the Christmas Market was busy, the candy shop promised to be busy as well.

I knocked the snow that had fallen overnight off my boots before I stepped into the gazebo. A string of lights hung listlessly to my right. I touched the cord and saw where it had been ripped down from the nail. It didn't look very hard to fix. I only had to find the end.

My glove-covered hands moved down the cord as I turned to the middle of the large gazebo. I dropped the cord of lights as if I had received an electric shock.

Rocky Rivers lay in the middle of the gazebo with a cord of twinkle lights wrapped around her throat twice over. Her unusual gray eyes were drained of any life. Long moments passed before I saw Eric standing over her, looking as guilty as sin.

Chapter 5

"Bailey, please, you have to help me. It's not what it looks like." Eric's voice wavered as he spoke.

I asked myself, What did it look like? It looked like Eric had strangled a woman with Christmas lights. That was exactly what it looked like. I took a step back to the safety of the gazebo steps. I should run away, get as far from Eric and the dead woman as possible. I couldn't process this. Eric had killed someone. Even when I thought I was in love with him, I knew Eric was capable of bad things, but I never would have guessed *this*. I never would have thought him capable of such violence. It wasn't possible for me to be attracted to someone who was capable of such a horrible act.

"I have to call the police," I mumbled as I backed away. The soles of my boots slipped on the gazebo floor, which was slick from the blowing snow.

Eric grabbed my arm. "No, wait. Don't! Give me a minute to get my story straight."

I wrenched my arm out of his grasp. "Get your

story straight? You mean make up a story as to why you killed her? Is that what you mean?"

"No, no! I didn't do anything to Rocky. I would never hurt her!" He was white as a sheet, which was quite an accomplishment considering his expertly applied spray tan.

"Really? Then what are you doing here?"

Eric's breathing was shallow. "I . . . I knew she was meeting with you this morning, and I wanted to be in on the meeting. She has no right to meet with you alone. If it weren't for me, she wouldn't even know that you existed. I didn't want her to make you any promises that I didn't know about. This Christmas special was my idea and should go off the way I want it to."

I stepped away from him. "So you killed her? Because she made a meeting with me and you didn't like it?" I was on the edge of the gazebo steps now. I could run away, and Eric would never catch me before I reached my candy shop across the street.

"Bai, please, don't look at me like that." Eric sounded as if he was on the verge of tears.

"Look at you like what?" I asked as I took another step back. If I wasn't careful, I was going to fall down the steps and onto the snow-covered grass.

"Like I killed someone." His voice was tight.

I didn't argue with him, because that was exactly how I was looking at him.

"I didn't kill her." His eyes were pleading with me. "I promise you."

I wanted to believe him, but Rocky was dead and he was standing right there.

"You know I couldn't do this. Do you realize how

murdering the executive producer would ruin my television career if not my entire life in New York? Don't you see how something like this would destroy everything that I have built for myself?"

I was about to take one more step backward and fall out of the gazebo when his comment made me freeze in place. "A woman is dead, Eric, and all you can think about is yourself."

He ran his hand through his hair. "But doesn't my selfishness prove I wouldn't do something this stupid? I would never do something that could end my career. Bai, you know better than that."

Eric had a point. Killing Rocky would not advance his career in any way, and to Eric, his career always came first. I'd learned that the hard way when we were together. Still, I was hesitant. Eric might not have entered the gazebo with the intent to kill Rocky, but murder wasn't always planned. "Maybe it was an accident. You said that you came in here planning to confront her about speaking to me alone."

The flush on his face deepened. "Of course I was going to confront her about it. This is my show! I should know the deals that Rocky offers you. Just because she works for the network, she thinks that she can tell me what to do. I don't answer to anyone. I told the network that when I signed this deal in the first place." He sounded angry.

"That's a motive, Eric," I said quietly.

"Motive! You have to be kidding."

"You just said she bossed you around and you hated it. That's motive. If you got mad enough, you could have killed her in a fit of rage." As I said this I realized how small the gazebo was. My heels hung over the edge of the steps, and I placed my hand on my phone in my coat pocket. This conversation had gone on long enough. I had to call Aiden and the police. I needed them to take over from here.

Eric must have seen my reaction, because he said, "Bai, come on, you know me. You know I wouldn't do anything like this."

"I do know you, Eric, but I never knew you as well as I thought I did, not even when we were together."

"Listen, you know I wouldn't do this. Think of all the bad press this is going to create. The Christmas special is surely off the table now, and there is a good chance that my show will tank altogether. Rocky was the driving force behind it with the network. The other producers have their own pet projects to pitch. No one is going to want to take my orphan. Rocky's death hurts my career."

My stomach knotted. It was impossible not to think of the woman whose unseeing eyes stared back at me. She was more than just a means to an end for some TV show. She was someone's daughter. Maybe a mother or a sister. She was bossy and maybe crafty, but on a bone-deep level, I knew she wasn't bad. She certainly didn't deserve this. No one did.

"Bailey, I swear I didn't do this!"

I needed to get away from Eric. All I had to do was run down those stairs and back to Swissmen Sweets.

But Eric was right—I did believe him. As callous as it was, I knew Eric wouldn't do anything to jeopardize his career. He'd worked too hard to get where he was. That was something Eric and I had in common, or at least we used to until I left the fast-paced life of New York behind. Now I measured success differently.

"I believe you," I said.

He dropped his hands and sighed with relief. I could be mistaken, but I thought I saw tears in his eyes. "I want you to believe me, Bai. You can't know how much it means to me." He took a step toward me.

I held up my hand, silently telling him to stop. "Someone did this to Rocky, and the sooner we find out who, the better." As I said the words, I found myself scanning the square. The tables and booths were set up for the day. A manger had sprung up overnight to my right. All it needed were the people and animals to complete the scene. Straw lay on the inside of the makeshift structure, and snow covered the small shelter's roof. This was not a place you would expect to find a dead woman. I wished I could say it was the first time this had happened to me.

"The sheriff's department needs to be informed as soon as possible," I said more to myself than Eric. "I have to report this to the police."

"You mean Deputy Brody," he said with a curl to his lip.

I gave him a look. "Deputy Brody is the finest officer on the force. I'm certain he will be investigating this crime."

"You speak very highly of him," Eric grumbled.

I ignored his dig. "What's your story?" I asked instead. I was inclined to think that Eric wouldn't kill an innocent woman, simply because he was too careful to risk killing his own career in the process. But that didn't mean I could be certain.

"It's what I've already told you. I came here to meet with you and Rocky. I know you well enough to know that you would come to at least hear her out. You're too savvy to let an opportunity like this pass you by."

I ground my teeth. It bothered me that he'd pegged me so well. "How long have you been here?"

"I arrived just a minute before you did, and I found her." He glanced back at the body. "I found her just like that. When I saw her, I couldn't move. I froze. I . . . I've never seen anything like this before. I mean, I have seen dead people at funerals, but not . . . not like this."

"Did you touch anything?" I asked.

"No, of course not, except . . ."

I narrowed my eyes.

"Except the light cord. I picked it up. I thought it had gotten knocked down. I didn't know she'd be at the end of it."

I grimaced. "I planned to do the same thing."

"Yes, but the deputy won't believe that *you* have a reason to kill Rocky. He will believe that I do. I could be in real trouble, Bailey."

He was right. He *was* in real trouble.

I took a deep breath and then another quick look at the body. That's when I noticed the crumpled pieces of cellophane near her feet. There were at least five of them. I recognized them immediately. They were the pieces of cellophane that we used in the shop to wrap many of our candies, including, I recalled, the peppermint meltaways that the sound guy had gushed about and had eaten by the handful.

"I need to call the police, and we shouldn't be in here with the bod—Rocky." I turned and hurried down the steps. I was relieved when Eric followed me out of the gazebo.

By the time my first step landed on the grass, I'd called 911 and was put through to the dispatcher. Unfortunately, this was not the first time I had called the police in Holmes County to report finding a dead body, so I knew the drill. I rattled off what I'd found, and the dispatcher promised to send a deputy out immediately.

As Eric and I waited by the gazebo, a group of Amish men arrived to finish setting up for the Christmas Market, which was scheduled to open at noon. That was assuming that the Christmas Market would go on despite this latest development. I bit my lower lip.

I paced while waiting for the deputies and wasn't the least bit surprised when Aiden and his young partner, Deputy Little, were the first to arrive on the scene. The temperature seemed to drop as a light snow began to fall.

Aiden jumped out of his cruiser and pulled up short when he saw me pacing in front of the gazebo while Eric hovered over his phone. I wondered whom he was texting. Should I have stopped him from doing that? Could he be warning someone? Who could it be?

"Bailey!" Aiden cried. "Are you all right?"

I stopped pacing as he jogged over to where I stood. "I'm fine. A little shaken." I closed my eyes. "That poor woman. I'll never get used to this sort of thing."

"I don't ever want you to get used to this sort of thing," he said. Aiden's whole body sagged as he ex-haled in obvious relief. "I was so worried," he added just loud enough for me to hear. "Thank God, you're okay."

I shivered.

"Why are you shivering?" he asked.

"I'm outside and it's snowing. Oh, and finding a dead body will make you shiver too."

"Who is it?"

"I thought the dispatcher would have told you. I told her who it was, or at least I think I did. I can't really remember. I might have not remembered to share that detail."

He touched my arm. "Bailey, who has died?"

I shook my head as if to dislodge cobwebs from my mind. "It's Rocky Rivers. It's just awful. I didn't know her long, but I could tell she was a force. I'm sure she had to be to become so successful in her chosen field."

Aiden's gaze darted over to Eric, who was tapping on his phone. "And what does he have to do with it?"

"He . . . he . . ."

"What do you want me to do, Deputy Brody?" Deputy Little asked. He stood at attention, ready to follow orders and eager to please. In the few months that he had been a rookie in the sheriff's department, he had always seemed to look to Aiden for guidance.

Little was a few years younger than I and was several inches shorter as well. He was a compact man, whom I imagined had spent a lot of time perfecting the precise part in the middle of his hair. The style made him look old-fashioned and vaguely Amish. Not for the first time, I wondered if Little had been born an Amish man and had left plain life behind for the English world. If he had, he hadn't traveled very far, since he still lived in Holmes County.

Eric stopped messing with his phone. "Are you going to ask me if I am all right, Deputy, or is that only for Bailey?"

Aiden narrowed his eyes. "If it weren't for you, Bailey wouldn't be in this mess. So excuse me if I don't care how you are."

I placed a hand on Aiden's arm. "Aiden, please."

"Yes, Aiden, don't make a scene." Eric sneered. "There are Amish watching."

I dropped my hand from Aiden's arm. "Don't you make a scene either, Eric. You're in enough trouble as it is."

Eric opened and closed his mouth as if he was going to argue with me but then thought better of it.

Aiden shifted his focus to me. "Where is the body?"

"In the gazebo," I said, nodding behind me.

Aiden turned to Little. "Secure the scene."

The young deputy nodded and climbed the steps into the gazebo with crime scene tape in hand.

"And it's Rocky?" he asked when his deputy was out of sight. "You're sure."

I swallowed as I remembered the cord that had been wrapped twice around her thin neck. "I'm sure. It's Rocky." The image of those unseeing gray eyes came back to me.

A second sheriff's department vehicle rolled up alongside the square. It wasn't the standard-issue cruiser like Aiden's but a fully loaded SUV. I inwardly groaned. There was only one man in the county who drove such an obnoxious departmental car.

Sheriff Marshall climbed out of the SUV, and if his steely glare meant anything at all, he was as happy to see me as I was to see him.

Chapter 6

Aiden murmured a curse under his breath. The sheriff and Aiden, who was the department's second-in-command, had a strained relationship, but according to Margot Rawlings it had only become worse since I'd moved to the village.

Aiden had the utmost respect for the Amish in the county, while the sheriff viewed the Amish community as a nuisance and thought the only value they brought to Holmes County was the number of visitors they attracted. If it had not been for tourism, I had a feeling it would have been the sheriff's personal mission to run the Amish out of the county altogether. Even if he'd wanted to chase the Amish away, it would be a nearly impossible task. Holmes County had the largest Amish population in the world, even bigger than Lancaster, Pennsylvania, which was more widely recognized by many *Englischers*.

Little wound crime scene tape around the gazebo with abandon.

"Little," Aiden said. "Come over here."

The younger deputy tore off his crime scene tape and set the roll on the frozen ground.

"Stay with Bailey and Mr. Sharp. I need to meet with the sheriff."

Little's eyes went wide. "Yes, sir."

"The two of you stay here. I'll be right back," Aiden said to Eric and me before he walked over to the sheriff, who leaned again his car and waited.

Little shifted from foot to foot and shot furtive glances at the sheriff. From his demeanor, I suspected he was terrified of Sheriff Marshall. I was a little afraid of the big, burly sheriff too, but I would never admit that to anyone other than myself.

Eric glowered at the young deputy. "Are you going to do any investigating, or just make us stand out here in the cold while poor Rocky is inside the gazebo?"

"I . . . I can't do anything until I know what Deputy Brody wants to do. I mean, I can't do anything until I know what the sheriff wants to do." Little glanced at the sheriff and Aiden, who were in the middle of a tense conversation with what seemed to me to be an excessive number of hand gestures. Huh, apparently Ohioans talked with their hands too. I wished I could hear what they were saying.

"You're a cop too. Can't you do something? I can't wait here all day. Someone has to tell the network what happened." Eric ran his hand through his spiky hair. "This is going to be such a nightmare. What do I do? Tell the crew to go home?"

"Eric, chill out," I said. "Not everything can work on your personal timetable, especially an investigation into a woman's murder." I turned away from

him. It was as if Eric hadn't even absorbed the fact
that Rocky was dead. Maybe he was in shock. Maybe
he really was so self-centered that he couldn't see
beyond his own ambitions. Or—I gulped—maybe
he was guilty.

"I know that a woman is dead," he said softly.

I turned back to face him, and much to my surprise I saw tears in his eyes. "I knew her. She was my
producer, my friend, she once was . . ." He didn't
finish the sentence.

"Once was what?" I asked.

He closed his eyes as if willing the tears back. Eric
shook his head.

"Who were you texting a minute ago?" I asked.

"When?"

"Just now before Aiden arrived. I saw you messing
with your phone."

"I wasn't texting. I was on the Internet," he said,
but in such a way that it made me believe he was
lying.

I let it drop for the moment as a crime scene van
and the coroner's car pulled up to the square along
with another sheriff's department car. It seemed as
if all the law enforcement vehicles in the county had
descended on the center of Harvest. Two Amish
buggies slowed as they rolled down the street to take
in all of the commotion, and the Amish men who
were there to finish the market setup stared at us. It
wouldn't be long before the entire county knew
something was amiss in Harvest . . . again.

The crime scene techs and the coroner got out of
their vehicles and consulted with Aiden and the
sheriff for a few minutes. Then Aiden, the sheriff,

the coroner, and the techs all went inside the gazebo after removing the two layers of crime scene tape that Little had put there to block the entrance. I winced as I remembered what I had found inside and what they were seeing.

I walked to the edge of the gazebo, but Little stepped in front of me. I frowned at him.

He cleared his throat. "I'm sorry, Bailey, but Aiden is not going to want you to listen in."

Aiden wouldn't, or the sheriff wouldn't?

Minutes ticked by as we waited for the sheriff and Aiden to reappear. The Amish men who had been working on the square went back to their tasks. I knew that they must be curious, but being Amish they didn't pry, especially when police were involved. With each minute that went by, Eric became increasingly more agitated. He paced and ran his hand through his hair and over his eyes. "I can't take this anymore. I'm going to text Linc. He needs to be here. I shouldn't be dealing with this alone."

"Who's Linc?" I asked.

He ignored my question.

I was just about to ask him again when Aiden and the sheriff stepped down from the gazebo. I wrapped my arms around my waist and steeled myself for the sheriff's approach. However, much to my surprise, the sheriff walked by me on his way to his SUV without so much as a sneer in my direction. He revved the SUV's engine before he drove away.

Aiden waited a few feet away from us in silence until the sheriff's car disappeared around the corner onto Apple Street; then he approached us. "I need to speak to you both privately and one-on-one," Aiden said. "I have a number of questions for each of you, and it would be best to ask them separately."

Eric laughed. "You want to make sure we're telling the same story. Is that right, Deputy?"

Aiden pursed his lips.

Eric folded his arms across his chest. "No way. I'm not letting you question me alone. I'm not answering any questions until I have an attorney present. I know my rights."

I inwardly groaned. Was Eric trying to make himself appear guilty?

"That is your choice," Aiden said evenly. "Is there a reason you feel you need an attorney?"

"You're right it's my choice. I can have one here within the hour. I'm not going to get railroaded by a bunch of country cops. You forget that you aren't dealing with some unschooled country bumpkin. I know what I'm doing."

Aiden scowled at Eric. "I know exactly who I am dealing with. It would do you well to show a little more respect for the community here. You're not doing yourself any favors by calling us country and unschooled."

"Even if you are?" Eric challenged.

"This conversation is going nowhere," I interjected. "Aiden, if you have questions to ask me, I will answer them. Eric can call his attorney while we talk."

Aiden glared at Eric for a long moment. "Stay here with Deputy Little," he ordered Eric.

"I know you have been waiting to be alone with her," Eric said, clearly baiting Aiden. "Now is your chance."

"Watch your mouth," Aiden snapped.

Eric held up his hands in mock surrender. "I can see Bailey is a touchy subject. Maybe one we have in common."

"Eric," I said. "For goodness' sake, would you shut your mouth before your get yourself thrown into jail?"

Eric opened and closed his mouth.

I walked away from Eric to the other side of the gazebo. The high bushes blocked any view of the crime scene, and I was just fine with that. I sat on a park bench a few feet away and watched as the Amish men put together the large white tent for the Christmas Market. Would the market go on with the police there? The case wouldn't be solved by noon when the market opened.

The gazebo was decked out in its Christmas finery of white and blue twinkle lights, greenery, and red bows. Rocky had been right. Harvest was like a Normal Rockwell painting but not nearly as innocent. Murder had been committed here in this beautiful place. And even though I had known her only briefly, I had liked Rocky. I liked her determination and dedication to her work. Under different circumstances, we might have even been friends.

The sound of Aiden's footsteps crunching through the frozen grass and snow shook me from my dark thoughts. I couldn't dwell on how murder had once again disturbed Harvest's tranquil setting. There was no time for that. Someone had done this to Rocky, and we had to find out who was responsible.

Aiden stopped about a foot away from me. It was close enough for me to reach out and touch him if I wanted to. I would admit, if only to myself, that

I wanted to feel his warm hand in mine. But Aiden and I didn't have that kind of relationship, no matter what his mother might wish, and with Eric and so many other deputies running around, now was not the time to bridge the gap.

Aiden and I had been toying with the idea of dating for weeks, but as of yet neither of us had made the first move. I know it was mostly because he was trying to be sensitive to my feelings as I recovered from my breakup with Eric. The funny thing was, now that I was with Eric and could really see what he was like without the rose-colored glasses of infatuation over my eyes, the reliable and kind sheriff's deputy was that much more appealing. I don't know what had attracted me to Eric in the first place. I was ashamed that his money and personality had wooed me into ignoring so much that was wrong with our relationship. I was also ashamed that it had taken the media holding a mirror to my face for me to finally make the decision to end it.

Aiden studied me in the reflection of the gazebo's lights for a moment. "Are you really all right?"

"Yes," I murmured. "I'm shaken up, of course, but I'm all right. I just keep thinking about Rocky. I know I knew her for only a day, if that, but she was such a strong, vibrant woman. You could see that the moment you met her. She had accomplished so much in her career, and to die like this in a place that someone from New York would assume was safe. . . ."

Aiden sat beside me on the bench, leaving a foot of space between us and bracing his large hands over his knees. "I can't believe I am having another conversation with you about murder. It seems to be all we ever talk about."

"We talk about candy, too," I said, forcing a smile. "Since you make a point of dropping by the shop every day to get your sweets allotment."

"I don't just stop by for the candy, Bailey, you know that."

I watched the Amish men for a moment. Truth be told, his daily visit to Swissmen Sweets was the highlight of my day even when he was busy and could stay for only a few minutes. I couldn't seem to tell him that though.

"Would you prefer to go back to the station to answer my questions? It would be warmer there," he suggested.

"Not really. I don't feel all that comfortable there."

"I understand. Not that this particular location is much better."

I couldn't argue when I knew Rocky's body wasn't more than twenty feet from me.

"It's better if I take your statement now," he said, and removed a notebook from the pocket of his department-issued winter coat. "While the details are fresh. You may recall something that will be significant to our investigation." He crossed his legs and said, "Tell me what happened from the beginning."

So, I did. I told him that Rocky had asked me to meet her at the production van before the other members of her team arrived. "So I came to the square this morning to hear her out." I swallowed. "I found Eric standing over her dead body. Before you ask, I don't believe that he killed her. He said he arrived a minute before I did."

"You said that you were meeting her at the van. Why then did you go into the gazebo?"

"It was the lights. I could tell some of the twinkle lights had fallen off the gazebo. I assumed it was the wind. I went to the gazebo to fix them, and that's when I saw her. Eric claimed that he went into the gazebo for the very same reason."

Aiden pressed his lips together as if he was holding back something he wanted to say. He leaned back on the bench. "Did you know Eric would be on the square this morning?"

"No. Rocky wanted me to meet with her alone. It was supposed to be just Rocky and me without Eric. I think she believed she would have more success talking me into being part of the show if Eric wasn't there. She was probably right, but as you know, we never were able to have that conversation."

Aiden looked up from his notes. "Then why was Eric there?"

"He'd found out about my meeting with Rocky, and he was upset she'd excluded him. He wanted to be there for the meeting. He said that when he stepped into the gazebo, he found Rocky and she was already dead."

"How did you find out about your meeting?"

I shook my head. "I don't know. Maybe he overhead something or asked Rocky what her plans were. You will have to ask him."

"I will," Aiden said. "Why do you believe he's innocent?"

I peered around the side of the gazebo to where

Eric and Deputy Little stood. The young deputy kept taking off and putting on his gloves as if he didn't know whether his hands were too hot or too cold. Eric crossed his arms over his chest and stood as still as a statue. His face was an indecipherable mask.

"Bailey?" Aiden asked in a gentle voice.

I turned back to him. "I know Eric."

The deputy winced ever so slightly but enough that I noticed.

I took a breath and started again. "Eric cares about his career and his image more than anything else. More than he ever cared about anyone else, including me."

Aiden moved his hand as if he was about to reach out and comfort me but then changed his mind. At this moment, I wasn't his friend or potential anything, I was a witness to a crime giving my statement. A professional distance needed to be maintained. Though I knew that, I still wanted him to reach across the invisible divide and comfort me.

He made another note in his book.

"I can't believe," I went on, "he would do anything that would jeopardize his career. For all his faults, Eric is a very hard worker. He came from nothing. He earned everything that he has. He wouldn't risk losing it all by killing anyone. He especially would not kill the television producer who had the power to catapult his career to the next level, whatever the next level for Eric might be."

"Do you have anything else to add?"

"Did you see the candy wrappers near the body?"

He nodded. "I did."

"Those are from my shop." I held up my hand

before he could ask the expected question. "No, I don't know how they might have gotten there, but they made me think of Pike."

"The kid doing sound for the show?"

I nodded. "He was eating those wrapped melt-aways by the handful in the shop yesterday after Eric first arrived. He said peppermint was his favorite candy, and *Maami* gave him a bag."

Aiden made another note and then asked, "Why did you agree to meet with Rocky about the show? Before you left the square yesterday, you said you weren't interested."

I adjusted my gloves on my hands to give myself time to think of the right answer. "I wasn't interested in the rekindled romance angle with Eric." I felt my cheeks grow hot. "But I can't deny that being part of Eric's show on Gourmet Television would be good for my family's business. When Rocky asked me to meet her this morning, she also mentioned that she would remove the romance piece." I watched the Amish men again. The tent was up, and now they were hanging white Christmas lights around the entrance. I wondered if I would ever look at Christmas lights the same way again after seeing how they had taken Rocky's life. I shook my head and corrected myself. The lights hadn't taken Rocky's life, the person who'd used them as a deadly weapon had.

Aiden raised his eyebrows. "And you believed her?"

"I was willing to hear her out. But ultimately I planned to tell her it wasn't my call. My grandmother said that she would have to get permission from her district elders to do the show. You know being on television isn't very Amish. As of yet, we don't know what their decision might be."

"I don't think I would have been so trusting of Rocky or Eric. They were going to do what was best for the show and ratings." He shook his head. "I know Eric was determined to have you play that part. He never would have gone along with your not participating. He's here to film his Christmas special, but he's here to win you back, too," Aiden said in a low voice.

I snorted. "You're crazy."

Aiden shook his head again and closed his small notebook, then tucked it back inside his coat. "Just keep this in mind, Bailey. A man doesn't travel hundreds of miles during the holidays to work with his ex-girlfriend. At least, no man that I know of."

"You don't know Eric," I said.

"I know his type." Aiden removed his department issue ball cap from the back pocket of his uniform and bent the bill a few times, but he didn't put it on his head. It might keep the top of his head warm, but it would do nothing for his ears, which were bright red from the cold. "What about a fit of rage or an accident? Could either of those have ended in your ex-boyfriend's committing murder?"

"I suppose anything is possible," I said. "Eric can get angry. I've seen him yell at his sous chefs more times than I can count—a lot of kitchens are like that. Most chefs see their staff as family, so it isn't done with malice, although there does tend to be screaming. Rocky told me that's why they were filming the Christmas special here. The network was trying to give him a softer image. Apparently, being a volatile chef is no longer so appealing to their viewing audience. But I never heard him threaten anyone with bodily harm. As for an accident, there is always a chance for an accident, but wrapping an electric cord around a woman's throat twice doesn't seem very accidental to me."

"Nor does it to me." Aiden stood up and then held out his hand to help me to my feet.

After a brief moment of indecision, I gave him my hand and let him pull me up. He squeezed my fingers tight before letting go.

Chapter 7

Aiden and I returned to where Deputy Little and Eric waited. Eric waved his arms in the air. "It's about time. While the two of you were over there making moon eyes at each other, I have been freezing to death."

Seeing as how we were on the opposite side of the gazebo, seated, and masked by snow-covered shrubs, I doubted Eric had seen much of anything.

Aiden scowled. "Have you called your attorney?"

Eric scowled in return. "I have. He's on his way to the airport. Should be here in three hours."

"You must be an important client for him to drop everything and fly to Ohio."

"It doesn't matter if I am important or not," Eric said. "I'm rich, so when I call, my attorney comes running."

I pressed my lips together to hold back a smart remark that was on the tip on my tongue.

"You aren't under arrest," Aiden said. "I would just like an account of how you found the body."

"I'm not saying a word about it until my attorney

arrives." Eric was defiant. Part of me wanted to whisper to him that he wasn't doing himself any favors by being so difficult.

Aiden was looking as if he wanted to argue with Eric when a large, white SUV screeched to a halt by the green, blocking in the coroner's car. The driver of the SUV flung open the door, banging it against the other car in the process. I winced.

The driver, a round man with a black mustache, did not seem to notice. "What is going on here?" he bellowed. "Where's Rocky? I knew this was going to be a disaster. I told the network that we should film the entire Christmas special in New York on the set, but did Rocky listen to me? No, of course she didn't. She never listens!" His face was bright red by this point, a shade that only darkened as he slammed his car door.

Cameraman Roden got out of the passenger side of the car, much more slowly. He hung his camera bag over his left shoulder. There was no one else in the car. It made me wonder where the sound guy Pike was. Wouldn't they need both of them if they planned to do some filming this morning on the square, assuming that was the reason they were there?

Aiden and I shared a look. If there were a comic book bubble over Aiden's head in that moment it would have said, "Suspect!" I couldn't agree more.

Aiden approached the men, and I followed him. He didn't even bother to tell me not to. He was a smart man. Maybe he knew it was pointless.

"Can I help you?" Aiden asked.

The mustached man rounded on the deputy. "Who are you? Where's Rocky?"

Aiden hooked his thumbs through his duty belt. "I'm Sheriff Deputy Aiden Brody. Who are you? I don't think we have had the pleasure of meeting."

The other man swore. "There is no pleasure in meeting me or in me being in this godforsaken place. I'm looking for Rocky Rivers."

Aiden's brow went up. "You know Rocky."

"Yes," the man snapped. "I know Rocky. I'm her producer, Linc Baggins. I'm her producer, although it should be the other way around. I should be the executive producer on this project. Everyone knows that. She stole—"

"Baggins? Like the hobbit?" Little injected.

Linc glared at him, but I couldn't blame Little for asking the question. I had made the same connection, and it seemed apt because Linc was a short, thick, hairy man. Little's question made perfect sense.

"Where's Rocky?" Linc asked.

"I have something to tell you," Aiden said.

Linc wasn't listening as he looked around. "What's going on here?" he demanded. "This place is crawling with police. Why is that? Don't tell me we're being evicted from the square. Rocky told me that she had taken care of all the necessary permits. If she didn't, it just proves to me once again that that woman is a liar at the core." He took a breath.

"Mr. Baggins," Aiden said quickly before Linc could start up again.

Linc rounded on him. "What?"

"There's something I have to tell you about Ms. Rivers."

Linc threw up his hands. "She didn't get the permits, did she. I knew this would happen. I told the network this would happen. That's what happens when you give a job to an amateur instead of a seasoned professional like myself. I climbed my way up the ladder the hard way with hard work and sweat—"

"Sir," Aiden interrupted Linc. "There has been an incident."

Linc pulled up short. "What do you mean?"

"I'm sorry to have to tell you this, but Ms. Rivers is dead."

The blood drained from Linc's face, and his complexion took on a gray cast. "Dead? But how is that possible? What happened? Was it a car accident?" He glanced around the square as if looking for the remnants of automobiles.

Aiden shook his head. "No."

Linc covered his mouth and shook his head back and forth. "No, no, that's not possible."

"Are you all right?" I asked. I knew it was a stupid question. Clearly, the man wasn't all right, but I didn't know what else to say or do. "Is there someone we can call for you?"

Linc looked in my direction with wild eyes as if he were seeing me for the first time. Maybe he was.

"Dead?" Linc repeated. "How could she be dead? She was the healthiest woman I knew. She ran the New York City Marathon, for God's sake. There is no way she is dead. People like her don't just drop dead. It doesn't happen."

Aiden studied the short, sweaty man. "She didn't just drop dead. We believe she was murdered."

When Aiden said that, Linc fell like a freshly cut Christmas tree into a dead faint.

Eric stared down at the prostrate man on the

frozen grass. "Maybe we should leave him there for a bit. It's the most peaceful I've ever seen him. And he is always sweating—disgusting trait—maybe the frozen ground will cool him off a bit."

"We can't leave the poor guy lying on the cold ground," I said.

"He will come to eventually," Eric said. "It's not as if he dropped dead."

I resisted the temptation to smack Eric. By the twitch of Aiden's jaw, it seemed to me that Aiden was resisting the same temptation.

At moments like this—*okay*, at most moments with Eric—I was the one in need of a smack upside the head. Really, what *had* I been thinking? Oh, Eric's looks were as tempting as chocolate peanut butter fudge, which I had a weakness for. But once you looked past his appearance and charm . . .

Aiden waved at an EMT who was jogging by in the direction of the van. "A little help here, please?"

The EMT amended his course and jogged to where we were standing over prostrate Linc. "What happened?"

"He had a shock and fainted," Aiden said.

The EMT nodded as if that was a completely normal and acceptable way to react when a person receives a shock. I wasn't so sure. I had fainted only once in my life, and it had been back at JP Chocolates. Cass had been cutting lemons and nearly sliced the tip of her index finger off. There had been blood everywhere. All over both of us, the counter, and the floor. It had been amazing that a person as small as Cass could make so much blood.

The EMT squatted next to Linc. "What's his name?"

"Linc Baggins," Aiden said.

"Baggins? Like the hobbit?" the EMT asked in disbelief.

"Don't say that to him. He looks too hobbit-like in real life not to take offense," Eric said. "And I wouldn't bring up second breakfast either. You know, to be safe."

Aiden looked heavenward.

The EMT checked Linc's pulse and lightly patted him on the shoulder. "Mr. Baggins? Mr. Baggins?"

"Do you have smelling salts in the ambulance?" Eric asked.

"Eric," I hissed.

He sidled over to me and whispered, "I wonder if he's going to wake up and mutter about the One Ring."

I elbowed Eric in the ribs.

"Ow." He rubbed his side.

Aiden shot us both a look, and I felt my face grow hot. How was it that Eric could bring out the inner twelve-year-old in me, and in front of Aiden, no less?

Chapter 8

"Mr. Baggins?" the EMT said again.

Linc moaned and slowly opened his eyes. "What happened?"

"You fainted," the EMT said. "Does anything hurt? You hit the ground pretty hard." The EMT helped Linc into a sitting position.

Linc rubbed his forehead. "I think I'm all right. I've never done that before. It was so strange. I had a terrible dream. I thought someone told me that Rocky was dead, but that just can't be possible."

"I'm afraid to tell you, Mr. Baggins, but Rocky *is* dead," Aiden said.

"Oh," Linc moaned and looked as if he was ready to fall over again.

"Easy there." The EMT supported him under his arm.

"I'm going to need to question him before you take him in," Aiden said.

The EMT nodded. "It would be best if we did

that over by the ambulance, where oxygen is readily available."

Aiden nodded. He and the nameless EMT helped Linc to his feet, and when it looked as if Linc might tip over, they each put one of his arms over their shoulders and walked him in the direction of the ambulance.

"It's bad enough that he looks like a hobbit, but to have to share a name with one . . ." Eric shook his head.

I ignored him and turned to Roden, who had been standing off to the side throughout all the excitement of Mr. Baggins's faint. "Roden, when was the last time you saw Rocky?"

He frowned. "Last night at the guest house where we all are staying." He shot a look at Eric, and I couldn't help but wonder what that might mean.

"When was that?"

He played with the flap of his camera bag by opening and closing a small Velcro pocket on the front of it. The repetitive sound was grating, not quite as bad as fingernails on a chalkboard but a close second. "Sometime between seven and eight, I would guess." He shot another look in Eric's direction.

He removed an SLR camera from the case. "Mind if I get some stills of your shop?" he asked. "For PR purposes for the show."

I winced. I still hadn't heard from my grandmother about whether we could be part of the show, but there was nothing that I could do to stop Roden

from taking pictures of my shop. The photos were of
the outside after all.

I shrugged and watched as he changed the lens
on his camera and approached Swissmen Sweets as
if stalking a lion on the Serengeti.

The façade was very pretty, and I could see why he
would want stills of it. Swissmen Sweets looked like
the perfect little shop in the snow. The two large
windows on either side of the door were full of glass
jars of candies and boxes of fudge. Evergreens and
red ribbon wove around the displays for a little
Christmas cheer but not too much Christmas cheer.
As in all things, the Amish approached Christmas in
a plain way. They celebrated Christmas because of
the birth of Christ, but their gifts and decorations
were very minimal. Most Amish, including my grandmother, didn't even put up a Christmas tree in their
homes. However, this year, *Maami* was relenting
because I wanted one so badly. It just didn't feel like
Christmas to me without a tree.

I was sorely tempted to flee to the safety of my
cozy shop and away from the mess that Rocky's
untimely death had created. I would much rather
be making candy-cane peppermint fudge for the
Christmas Market than dealing with another murder
in Harvest.

Eric stood next to me. "Admiring your shop? It
would be great on television."

I glanced at him. "Do you ever stop thinking
about work, Eric? Your executive producer is dead,
and you might be in some serious trouble because of

it. Even so, it seems to me all you can think about is the next move in your career."

Eric's face clouded over for a moment. "I have to think about myself and my career. No one is going to do it for me. If I don't fight for the spot I earned, I will lose it. It's hard to claw your way to the top. It's even harder to stay on top." He swallowed. "That's something Rocky taught me. I know she wanted me to do the special with you to soften my image. The audience has tired of the angry chef persona. It seems nice guys like your Aiden are in, and guys like me are out."

I blinked at him. It was the most honest Eric Sharp had been with me in all the time I had known him. "I thought you said this was your idea."

"Seeing you again was my idea, not necessarily my image reboot." He scowled, and the vulnerability I'd seen on his face a moment ago cleared. "I know that deputy of yours thinks I killed Rocky. I can tell by the look on his face."

"You said you don't have a motive. You said that, in fact, Rocky's death makes things more difficult for you where the network is concerned. I told him that."

Eric looked at his shoes, reminding me of a grade schooler caught cheating on a math test.

I studied him. "You don't have a motive, do you, Eric?"

He looked up at me. "Linc is the one with the motive. The deputy should concentrate on that man as the prime suspect. He hated Rocky and was jealous of all her success."

I glanced back to where Aiden and Linc were in

the middle of what appeared to be a heated discussion. What I wouldn't give to be over there to hear what Linc had to say! "Why is that? Because he wasn't the executive producer on your project?"

Eric blinked at me. "How do you know that? Do you have some sort of information superpower?"

I shook my head. "Linc said something a little while ago that made me think so."

Eric shook his head as if in wonder. "I don't know how you do it, Bai, I really don't."

"Is there anyone else who might have wanted to hurt her?"

Again, he wouldn't look at me. "No."

I knew he was lying, just as I'd known he was lying when we were together and I asked him if he was seeing anyone else. He told me "no" then too, but I knew it was a lie. I just wanted to believe the lie. That's why I stayed with him as long as I did. Now I couldn't believe how stupid I had been. My face flushed with embarrassment just thinking about it.

Across the green, Linc threw up his hands and stomped away from Aiden, making a beeline for Eric. "You!" He pointed a finger at the pastry chef.

I hopped out of the way. It wasn't my job to protect Eric. He was a big boy.

Linc's finger shook. "This is all your fault, Sharp. If you hadn't told Rocky about this place, she would have never gotten the harebrained idea to film here and she would still be alive."

Eric glowered at the other man. "Calm down, Lincoln, or you might have a stroke."

Linc wiped a gloved hand across his damp brow. "How can I calm down? You know the tight schedule we're on. We only have three days to shoot all the footage we need in order to edit and package it to air on time. Do you even understand the kind of pressure we're all under? And now that Rocky is dead, the show might be cut entirely. How am I supposed to tell administration that our executive producer was killed in Amish Country, of all places? I suppose a pretty boy like you doesn't understand that kind of stress. You don't understand hard work."

My eyebrows went up at that comment. Eric had many faults, but his work ethic wasn't among them.

"I'm sure Eric understands the pressures you are under, but let's not forget a woman has died," I said.

Out of the corner of my eye, I saw Eric smile. I should have kept my big mouth shut. I'd only spoken to correct Linc's incorrect assumption about Eric. I can't help myself. I will always go to someone's defense when they've been wronged, even Eric Sharp's defense, apparently.

"Who are you?" Linc's face was bright red.

I backed away at his gruff tone.

Before I could answer, Eric spoke up. "Linc, this is Bailey King. I thought you would have recognized her from one of the photographs you've seen. She's the reason we're here. Not me, not Rocky, it's Bailey."

Linc sucked in a mouthful of air. "I'm so sorry. We're very happy that you have come on board to be part of this project," he said, tripping over his words to make amends with me. Under different circumstances, I might have found that amusing.

"I took a peek in the window of your shop yesterday evening after you had already closed," Linc went on. "If you had been open, I would have stopped in and introduced myself personally then. It looks like such a charming place, and I just know it will be the perfect setting for part of our shoot."

"My shop is charming, but—"

He adjusted the collar of his coat. "Good, good," Linc said. "At least something is going right today. We can start the shoot in your shop since activity on the square might not be appropriate to film until all the police vacate the area."

"I'm not—"

Eric interrupted me. "Bailey is happy to help, but I don't think we will be doing any filming today."

"No filming today?" Linc asked. "Are you insane? We only have three days to get this shoot done. We can't lose an entire day."

"Linc, Rocky is dead," Eric said. "Do you really think we can go on like nothing has happened? Someone has to talk to the network."

Linc turned slightly green. "I know that." He ground his teeth. "And it's your fault she's dead."

Eric rose to his full height, which was several inches above the squat television producer. "I'm not the one who wanted her job."

Linc glared at him. "I wasn't the one who was dating her."

I gasped. He was dating Rocky? This had to be the motive he had been avoiding telling me. If it had been a romance gone bad, that would be more than enough reason for him to strangle her. People have killed for less.

"Bailey," Eric said. "Don't look at me like that."

Look at him like what? I wondered. I felt my face was completely blank despite this latest revelation.

Aiden joined us then. "Mr. Baggins, I would appreciate it if you would return to the ambulance so that the EMTs can check you out further."

"I'm fine," Linc protested.

"I'm sure you are, but you still need to be checked out by the EMTs."

Linc finally relented and stomped to the ambulance bay, where an EMT strapped a blood pressure cuff onto his arm.

Aiden pulled me aside. "Bailey, go home. If I have any more questions for you, I know where to find you."

"What about the Christmas Market and the live nativity? Will those events go on as planned with . . ." I trailed off.

Aiden sighed. "They will. That's what the sheriff stopped by to tell me. He said in no uncertain terms that the events will go on as planned. That's why we have to work so fast to gather evidence. I was, thankfully, able to convince him to close the gazebo for the day, but no longer than that." He pressed his lips together, clearly not happy with the sheriff's decision. "Now, please go home so I can finish up here before the market opens."

"But—" I started to protest.

"Please. I'll talk to you later."

I looked from Eric to the gazebo, where Rocky's body remained. There was no way the police were going to let me inside the gazebo again even if I wanted to go, which I didn't. Seeing Rocky's dead body once was more than enough for me.

"I'll stop by the candy shop later to check in with you," Aiden said.

I looked up at him. "You promise?"

Aiden smiled. "Have I ever broken a promise to you before?"

I thought about that for a moment. "I don't think you have made a promise to me yet."

"Yet is the most important word in that sentence," he replied.

Chapter 9

I stumbled across the street to Swissmen Sweets. I was bone-tired. It was a phrase that my *daadi* used to say when he was exhausted. That was how I felt, as if I was so tired my bones seemed to have turned to licorice and could no longer hold me up. I had been awake for only a few hours, but it seemed like forty-eight at least, so much had happened in such a short period of time.

I couldn't get out of my head what Linc had said about Eric dating Rocky. I knew I should have questioned him more about it, but I was just too shocked. I knew it wasn't because I still had feelings for Eric; seeing him again had proved to me that I didn't.

I just was so surprised that he would date someone who was essentially his boss. It was such a risk to his career. Eric was a ladies' man, and I should have suspected a romance gone wrong. Was I really one to talk? I had dated Eric when he was on the selection committee for Jean Pierre's replacement at JP Chocolates. I shuddered at the thought. Not one of my proudest moments, but I'd been guilt-ridden over it and I'd certainly resisted Eric for a very long time before we commenced dating. *And* I could say that we had begun dating long before his involvement in the selection committee. Technicalities, perhaps, but I was going to cling to them, with both hands.

It was still before ten in the morning, so Swissmen Sweets wasn't open yet. I put my key in the lock as a voice said, "In trouble again, are you?"

I looked to my right and found Abel Esh leaning against the outer wall of Esh Family Pretzels smoking a pipe. I should have known it would be Abel. The scent of the sweet tobacco turned my stomach, and I moved so that I was upwind of the smoke.

I turned the key in the lock, but I didn't push the door open just yet. Something compelled me to stay and listen to whatever it was Abel had to say even though I knew it wouldn't be pleasant or complimentary. "What is it, Abel?"

He chewed on the end of his pipe. "You aren't being very neighborly with that attitude, Bailey King."

I cocked my head. I was tired, cold, sad, and in no mood for any of Abel's games. "I can't remember a time when you have ever been neighborly, Abel, so I don't see why I should be neighborly back."

"That's not very Amish of you." The pipe moved to the other side of his mouth as he spoke.

I looked down at my puffy winter coat and dark jeans and boots. "I'm not Amish."

He didn't say anything in reply.

I shrugged. "If that's all . . ."

Abel removed the pipe from his mouth and looked at it. "Another *Englischer* in Harvest has died because of you. You're building quite the reputation for that."

I stepped toward my shop.

He shook the pipe out on the sidewalk. Ashes fell to the ground like snowflakes. He pushed off the wall. There was less than a foot of space between me and the front door to Swissmen Sweets, and Abel moved into it, forcing me to step back and blocking my access to my own shop.

I folded my arms. "Can I help you with anything, Abel? If not, I suggest you get out of my way."

"I thought you would want to talk to me." He smiled.

"You thought wrong." I started to move around him toward the door.

He stepped aside. "Very well. I won't tell you what I saw on the square last night since it's not important to you."

I froze. After a beat, I looked at him. "You were here last night? Not at your farm?"

He smiled as if he knew he had caught me. We both knew he had. There were very few things that could have gotten me to turn around and speak to Abel, but the possibility that he might have witnessed activity on the green related to the murder was one.

He nodded his head. "There were a lot of comings and goings around the square last night."

"Who did you see?" I asked.

"Wouldn't you like to know?" He smiled again.

This was pointless. Able was treating our conversation like a game, a game that I wasn't interested in playing. "If you aren't going to tell me, why bother stopping me like this?"

He smiled.

I crossed my arms. "You can tell me, or you can tell Deputy Brody."

He scowled. "I'm not talking to your *Englisch* boyfriend."

My face reddened. "The deputy is not my boyfriend." I felt like a fifth-grade girl denying her crush.

"There is a rumor in the village that the two of you are getting married." He spat out the words as if he didn't like the taste of them.

I snorted. "You shouldn't believe everything you hear." I had the uncomfortable knowledge that the rumor had most likely been started by Aiden's own mother.

"I could give you the same advice."

"So I shouldn't believe what you are about to tell me. Then there's really no reason I should be talking to you right now." I took another step toward my door.

He frowned. "I was working late at the pretzel shop," he said, speaking quickly now. "One of the ovens broke, and I promised Esther that I would fix it a week ago. She had been barking at me about it for days, so I finally made the time."

I bit my tongue to stop myself from saying that Abel should do more to help his two sisters at the pretzel shop. I really didn't know what he did for work other than odd jobs around the village. The three siblings had inherited the shop from their parents years ago, but from where I stood, it looked like Esther and Emily did all the work to keep the family business afloat and Abel showed up only when it suited him.

I swallowed. "Who did you see on the square?"

"The red-haired woman. The one they are saying died. She was moving around the square a lot. There were a couple young *Englischers* there too, but it was clear that she was in charge."

"How many were there? Can you describe them?"

He exhaled into the cold air. Thankfully, I was still upwind and couldn't smell his breath. I willed myself not to wave the cloud away. He wanted a reaction from me, and I wasn't going to give it to him.

"It was really too dark," he said. "And by the way they were dressed, it was hard to tell if they were men or women."

He looked me up and down. I was wearing jeans, a green puffy coat, a turquoise scarf, and matching gloves.

"See, they were dressed like you. No one would know you were a woman from far away."

I frowned, but again I didn't say anything. Abel was just trying to get a rise out of me, as my *daadi* would have said. I wouldn't give him the satisfaction.

When I didn't take the bait, he said, "In any case, they were still there when I left our shop at nine. By the looks of it, I think they were going to be there for a while after that. I didn't stick around to watch. I have no interest in the comings and goings of *Englischers*."

That was an interesting thing for him to say since he had given me an almost full spy report on them.

"Everyone you saw coming and going on the square was English? You didn't see any Amish? Weren't there Amish getting ready for the Christmas Market?"

"It was far too late for any Amish to be out." He

said this as if even the suggestion was an insult. "Now, you tell all that to your boyfriend, and make it clear I have no interest in talking to him about it. I have no use for the police." He stepped away from me in the direction of the pretzel shop, giving me free access to my front door.

I told him that I would tell Aiden, but I knew it wouldn't do any good. Aiden was a thorough cop, and he would want to interview Abel himself.

I thanked Abel, but before I turned away I saw the curtain move inside the pretzel shop and caught a glimpse of Emily's heart-shaped face. She was frowning. My heart constricted when I saw her. Emily's face disappeared, and the curtain in the pretzel shop window fell back into place.

Abel looked behind him and then back at me. He smiled. "Emily is no longer a member of your fan club. You can't charm everyone in this village. The sooner you learn that, the better."

I turned away from him and stepped through the front door to Swissmen Sweets without a backward glance.

Nutmeg met me at the door. He meowed, demanding attention and possibly complaining because I hadn't let him out to run to Emily. I picked up the cat, and some of the guilt I felt over the situation with Emily dissipated. Emily had been the one to give me Nutmeg, or, more accurately, to beg me to take the kitten when her brother said she had to get rid of him. I would think of a way to help the girl. I'd make it up to her somehow. I set the cat back on the hardwood floor.

I removed my gloves and clenched and unclenched

my hands. Even with my gloves, my hands were cold from standing outside in the chilly air for the past couple of hours. Nutmeg rubbed at my ankles. I bent down and picked up the purring animal a second time. I buried my freezing fingers deep into his warm fur. The cat looked up at me and licked the tip of my nose. He always seemed to know how to make me feel better.

Maami and Charlotte came through the swinging door that led to the shop's industrial kitchen. My grandmother had flour on her apron, and Charlotte had a smear of chocolate on her prayer cap. It was a sure sign that the two of them had been working in the kitchen the entire time I was gone. Through the picture window, we had a clear view of everything that was happening on the square.

"Bailey, what is going on? We came out to fill the display case with trays of candies just a little bit ago and saw that the square is crawling with police," *Maami* said breathlessly.

I started flipping over the chairs in the front of the shop so that people could sit down and enjoy one of our sweet treats if they chose to. In winter, business was slower, but it picked up the closer we got to Christmas, or at least that's what my grandmother told me. It was my first Christmas at Swissmen Sweets. As of yet, I had not seen a large increase in business.

I put the last chair on the floor and told them what had happened.

Charlotte stared out the window. "That pretty woman is dead. She was so—" She searched for the word. "So lively. She looked like she was invincible to me. Like she could do anything. Like women in the movies."

Maami gave Charlotte a look. Although Charlotte had left her strict Amish district to be a part of *Maami's* New Order Amish one, watching movies was still frowned upon. However, even though she was twenty-one, Charlotte still hadn't been baptized in the church. She'd left her district for the love of the organ, which she played beautifully. Her old district would not let her play the musical instrument. *Maami's* district did not care about that, but as of yet, Charlotte had not made the full commitment to Amish life by being baptized, and as long as she remained unbaptized, she was in *rumspringa*, which meant she could do things like watch movies without getting into too much trouble. We all knew that there was a time coming soon when Charlotte would have to decide whether she wanted to be fully Amish or fully English. The Amish did not look kindly upon anyone who straddled the fence for too long.

"No one is invincible," *Maami* said. "Only the good Lord." She turned to me. "Does this mean these TV people will leave and go back to wherever they came from? I'm sure there are many Amish in the village who would be relieved if they did."

I winced. "Have you heard from the bishop or Deacon Yoder about Swissmen Sweets being part of the show?"

Maami sighed. "The deacon's wife, Ruth, telephoned and said she would be over before the Christmas Market. She will tell me the district's decision then. As you know, both the bishop and deacon are quite elderly. They no longer like to drive their buggies if there is a chance of snow."

The snow was falling steadily outside, so there was clearly far more than just a chance.

"Why didn't Ruth just tell you on the telephone, then? Does she really want to come to the village in this weather?"

Maami smiled. "*Nee*, she'd much rather make a huge production out of it and hold us in suspense. Even if that means driving her husband's buggy through the snow."

I shook my head. I knew that we hadn't gotten the official word just yet, but I would be shocked if the district elders agreed to the filming. It would be such a missed opportunity for the shop. I bit my tongue. I didn't want to say this to my grandmother. This was her shop and should be run the way she saw fit even if I didn't agree. Besides, I really didn't know how the TV special could go on after what had happened to Rocky. I felt sick. How could I be so callous and worry about a missed opportunity when a woman was dead? Perhaps I was more like Eric than I was willing to admit.

"Maybe Ruth will surprise us and say it's all right. I don't think the show was going to focus on the Amish much. Other than being taped here and including Amish recipes. In any case, I don't think the show will be able to go forward. They can't film here under the circumstances. I doubt the network would like the bad press."

"I am sorry that the woman was killed; that is truly awful, and I will pray for her family," *Maami* said. "But I sensed that there would be trouble from this.

There would be many Amish in Harvest that would like the television filming never to start."

Maami had just given me the idea that perhaps the murder hadn't been committed by someone from the production crew as I'd first suspected. It was very possible it had been committed by someone right here in Harvest, someone who would do whatever it took to shut down the production of a television show that might disparage the Amish community in the village. I found that prospect much more chilling.

Chapter 10

I tried the best I could to put the murder out of my mind as Charlotte and I made final preparations for the Christmas Market. We had made every peppermint treat we could think of. In addition to the peppermint bark, we had peppermint sticks, peppermint ribbon candy, peppermint patties, peppermint fudge, peppermint taffy, and a few others. It was literally a sea of peppermint in front of us on the counter as we packed everything up for the market.

"What if someone doesn't like peppermint?" Charlotte asked.

"Hold your tongue!" I said

She held a handful of candy canes suspended in the air. "I . . . I didn't mean anything by it."

I laughed. "I'm only teasing, and you make a good point. We can't assume that everyone coming to the Christmas Market likes peppermint. Let's put some plain chocolate and fudge in the cart too, just in case."

She laughed. "You got it, and you really scared me

for a second. Sometimes, I just don't get your *Englischer* sense of humor."

I smiled as I affixed a red bow to the top of a white bakery box of peppermint fudge. I had a feeling that after the Christmas Market ended, it would be a very long time before I touched peppermint again. The scent of it lingered in every corner of the shop.

Maami poked her head into the back room. "You girls are having far too much fun back here." She smiled. "The shop is picking up. I could use some help out front."

I added the last bow to the fudge boxes. "We are all set here. There is nothing more that we can do until we are able to go to the square and set up in an hour."

Maami nodded and ducked back into the main part of the shop.

Charlotte placed boxes of peppermint candies on the rolling cart that we used for market days. "I thought maybe we would have heard something more about the woman in the gazebo before the Christmas Market opened."

I tied an apron around my waist before I went out into the main part of the shop. "I don't think Margot Rawlings would let anything get in the way of the market. She's worked too hard." I paused. "I still think it's odd that I didn't see her this morning when the police were at the square. Juliet said she was working on a secret project, but that was yesterday."

Business was brisk that morning. All three café tables were full, and even more customers stood along the windows, staring out across the street into the square. Nutmeg held court in front of the shop accepting all the compliments and head scratches he could get. He also kept a close eye on the door, watching to see when he could make a break for it. I, in turn, was keeping a close eye on the wily kitten.

Part of me thought the shop might be so busy because of the Christmas Market that was to open in an hour, but the cynical part of me thought Swissmen Sweets had the best view of the gazebo where Rocky had died. Most of the talk in the shop that morning had been about the poor English woman who was murdered. Usually, these comments were whispered with furtive glances in my direction. I didn't know if the villagers knew of my connection to the deceased woman or if they just assumed a connection because of my unfortunate ability to find dead bodies in the past.

I did my best to ignore the whispers and looks. I wrapped in parchment paper the piece of mint chocolate chip fudge that a middle-aged woman had ordered and carefully tucked it in a white candy box.

The woman handed me her credit card, and as I put the card into the reader, I could feel eyes watching me. I handed the woman her card back and found Eric watching me from the front door. I looked away, and the customer thanked me as she accepted her fudge and receipt.

An Amish man who was a regular customer and next in line started to take a step forward in order to speak to me, but Eric cut in front of him.

I frowned at Eric. "I'm sorry. You can't cut in line. The man behind you has been waiting for several minutes, and there are others behind him, too, who have been waiting."

"I need to talk to you now," Eric said.

I shook my head. "That's not how it works."

"It's how it works today." His eyes pleaded with me. "Please, Bai, I have to talk to you."

The Amish man frowned but stepped back. It wasn't the Amish way to argue over who was really next in line. I gave the man an apologetic look. "Charlotte or my grandmother will be with you shortly. I'm so very sorry."

He nodded, and his long Amish beard dipped farther down the front of his black wool coat.

I walked to the end of the counter. "Eric, I'm working. Now is not a good time."

"I know that, but your grandmother and that girl," he said, referring to Charlotte, "can handle it. I need your help much more than they do."

"I—"

"Bai, please." He stared at me with those big blue eyes lined with dark blond lashes. The eyes that used to make my heart melt.

"Fine. We can talk in the kitchen." I knew if I didn't give in and talk to Eric now, he would be in my shop disturbing customers all day. I couldn't have that. I untied my apron and hung it on a hook behind the counter. I lifted the piece of wood that divided the front of the shop from the back counter and let Eric through before I replaced it. As I led Eric to the kitchen, my grandmother caught my eye and raised her brow. "I'll be back in a minute," I promised, hoping I was telling her the truth.

When we were in the kitchen, Eric looked around.

"Wow, I haven't seen mixers this old since I was fresh out of culinary school and interning at an Italian bakery in the Bronx."

"They still work great," I said defensively. "We might not have everything top of the line, but what we have does a good job."

He held up his hands. "I'm not knocking it. Mixers like that are workhorses. They're hard to find nowadays. What they make now doesn't last nearly as long. I wish I had one."

"Oh," I said, feeling a blush creep up the sides of my face. "I'm sorry for snapping."

"You shouldn't take everything I say as a negative, Bai. I hope that you can put our past behind you now, because I need your help. I just left the sheriff's department."

"Your attorney made it?" I asked.

He nodded. "He's checking into a hotel right now. I'm supposed to meet him there in an hour so we can plan a strategy."

"A strategy for what?" I braced my hands on the island in the middle of the kitchen.

Eric perched on one of the backless stools in the room. "The sheriff thinks I killed Rocky, and he is determined to make any arrest stick."

I wasn't surprised to hear that Sheriff Marshall thought Eric was behind Rocky's death. It would be so less messy for him if someone outside the county was responsible for the murder. The last thing the sheriff wanted was a mess on his hands.

Sheriff Marshall ruled the county with an iron fist and wasn't the kindest of men. He looked down on the Amish in the county and was generally disliked by almost everyone who lived there, both Amish and English. However, he'd just won his fifth consecutive election in November because for a fourth time he'd run uncontested. It seemed no one wanted to go up against the incumbent sheriff. I had thought for a brief moment that Aiden would challenge him. Aiden had spent most of his life in Holmes County, was a seasoned deputy, and was well liked by both the Amish and English, but in the end he'd refused to run. He told me that in law enforcement it was frowned upon to run against your boss, even if your boss was a terrible official. It probably wasn't a smart idea either, because Aiden and Sheriff Marshall's relationship was tenuous at best. If Aiden ran and lost, I could only imagine what the sheriff might do to Aiden to retaliate.

If the sheriff thought that Eric was behind Rocky's murder, the pastry chef really was in trouble, and if Aiden agreed with the sheriff, I thought Eric didn't stand much chance of getting out of that trouble. However, I knew that Aiden wouldn't come to a final conclusion until he investigated all possibilities, despite the fact that he'd disliked Eric on sight.

"Is it because you dated Rocky?" I asked.

"You heard that?"

"How could I miss it? Linc yelled it at the top of his lungs." I walked to the other side of the island, putting it between us.

"That annoying little hobbit," Eric muttered.

I gave him a look.

"He's been terrible to work with the entire time. I don't even know why he's here. Rocky was more than capable of handling everything. Rocky was . . ." He trailed off.

I stared at Eric. Was he about to cry? Did he really care about Rocky? This was quite a revelation if it was true, and my heart softened toward Eric just a little. If he'd lost someone he cared about, he deserved my sympathy, no matter what our past might have been.

He swallowed and walked over to my spice shelf. He ran his finger along the containers of spices. "Will you help me, Bai?"

"I think you need to be honest with me before I can make up my mind about that. If you have or had a relationship with Rocky, you have a motive, and Aiden will definitely follow up. It's best to be honest."

"Oh, I know Aiden is Mr. Perfect. You don't have tell me that." He curled his lip in disgust.

I scowled. "You're not helping your case by keeping information from me. I don't know how I can help you anyway."

He dropped his hand from the spice shelf. "You can help me because you have an in with Mr. Perfect. You can whisper into his ear. I know he listens to you."

I folded my arms. "This conversation is going nowhere. I don't know why I let you come back here in the first place."

I walked toward the swinging door and was about to push it open when he said, "Bailey, wait, I'm sorry." His shoulders sagged. "I know that acting like this isn't helping my situation. You probably think that being a suspect in this murder doesn't bother me, but it does. Bailey, I'm scared, and you are the only one who can help me. I don't have anyone else here."

"You have your attorney."

He shook his head. "His advice is for me to go back to the guest house where I'm staying and keep my head down. I can't do that, Bailey. Don't you see? The sheriff has made up his mind. I have to prove him wrong, or I might be stuck in Ohio forever."

It was truly terrifying to think that Eric might never leave Ohio. Although his never leaving Ohio State Penitentiary was certainly an even more terrifying thought! The sooner he went back to New York, the sooner I could get on with my real life. Without him. "Then start talking. How did your relationship with Rocky start?"

He sighed. "You know the network was finalizing the plans for my show just about the time you and I broke up."

I nodded for him to continue. I had no interest in going back down our personal memory lane.

"I met Rocky a year before that at a city pastry show. She was walking around the arena, and she approached me. I had just torn the head off of one of my sous chefs for messing up the custard for my tarts."

I winced, thinking of that poor sous chef. I had seen Eric in the kitchen, and he accepted nothing less that absolute perfection from his employees. Anyone who fell short was in for it.

"Rocky approached me then and told me the name of the network she represented. She said they were looking to change their image, and she thought I was the perfect chef to help transform the network."

"Because you screamed at a poor nineteen-year-old kid who made a minor mistake? Lovely." I folded my arms.

"Screwing up the custard is not a minor mistake." Eric looked aghast. "You know that as well as anyone."

"I would never yell at someone the way you do," I said.

He frowned. "I know you wouldn't, and it seems the viewing audience now wants a kinder, more wholesome Eric Sharp, which is what Rocky and I were trying to give them with this special program."

"It's just an act though. You are doing it only for ratings." I found I was disappointed in him when I made that realization.

"I suppose Mr. Perfect would never yell at anyone either." His blue eyes narrowed.

"You're right. Aiden would never treat anyone so poorly."

"Ah, so he *is* Mr. Perfect, at least to you. You're infatuated with him. You were never able to hide your true feelings, Bai, especially not from me."

My face grew hot. "I'm leaving. I have a business to run."

He stepped between the door that led back to the front of the shop and me, and I wondered if I had made a horrible mistake in trusting him one last time.

Chapter 11

"If I start screaming, half the village will come running," I said as evenly as I could. "Besides, I can just go out the back door, which leads into the alley. You can't block both at the same time, and you can't trap me in here until I agree to help you, if that's what you're thinking."

"I know that, but I'm hoping your compassion will prevail and you won't leave. I really do need your help. If you help me, I promise not to make any more comments about super country cop."

I glared at him.

He held up his hands in a Boy Scout salute.

"That is meaningless. You never were a Boy Scout."

"That's where you're wrong. I made it all the way up to Eagle Scout. There is much that you don't know about me, Bailey King."

"I don't doubt that in the least." I sighed and leaned on the island again. "Okay, then tell me more about the motive." I waved at him with my hand, telling him to get on with his story. "You and Rocky dated. Were you still dating when she died?"

He looked down at his shoes. "No. We broke up about a month ago. It was a bad breakup, but we decided to keep it secret from the rest of the production team and the network. We both had too much at stake in my show. I had been waiting for this moment to have the media spotlight, and she had worked her way up in the chain of command within the network. We both had too much to lose. Or at least I thought that was the case until she lost it."

"Lost it how?" I asked.

He frowned as if remembering it was painful. "Last night at the guest house. She yelled and screamed at me."

"Out of the blue? What made her so upset?"

He wouldn't meet my eyes.

I made a move for the back door, which would lead me to the alley and away from Eric.

"Wait!" he cried. "I'll tell you."

I paused at the door. I shouldn't have. What I should have done was leave or, even better, kick Eric out of my shop.

There was no reason for me to help Eric. I didn't need to hear him out. There was no reason for me to help him, other than that I thought he was innocent. I knew he was innocent. The Eric I knew wouldn't do anything that would endanger his career. Even if he wasn't found guilty of the crime, this murder had the potential to ruin his career because Rocky's death would always haunt him. It was something that those in New York would always talk about, and in a city where reputation was everything, Rocky's death could topple Eric's empire. Was I going to stand by and let that happen? Part of me wanted to, part of me knew that he deserved whatever he got, but in the end I asked my question again. "What made her so upset?"

He scrunched up his nose. "Does the reason really matter?"

"If you don't tell me, this conversation is over." I put my hand on the doorknob.

"Okay, okay, don't leave. She lost it because she found out I was dating someone else."

"She had to know that you're a playboy. She shouldn't have been surprised if you were dating someone else after you broke up. Why was this news so earth-shattering to her?"

"Because she found out that I was dating some-one on this production team."

"Who?" But I could guess. There was only one other woman who was part of this production. "Josie." The young girl's pretty face came to my mind. I could see why Eric had been attracted to her. "So, there is a jealous hairstylist girlfriend on the production crew," I said.

He swallowed. "Exactly. I think my girlfriend might have been the one who killed Rocky. She can be volatile."

"In what way?" I asked,

"She's an expressive person. Vibrant. She feels deeply," he said vaguely. "I would never believe that she planned to kill Rocky, but if she got mad enough, yeah, she would do it."

"How long have Josie and Rocky known about each other?" My head was spinning with Eric's romantic entanglements.

"Josie knew about Rocky for a while. She noticed how Rocky and I acted around each other and called me out on it. I think that was what attracted me to her from the start—that she was clever enough to figure that out, because Rocky and I were so careful to keep everything professional. Rocky, however, didn't know that Josie and I were seeing each other until last night. Anyway, Rocky came into the house with a huge chip on her shoulder and yelled at Josie. She told her she was fired, that she could ruin Josie's career."

"Who knows about this fight?"

"Everyone on the production crew. It wasn't like it was done quietly. They were both screaming their heads off."

"So the police already know about it?"

"If they don't, they will as soon as they start interviewing the production crew."

"Why was Rocky so mad at Josie but not at you?"

"She was mad at me, plenty mad, but she needed me for the show. Josie was expendable. Rocky fired her right there for acting in an unprofessional manner and refused to give her a reference for another job. She said that if a future employer called the network, she would ruin Josie's reputation. This was Josie's first professional job, so she really needed a good reference."

"So basically Rocky planned to destroy this girl's professional life for dating you."

"Pretty much." He sighed. "Rocky was an impressive and powerful woman, and she used all of her means to get where she was in her career. She made a lot of sacrifices along the way, as we all have." He gave me a look.

I didn't respond to his comment, but instead I said, "It sounds to me as if Josie is a much better suspect than you are."

"I agree, and I wouldn't be surprised if she did it."

"You'd say that about your own girlfriend? That she was capable of murder?"

He shrugged. "I don't know her that well, and we've only hung out a handful of times."

I scowled at him.

"It's not like I ever thought you were capable of murdering anyone, well, murdering anyone but me. I could see you doing that."

I frowned. "Not a funny joke under the circumstances, Eric."

"Sorry," he muttered. "Will you help me or not? Will you save me from some Podunk prison in the backcountry?"

I sighed. "Did you tell Deputy Brody all this?"

"I would, but I don't think he or the sheriff would pay much attention to me. They still think I am the prime suspect."

"I think you need to give Aiden a little more credit."

"So what do I do now?" he asked.

"You don't do anything. You should follow your attorney's advice and go back to the guest house."

"Please just tell me your answer. Will you help me?"

I sighed because I knew the answer I was going to say all along. It was the answer I was going to give even before he asked, right from the moment I found him in that gazebo standing over Rocky's dead body. I was going to help him—of course I was—and I kicked myself for doing it. "Yes," I said. "I'll help you, but it is as much for Rocky as it is for you. She seemed to be an interesting woman. I wish I had gotten the chance to know her better."

He rushed at me and threw his arms around me. I didn't have time to run away. I didn't even have time to react as he hugged me tight. "Bailey, I always knew—"

The door to the kitchen swung in, and Charlotte froze. "Oh!" She covered her eyes with her hand. "I'm so sorry. Clara just sent me in here to get my peppermint extract for the peppermint rolls." Her face was turning the same shade as her bright red hair. "I'm so sorry to interrupt. I didn't know that you were in here." She stared at the tops of her sneakers.

I pushed Eric away from me. "You weren't interrupting anything, Charlotte."

Charlotte still wouldn't look at me and concentrated on the tops of her black sneakers. I walked over to the shelf where we kept the bottles of extract. I took the peppermint extract bottle off the shelf and handed it to her. "Here."

She took the extract from my hand. *"Danki."* She spun on her heel and disappeared through the door.

After Charlotte left, Eric started to laugh. "Are they

going to kick you out of Amish Country for touching a man?"

"No," I said, already regretting agreeing to help him. "But they might kick you out if you're not careful."

"I wish they would," he said wistfully.

Chapter 12

Through the swinging door that led into the shop I heard excited voices. "Is Bailey here?" a loud, high-pitched southern voice asked.

My mind immediately went into panic mode. The last thing I wanted was for Juliet Brody to find me alone in the kitchen with Eric. Our meeting was completely innocent, but I wasn't sure Juliet would see it that way, seeing as how she had been planning her son Aiden's wedding to me since the moment I set foot in Holmes County. Aiden and I weren't even officially dating, but I still didn't want his mother to overreact to finding me with Eric.

"You have to go," I said in a harsh whisper. I grabbed Eric by the arm and started to pull him in the direction of the back door to the building.

Eric dug his heels into the polished wood floor. "Wait, what? Why are you sending me out the back door like I'm some kind of criminal? I thought you were going to help me."

I tugged on his arm until he started moving

again. "We don't want you to create a scene with the customers. It's just easier if you go out the back."

He stopped again. "Easier for me or easier for you?"

"Easier for both of us. Now go!"

He laughed. "I don't remember your being this bossy when we were together, Bai."

"Maybe Ohio has changed me. Now please leave before she sees you." I pushed him a little harder toward the door.

"She? She who?" He looked around. "We are the only ones in the kitchen. What's going on?"

"I need to talk to Bailey right away. I have a wonderful idea to share with her. Bailey is always willing to listen to my ideas." The kitchen door started to swing inward.

I threw the deadbolt on the back door and opened it. Eric was still standing in the same spot. "Who's at the kitchen door?" he asked.

"No one," I answered in a harsh whisper. "Now you need to go."

The door pushed in farther, and I saw Jethro's snout poke around the bottom corner.

"Juliet," Charlotte's voice interrupted. It sounded a bit closer than Juliet's. "You know that you can't take Jethro into the kitchen. Bailey has told you that a bunch of times."

"Fiddlesticks," the pig owner shot back. "Jethro is nothing to worry about. He is cleaner than most people, and you let the cat in the shop."

"Nutmeg knows he's not allowed in the kitchen," Charlotte said.

"What's going on out there?" Eric asked.

"Is Bailey in the kitchen?" Juliet asked in her singsong voice.

Charlotte was quiet. I knew that she wouldn't lie directly to Juliet's face about where I was. "She's . . . she's occupied."

Juliet laughed. "She's not too occupied to have a visit from Jethro and me, especially when I have such a terrific idea. She is going to absolutely flip over it. I'll only be a minute."

Just as Juliet pushed inward on the kitchen door, I shoved Eric out the back door.

"Hey!" he cried. "You can't—"

I slammed the back door closed and bolted it before he had a chance to get out the rest of his protest. For the briefest moment, I hoped that he hadn't hurt himself as he tripped down the back stoop, but my worry was brief. Juliet stood in the middle of Swissmen Sweets' kitchen with Jethro tucked like a football under her right arm.

"Juliet!" I said as if I was delighted to see her. "What are you doing here?"

She came toward me and gave me a hug, squeezing Jethro between us. The small pig snorted in protest. "It's so nice to see you, sugar. You grow prettier every single day. I was just telling Aiden that when I ran into him by the gazebo. He didn't take much time to stop and talk with his mama. You know that boy works so hard. He will make a fine husband. You can bet on it. And you will be an absolute vision as a bride."

"Umm," I didn't know what to say to that. I swallowed and stepped away from her. "It's very nice to see you here, Juliet, but you know Jethro can't be in the kitchen. The candy shop could get into trouble if the food administration decided to make a surprise visit."

"They are too fussy," she complained.

"Even so . . ." I trailed off.

"Ridiculous." She adjusted Jethro in her arms. She was wearing the same polka-dotted coat that I had seen her in the day before. She was very partial to polka dots because they matched Jethro, of course.

According to Aiden, Jethro was technically a comfort animal for Juliet, which was why she had permission to take him everywhere she went. Few places were off-limits to Jethro, but one of those few places was the kitchen of my candy shop.

"I'm sorry, Juliet. My hands are tied. It's the law that farm animals aren't allowed in working kitchens."

"Jethro hasn't slept on a farm one day in his entire life."

"I know but—" I motioned her back toward the swinging door that led into the main room of the shop.

"Why don't we talk out back?" she asked, and started to maneuver around me to the back door.

"No!" I said a little too quickly, stepping into her path.

She blinked at me.

"I mean, the Dumpster is back there. It's not the most pleasant place to chat. I know Jethro has a sensitive nose. The smells might bother him." I put the most understanding look on my face that I could muster.

"Oh, Bailey." She squeezed my arm. "You are always on the lookout for little Jethro. I feel like the experience the two of you went through together a few months back bonded you for life. We really are like a little family."

When all else failed with Juliet, it was best to appeal to her pig's comfort. She was even more concerned about Jethro's happiness since he had been lost for a few days back in October. It was hard to believe that it could be possible, but she had started babying the little bacon bundle even more after he was found. Everyone in Harvest had given a sigh of relief that Jethro *was* found. Juliet had not been quiet in her dismay while he was gone. Not that I could blame her. He was awfully cute, even if he was known to bite from time to time. She called his bites love nips, but I didn't think love had anything to do with it.

"Where should we speak? I'm not sure I want the whole village to overhear what I am about to ask." She lowered her voice. "You know how they talk, and this has to remain between us until we are absolutely ready to spread the news."

I did know this. The Amish gossip machine had more dirt than any of the most scandalous tabloids in New York. If the tabloids wanted to really ramp up their business, I would suggest that they hire some Amish gossips. They would never fear going out of business then.

"If it's quick we can talk here, just please don't set Jethro on the floor," I said.

She hugged the pig a little closer to her body. "I won't. The reason I have Jethro with me is because I want to talk to you about him."

"You do?" I wasn't sure I wanted to hear it. The

last time Juliet had a problem with Jethro, I had gotten locked in a mausoleum with the pig and was almost killed by a madman. It wasn't an experience I wanted to repeat. Ever.

"Yes! Aiden tells me that you know the people here from New York, the TV people," she added, as if there might be anyone else from New York in the tiny village of Harvest during the holiday season.

I winced. I wondered how much Aiden told her about how well I knew them, particularly Eric. However, I couldn't see Aiden talking to his mother about my ex-boyfriend. From what I had observed of their mother-son relationship, Aiden was much more the parent than Juliet seemed to be. Upon reflection, that must have been different when Aiden was growing up . . . or maybe not. Aiden was the type of man who was born responsible.

"I know some of the people from New York, but not all of them."

She beamed at me. "That's all I need to know, and it makes me realize how lucky Jethro and I are to call you family, well, almost family. You and Aiden have to get engaged to make it official. Have the two of talked about that, or when you would like the wedding to be?" She squeezed the pig closer to her chest. "Oh, I cannot wait for that day. Spring weddings are always nice."

I stared at her. She couldn't possibly think that Aiden and I were getting married anytime in the near future. We still couldn't decide if we wanted to go out on a single date. I felt that much of our hesitation stemmed from the very situation I was in at the moment. Juliet wanting us to get together so badly was putting us both off. The only times I saw the deputy was when he came into the candy shop and when there was a dead body involved. That didn't really add up to the makings of a great marriage to me.

"I know you are the right one to talk to since you know the right people." She smiled even more brightly at me. "Can we make Jethro a star? I really think he has what it takes. Can you imagine how wonderful he would be on the small screen? Why, he might even jump to the movies. The next Wilbur in *Charlotte's Web*, and it's been a long while since there has been a great pig movie like *Babe*. He would do so well in a role like that."

I took a breath, which was just long enough for me to register what she had said. Jethro in a movie?

The pig stared at me and licked the tip of his black and white polka-dotted nose.

"A star?" I asked.

She nodded. Juliet held the toaster-sized pig to my face. "Do you think that Jethro could have a part in the cooking show? I think I have always known that he could be a star if given the right opportunity. I know that he would be a perfect fit, and if they really want to show a true Amish Christmas, then they need to add Jethro to the program. He will bring the show together and help it stand out from all other holiday programs on television.

"Pigs aren't really Christmas animals," I said. "I mean, I've never thought of them that way."

She wrinkled her small nose. "Of course they are! You should see Jethro in his Christmas sweater. He is the toast of the town during the holidays."

Juliet thought that Jethro was the toast of the town for every holiday, not just Christmas, so I wasn't putting much weight on her pronouncement. And I didn't add that it wasn't very Amish to dress up a pig in a sweater either. The Amish saw pigs as food and little else. I'm not sure what Jethro, sweater or not, would add to the Amish Christmas aspect of Eric's special.

"What would you like me to do?" I asked. I didn't see much point in fighting it. Maybe if I concentrated on making Jethro a star, Juliet would lay off the idea of my marrying her son. Probably not, but I was willing to try.

"If you could, I would love you to speak with the television people and ask them to give Jethro a part on the show. I know deep down he's got what it takes. He has so much talent, and no one can dispute that he is the most handsome pig in the state, if not the country." She held Jethro up in my face as if challenging me to question the little pig's star power. I had to admit he was a cutie, but that didn't mean he had what it took to be a television star. Also, there were the love nips to contend with. I guessed one nip on the back of the leg of producer Linc would be all it would take to get Jethro banished from TV forever.

"You want me to talk to the production crew?" I asked. "I don't even know if the special is going on. You must have heard what happened."

She shook her head sadly. "I did. It is a horrible thing. I can't believe that such a beautiful woman was killed. She seemed so vibrant and put together. She was a real working woman."

I did my best not to make a face at the working woman comment. I was a working woman, too, as was my grandmother, and almost every other woman I'd ever met, including Juliet.

She smiled. "But as sorry as I am over what happened to that Rocky woman, I'm so happy that I'm the one who gets to tell you—the production is definitely going on. I heard that from Aiden himself."

Aiden tended to be a good resource when it came to investigations and information in the county, even more so than the sheriff. Not that I would ever speak to the sheriff without being forced to. "Did Aiden say why the production is continuing? It seems . . ." I searched for the right word. "It seems a bit callous to go on as if nothing's happened. A woman is dead."

Juliet nodded solemnly. "It's true, and it is horrible. But Margot was very insistent that the production would go on, and the TV people thought it would be a great thing to do in Rocky's honor since she was excited about this special. I think Margot made some calls. You know how she can be." She laughed.

I bet Margot made more than a few calls. I can imagine the network giving in to her just to stop the incessant calling, a little sarcastic voice in the back of my brain whispered.

"Did Margot tell you where she was all morning?" I asked. "You said before she was on some kind of secret assignment."

"She didn't say," Juliet said. "The only thing she said about this morning was 'Mission accomplished.'"

I was terrified to learn what the accomplished mission might be. I just hoped that it didn't involve me.

"As you can imagine, I have already spoken to Margot about getting Jethro on the television program, and she thinks it is a fabulous idea. She says it would be great for the village to include as many residents of Harvest as possible, even the animal residents, because it will make tourists want to visit here."

"Why doesn't she talk to the television people, then? She seems to have the right amount of pull with them."

"Oh, she will, but she suggested that I speak to you about it. She said that you were close with someone on the show. Who are you close to?"

I winced. I had a feeling that Margot was having a little too much fun stirring the pot. "I know people who are associated with the production." That was one way to put it, I thought. "But I'm not close to anyone on the show at the moment." I thought my comments were just vague enough to avoid lying. The last thing I wanted was for Juliet to know that my ex-boyfriend was the star of the show. I'm not sure what she would do if she thought I was betraying Aiden, even if it was only in her mind.

"Oh." Her shoulders drooped. "I just thought you could help me get Jethro's talent recognized." She looked as if she might actually cry over it.

I sighed. "I'll see what I can do."

She looked at me with her big blue eyes. "Really?"

"I'll try," I said finally. "But I can't promise that

anything will come of it." I scratched Jethro's head. The pig was half asleep, getting a jump on his afternoon nap.

She threw her free arm around me and crushed the three of us into a massive hug. "Thank you, Bailey, thank you so much. I just can't wait for Jethro to have his big television debut, and I can't wait to call you my daughter. I will have to tell Aiden to hurry up. I'm not getting any younger, and I want grandchildren!"

I grimaced.

Juliet hugged Jethro into the curve of her neck, and the pig made mournful eyes at me. "I have the perfect idea," she said. "This afternoon I have choir practice at the church, and before that, Reverend Brook and I are meeting to talk about the Christmas services. He likes to have my input on these things. I always tell him that he's the pro. Nevertheless, he likes me to lend my support. You know, over the holidays there is so much going on all the time."

I suppressed a smile as I always did when she spoke about the reverend. Juliet and Reverend Brook weren't fooling anyone. Everyone in the village knew that they were sweet on each other.

"Why don't you take Jethro while I'm busy at the church and go talk to the television people? I think if they saw him, they couldn't say no." She held the pig up to me for a third time. "Who could say no to this face?"

Jethro licked my chin, and I stepped back. Pig slobber. "I have no idea," I said as I ran my hand under my chin.

"Then it's settled. I'll drop Jethro here at the shop before I head over to see Reverend Brook. And I'm afraid it's going to be a long choir practice. Everyone wants to make sure that we run through the music for Christmas Eve onstage. It has to be perfect. It's the biggest service for the church every year. I know Reverend Brook is feeling the pressure. Poor man." She spun on her heels to face the kitchen door. "Now I must be off. There is much to do. There's no time to delay, not even a moment!" And she was gone.

I stared at the door as it swung back and forth in her wake. What had I gotten myself into this time?

Chapter 13

After Juliet left, I found I was more worried about promising Eric I would help him, essentially promising that I would solve Rocky's murder, than worried about making Jethro a star. However, making Jethro a star was a worry in the back of my mind too.

I had promised Eric that I would help him, but I wasn't entirely sure how I would do that. If he'd already told the police his suspicions about Josie, there wasn't much else I could do unless Josie was innocent. That was more than possible, but if she was obviously guilty, I knew the sheriff would have arrested her by now. He wanted this case closed so that Holmes County could go back to being the picturesque place portrayed on the postcards in all the local gift shops—postcards we too displayed for sale at Swissmen Sweets.

As much as I may have wanted to help Eric, I had to focus on the Christmas Market. I held the front door for Charlotte as she pushed our cart, filled to the brim with peppermint treats, over the threshold and to the street's edge.

I waved at my grandmother before I let the glass door close.

"You girls have fun!" she called from her post behind the counter.

I waved again and closed the door.

"Think we made enough peppermint candies?" Charlotte asked as she pushed the heavy cart over the curb's edge and onto Main Street.

I laughed. "This is a two-week event. We might have to make more."

"Ugh. I'm over peppermint."

I patted her arm as we crossed the street. "Me too."

When we reached the square, I looked for any evidence of the trouble that had fallen over Harvest that morning. The one sign that something was amiss was the crime scene tape that blocked the entrance to the gazebo. It was the only thing that marred the lovely holiday scene. At least a dozen vendors peppered the square on the right side of the gazebo, selling everything from baked goods to quilts. An Amish man stuck a sign in the ground outside of the group of freshly cut Christmas trees that read TREES $35–$50. KEIM CHRISTMAS TREE FARM. A teenaged boy strung large-bulb Christmas lights from the posts that surrounded the trees. Even though the bulbs were three times the size of the ones on the string that had killed Rocky, they still brought back the memory of how her body had looked when I'd seen her this morning and how guilty Eric had appeared standing over her body.

To the left of the gazebo, straw had been strewn over the snowy ground for the live nativity scene. I saw a horse, a cow, and a goose there so far. I hoped that Margot had thought to have someone watch over those animals. No one wanted a goose loose at the market, or a cow for that matter.

"There's our table." Charlotte pointed to a table that was in the middle of the market. Most of the other vendors were already set up for the sale.

I helped her push the cart over the frozen grass. "I don't think the cart was made for this kind of terrain," I said.

Finally, we got it into place and began to unload.

I knelt in the snow to attach a plain navy table-cloth to the underside of the table so that it wouldn't blow away in the December breeze.

"That sure is a lot of peppermint you have there," a woman's voice said above me.

I banged my head in my rush to get out from under the table. I knew that voice. "Cass?!" I jumped to my feet and threw my arms around her. "What are you doing here?" I asked. "You can't be here!"

"Sure, I can," she said, seemingly unconcerned about my outburst. "It's a free country—I can go wherever I please."

She wore her signature head-to-toe black, from her wool coat to her high-heeled boots. Her black hair was silky straight and fell to her ears, except for her extralong bright purple bangs that fell over her right eye. She didn't wear a hat despite the below-freezing temperature. Cass didn't do hats. She certainly wasn't sporting the traditional Holmes County look.

I gave Cass another hug before letting her go. "I still don't know how you got here or why you are here. I'm thrilled to see you, but what on earth is going on? Why have you come?"

"When I got your text this morning, I told Jean Pierre the situation, and he offered me his plane."

"But, but, you are the head chocolatier now at JP Chocolates," I protested. "This is the busiest time of the year. They need you in New York."

She smiled. "I'm not denying that they need me. I am hard to replace, but Jean Pierre is the worst retiree ever. He's been itching to get back into the shop and fill all the Christmas orders. I swear he's been at the chocolate shop every day since he retired. I think he was happy to be rid of me, really. Plus Caden, for whatever he's worth, is there and can do the heavy work for Jean Pierre."

Tears gathered in my eyes.

"OMG, Bailey, are you crying? Why are you crying?"

"I . . . I'm not crying." I sniffled. "I just . . . you don't even know . . ."

"I don't even know what?" She looked around the square. "Is Eric here? Did he hurt you? I'll kill him."

Charlotte gasped.

I wiped tears from my eyes. "She doesn't really mean that."

"Says who?" Cass asked. "Where is the little rat?"

"Eric's not why I'm upset," I said. "Well, not entirely."

"What is it, then? What could be worse than that rat coming back into your life? I knew he was never good enough for you, but I won't say anything more about it because that's all in the past."

I highly doubted that Cass wouldn't say anything more about it. That wasn't her style.

"I found a dead body this morning." I just came out and said it. With Cass, that was one of the best ways to share information. You had to be quick before she moved on to the next thing.

"Another dead body?" Cass yelled loud enough for every shopkeeper on the square to hear.

The goose honked a reply. Perhaps she thought Cass was yelling at her.

I winced. "Yes, and it's the executive producer for Eric's show."

"Are you kidding me?" She peered into the cart. "Do you have anything stronger than fudge in that cart?" Cass asked. "Because that's not going to cut it this time."

Charlotte shook her head.

"Who's the quiet one?" Cass asked, smiling at Charlotte, who still had her mouth hanging open. She held a bag of peppermint puffs in her hand as if she'd been frozen in time by my best friend's appearance.

"This is my cousin Charlotte."

Cass smiled. "You're the organist, right?"

Charlotte only nodded, as she seemed to have been struck dumb by Cass's appearance.

Cass just shrugged when Charlotte didn't speak. "I hope she plays better than she talks." Cass turned back to me. "Does Hot Cop have any suspects for the murder?"

"Cass, please lower your voice. I don't want anyone to hear you referring to Aiden as Hot Cop."

"I don't know why that's a problem. I'm just stating the obvious about him."

"The police think that Eric killed Rocky," I said. "So I have—"

She shook her finger at me. "No, no, no, no, no."

"No what? And for goodness' sake, get your finger out of my face."

"I'll get my finger out of your face when you tell me that you are not helping Eric out of a murder rap."

"I can't tell you that," I said.

"You cannot help him. You have no reason to help him. Let the county sheriff run him up river. It would do him good to learn a lesson for once. It would do him good not to think he rules the world."

"I can't do that if he's innocent. And I know he wouldn't do this."

"How do you know?" Cass asked. "You can't possibly trust him after what he did to you."

"I don't trust him, but I know that he didn't kill Rocky Rivers."

"Rocky Rivers? Is that a joke I don't get?"

"That's the producer's name."

"That is so not the name she was born with."

I didn't disagree with her, because I had thought the same. "But I know that Eric didn't kill her, because it could ruin his television show. He worked too hard and too long for that. He's too selfish to have killed Rocky."

She nodded. "Okay, you have point there, but that still doesn't mean you have to help him in any way. Hot Cop—" She held up her hand. "Okay, Aiden is a good cop, right? He won't arrest Eric unless he has airtight evidence. The last thing he would want to do would be to accuse the wrong person, even if the wrong person is Eric." She touched her cheek with her black leather glove. "Then again, maybe I'm wrong on that. He can't like the guy after the way

Eric treated you. Scratch that. Aiden definitely would like to lock him up and throw away the key."

"Not helping," I said.

"Well, if this"—she moved her hand back and forth between us—"isn't helping, what do I have to do to help? Because dead body or not, that's what I'm here to do."

"Thank you." I hugged her again and sniffled.

"Don't you dare start crying again!" Cass ordered.

And I swallowed my grateful tears.

Chapter 14

After Cass's arrival, she and I helped Charlotte set up the rest of the table, so that we would be ready on time for the Christmas Market. The market would run from noon to four, which would give the vendors plenty of time to close up shop before the sun was fully set. The live nativity would take over at that point.

As we walked back to Swissmen Sweets, I filled Cass in with as many of the particulars of the murder as I could. Just as we reached the door, I finished the recap.

"Eric wants you to prove that his current girlfriend, Jane, killed Rocky to get him off the hook," Cass concluded.

"Josie. Not Jane," I said.

"Whatever. It's a terrible thing for him to ask you to do."

I put my hand on the doorknob of Swissmen Sweets and turned it. "I'm going to find out who murdered Rocky, no matter who it is, even if it turns out to be Eric. Rocky deserves that." I pulled open the door before Cass could reply.

"Cass!" my grandmother exclaimed as we stepped into the crowded shop. Christmas shoppers, mostly English but a few Amish, filled the room. *Maami* hurried around the counter. "It is so good to see you!" My Amish grandmother gave my purple-haired best friend a tight hug.

Cass hugged her back with just as much feeling.

The customers in the shop stared at them open-mouthed. They must have looked like an odd pair.

"What brings you to our little corner of the world?" *Maami* asked.

I gave Cass a look. My grandmother still didn't know about my history with Eric in New York, and I wanted to keep it that way.

"I just wanted to surprise you all before Christmas."

Maami clapped her hands. "Well, this is a lovely surprise. We're so glad you are here. Many of Bailey's friends have come to Harvest for this special season. I am very glad that she has people who care about her so much that they would travel so far to see her." *Maami* reached out to me and squeezed my hand. "I know it was a hardship for her to leave her life in New York behind for me and Swissmen Sweets, but I am forever grateful to my beloved granddaughter that she did."

"It wasn't a hardship for me to leave New York, *Maami*. I have told you that. I miss Cass, of course, but this is where I belong now. It's where *Daadi* would want me to be."

My grandmother's eyes filled with tears when I

mentioned my grandfather. "I am sorry." She removed a handkerchief from the pocket of her apron. "This is the first Christmas since . . . It is a hard season for me."

I hugged her. "It is a hard season for all of us."

"We will make the most of it," Cass said.

"*Gut!* I'm so glad. Now, I must get back to the counter and help everyone find their Christmas treats. The peppermint candies are a huge success. We are almost sold out of what we have here at the shop. I have been directing customers across the street to our Christmas Market table."

I gave her a half smile. I was so over peppermint.

My grandmother went back behind the counter, and Cass turned to me. "What's the plan? How are you going to help Eric? Because even though I think it's a stupid idea, I'm going to help you as long as I'm here. That's what a best friend does."

I gave her a big hug just as my grandmother had. "You are the best."

"Please don't ever forget that." She smiled, taking the edge out of her words.

The door to the shop opened. "Bailey, thank goodness you are here!" Juliet flew into the shop and thrust Jethro into my arms. "Can you take Jethro now? I know it's earlier than we discussed, but I have been called into an emergency live nativity meeting."

"An emergency live nativity meeting?" Cass asked. "Did Joseph go AWOL?"

"Oh!" Juliet said when she saw Cass standing in the shop. "You are . . . ?"

"Cass," Cass said.

"Yes, of course," Juliet said. "It's so nice to see you again." She turned her attention back to me. "Can you take him now?"

"I don't see why not," I said, well aware that all the customers in the candy shop were watching our exchange.

She pressed Jethro and me into a three-way hug. Jethro snorted. When she let go of me, I found Jethro in my arms, and I didn't even know how she'd managed to put him there.

"Thank you, Bailey. Thank you so much. You are the best daughter-in-law any mother would ever ask for."

"Wait," Cass yelped. "Hold the phone! Daughter-in-law?"

I merely shook my head and mouthed, "Tell you later."

"You got married and you're going to tell me later?" Cass hissed.

"I'm not married," I said.

Juliet smiled at me. "I know those TV people will take one look at my little pig and want to sign him on the spot. Isn't that what it's called in showbiz? Signing? I need to learn all the terminology if I'm going to be Jethro's manager." Her eyes glistened with happy tears. "Or maybe you can be his manager, Bailey?"

The pig looked up at me, and I would be lying if I didn't say that it looked like he shrugged at me. As if to say, "What's to be done with her?"

I didn't know how to answer that question. I suspected that it was one Aiden asked himself on a regular basis.

She fondled Jethro's ear as if she was reluctant to leave him. "You knock them dead, kiddo. You can do this. Bring home the bacon."

I winced. Under the circumstances, I thought it was a poor choice of words, but that was just me.

"Now, I really must scoot," Juliet said. She ducked her head and gave Jethro a kiss on the top of his snout. "You be good for your sister, all right, sweetheart?" With that she went out the door.

Cass put her hands on her hips. "Clearly, there is some stuff you need to tell me."

I sighed and set the pig on the floor. He pressed his nose to the hardwood, inhaling all the scents. "I'm not married. Jethro is not related to me at all. That's all wishful thinking on Juliet's part."

"Well, that's a relief, because I had better be told well in advance if you plan to tie the knot."

"I'm not tying anything up with anyone any time soon."

Cass still had her hands on her narrow hips, and she looked down at Jethro. "Juliet wants you to talk to the production team about him, to make him a star. Is that right?"

"Yes," I admitted.

"Perfect!" she said.

"Why is that perfect?" I couldn't see anything good coming out of my toting Jethro around as if I were a farmyard animal talent agent.

She pointed at Jethro. "The pig is our ticket."

"Our ticket where?"

"I'll tell you on the way." She opened the door to Swissmen Sweets. "Let's go."

"Where are we going?"

She looked back at me. "To solve a murder, of course."

Chapter 15

It wasn't until I was behind the wheel of my car, which had been parked on Apple Street away from the commotion of the Christmas Market, that Cass told me what we were doing.

"We need an excuse to talk to the production team, right?" she said.

I nodded. "We could use one, sure."

She pointed at Jethro, who was in her lap in the passenger seat. "Excuse."

Jethro grunted.

"Don't be sensitive," she told the pig. "It's for a good cause."

"It's an idea," I said, starting the car.

"It's a brilliant idea," Cass exclaimed. "Do you know where they are staying?"

I nodded. "Eric told me it's a guest house out on Tree Road. I was surprised that they picked a place so remote."

"The plot thickens," she said, twirling an imaginary mustache. "Onward!"

Twenty minutes later, my car bounced out of

another snow-covered pothole as I finally made the turn onto Tree Road on the outskirts of Harvest.

Cass and Jethro bounced in their seat next to me.

"Geez," Cass complained. "Are you aiming for the potholes?"

"No," I said defensively. "I just can't see them because of the snow on the road. These rural roads don't get as much attention as the main highways."

"You might want to get the Ohio governor on that," Cass said as we rolled through another hole.

"Sure, I'll call him right up."

Cass laughed.

As I drove along the road, it began to snow large, white flakes. "I hope we can get out of here before the weather turns too bad," I said. "This would not be a good place to have a car break down."

"Why would you even say anything like that?" Cass asked. "You're just asking for trouble when you do that. Besides, we will be quick: We get in, ask them to make Jethro a star, ask which one of them killed Rocky Rivers—so not her real name—and then we get out. Easy-peasy."

"Right," I said. "Easy-peasy."

Through the increasing snow I saw a hand-painted sign on the side of the road. It said, CHRISTMAS TREES! and pointed forward.

"There must be a Christmas tree farm out here," I said. "I wonder if it's the same one that is selling trees at the market in the village."

Cass shrugged as if that didn't matter.

I sighed. Tree Road was long, and we passed the Christmas tree farm before reaching the guest house. I was happy to see that my guess had been right and the farm on the road was Keim Christmas Tree Farm, the same one selling trees at the Christmas Market.

We drove another mile down the road until we saw a second building. It was the guest house, a huge, white-framed farmhouse in the middle of a field. A clothesline was holding a lone patchwork quilt that flapped back and forth in the brisk wind. If the quilt was left out there much longer, it would be frozen stiff.

A buggy without its horse stood in the middle of the driveway, and the production van that had been a bone of contention between Eric and Aiden the day before was parked in the middle of the snow-covered yard. Behind the parked buggy was an SUV with GOURMET TELEVISION and the network's logo emblazoned on its side. I knew I was in the right place, but what was clearly an old farmhouse was the last place on earth I'd thought I would ever find Eric Sharp. Eric stayed at places with a doorman and a high-end fitness center. Not that the small village of Harvest had one of those. But knowing Eric's tastes, I thought he'd elect to stay somewhere five star and demand that a helicopter fly him to and from the set.

I parked on the lawn next to the van. It would be an easy spot to leave in case we needed to make a quick exit. Usually, I didn't think of such things, but Cass was with me on this excursion. It was best to consider all possible contingencies. And Jethro. Heaven forbid something should happen to Jethro.

I turned to Cass and the pig. "You guys ready for this?"

They both showed me their teeth, which I didn't find particularly comforting, especially in Jethro's case.

I climbed out of the car, and Cass followed suit with Jethro in her arms. I shoved Jethro's leash into my pocket. I wasn't sure how the production team would react when Cass and I showed up at the door with a pig in tow. I was certain this was never a concern that Juliet had when she carried her pig around the county. She expected everyone to welcome Jethro with open arms.

White, wooden rocking chairs lined the porch. Cass tucked Jethro under her arm like a football and walked up to the door first. She waited for me by the door before placing her hand on the doorknob. "It's locked," she said.

I knocked and waited for a long moment. No one came to the door. I tried the doorknob again, and again, nothing happened.

"What?" she asked me. "You didn't believe me when I said it was locked?"

"I believed you."

To my left, the half-frozen quilt whipped back and forth on the line, making an eerie snapping sound. I wondered if the quilt would shatter if it eventually did freeze solid.

I knocked on the door again, and a moment later it opened. I had expected to be greeted by the Amish owner of the home, but instead we were greeted by Pike, the sound guy from Eric's production team.

I guessed his age to be close to twenty. He wore a gray T-shirt and jeans. He had dark circles under his eyes that seemed out of place on someone so young. There was stubble on his face as if he hadn't shaved for a couple of days. I didn't know if that was by design or just the result of his obvious exhaustion. He also held a half-eaten candy cane in his hand. He blinked at me. "You're Eric's Amish girlfriend." He glanced at Cass. "She's holding a pig."

"I sure am," Cass said, and stepped forward with Jethro pointed outward from her body like a battering ram. "You don't care if we step in from the cold, do you?"

He stumbled back, making sure to hold his candy cane out of the pig's reach. "Umm, no?"

"Said with so much confidence," Cass quipped, and crossed over the threshold.

I followed her inside and held out my hand to Pike after closing the door behind me with my foot. "I don't think we formally met back in the candy shop yesterday. I'm not Eric's girlfriend. I'm Bailey King."

He limply shook my hand with his free one.

I broke off the handshake, and it took all my willpower not to wipe my hand on the thigh of my jeans to remove the feel of his limp, damp flesh on my palm.

I found myself in a tasteful, country-style living room. It was plain and simple, but not in an Amish way. There were a few ceramic knickknacks on the tables and framed photographs on the wall. It looked like an English country home.

Pike noticed me looking around. "It's an Airbnb

place. Rocky found it on the Internet. It had enough rooms for the entire crew, so none of us have to bunk together, which is a nice change. I usually have to share a room since I'm the low man on the totem pole, so to speak. It's been nice having my own space. We have to work long hours to get this show done in time to air, so Rocky thought it would be best to rent the whole house." He frowned. "But I don't even know if there is still a production to run sound for."

"I heard that the show is going to go on," I said.

He shrugged. "If you did, that's news to me. As far as I know, no one on the crew knows. Well, I guess that's just me and Roden. Oh, and Josie, if she counts." He said this as if she might not, at least not in his estimation.

"The three of you are the entire crew?" Cass asked, and set Jethro on the floor.

"Umm," Pike said, holding his candy cane high and staring at Jethro as if he might bite him—which he might, but I wasn't going to tell the young sound guy that. "I don't think we are supposed to have animals in here. You're going to have to put the pig outside."

Cass waved away his comment. "The pig is fine. He's used to being inside. He will be a perfect, portly gentle swine."

Pike looked down at Jethro as if he wasn't so sure about that. I silently agreed with the sound guy.

"There is no one else on the crew?" I asked, getting the conversation back onto the murder and away from the pig.

Pike blinked at me. "It's a small production. Just six of us came out, and that includes the talent."

"You mean Eric?" I asked.

"I wouldn't call him talent," Cass whispered to me.

I made a motion as if I was going to step on her foot, and she moved away from me. She had learned from the last time she'd visited me in Harvest.

He nodded. "Is that why you're here? For Eric? He's not here. He left a little while ago with Josie. I don't know when they are coming back."

It was interesting that Eric would go anywhere with Josie when he thought she was the killer.

Pike popped his candy cane in his mouth, and the end hung from his lower lip like a cigarette. This reminded me of his affinity for peppermint and the candy wrappers that were found around Rocky's body.

"You seem to very fond of peppermint," I said.

He grinned, taking the candy from his mouth. "I love the stuff. I think that's why Christmas is my favorite holiday, because you can find peppermint everything."

"You know what happened to Rocky."

His candy cane drooped in his hand. "Yeah, it's terrible. She ran a tight ship, but she was a good boss. I always knew what was expected of me. I can't say the same about other producers." He made a face and popped the end of the cane back in his mouth.

"Candy wrappers from my shop were found near her body. Did you know that?"

He removed the candy cane from his mouth again. "The police asked me that too."

"And what did you tell them?" Cass asked.

He shrugged. "I don't know how the wrappers got there. Roden and I went back to the square close to six, I would say. We wanted to get some exterior night shots of the lights on the gazebo and the rest of the village. We thought it would be a great opening to the program. I captured some sounds from the gazebo. A buggy was driving by, and the clip-clop of the horse hooves was really clear on the still night. I love it when I catch crisp sounds like that. Working in television is fine to pay the bills, but I really want to be a Foley artist."

Cass frowned. "What's a Foley artist?"

"The guys who make sound effects for movies like *Star Wars*. Movie soundtracks really need the sounds to be crisp." He paused. "I was so focused on capturing the pure sound of the buggy, the candy wrappers must have fallen out of my pocket while I was recording and I didn't notice. That's my best guess."

"Were the twinkle lights disturbed when you were recording your sounds?"

He shook his head. "They were perfectly in place when we got there and when we left."

"What was Roden doing while you were in the gazebo?"

"I wasn't paying much attention to him. I guess he was shooting film and stills of the square at night." He shrugged again.

"And when did you leave?" Cass asked.

"I don't know exactly, but we weren't very long. When we got back to the guest house, Rocky and Josie were in the middle of this giant fight."

"Did you know what the fight was about?" I asked, even though I already knew.

He shook his head. "Don't know. Don't care. I'm not one for drama. I saw that they were in the middle of a fight and went straight up to my room to escape. I cranked up my music and fell asleep at some point. I didn't know Rocky was dead until late this morning."

"When was the last time you saw Roden?" I asked, realizing that I hadn't seen him since that morning with Linc, when I'd lost track of him in all the confusion.

He shrugged again. "Maybe an hour ago? He said he was going to run to Millersburg to buy a few groceries for us since we don't know how long we'll be here. He has his own rental car."

I made a mental note to track down the cameraman. Maybe he'd seen something on the square that Pike had missed when he and Pike were there last night. Although I wasn't sure why it would matter. Pike said Rocky was very much alive and fighting with Josie when Roden and Pike returned to the guest house for the night. Rocky had died sometime between when she'd stormed out of the guest house and the next morning, when Eric had found her body in the gazebo. It was close to a twelve-hour window. A lot could have happened during that time. Murder being one of the events.

"Is anyone else from the production team around?" Cass asked.

It was a good question, I thought. I asked, "Is Linc Baggins here?"

Pike's eyes widened. "Man, are you sure that's who you want to talk to?"

"Man?" Cass asked. "We are clearly ladies."

Pike's ears turned bright red.

"Is there a reason we wouldn't want to speak to him?"

He shrugged. "It's your funeral. He's in the production room."

"Production room?"

He pointed with his thumb behind him. "That's what we're calling it, but I think it used to be a dining room."

I thanked him and walked through the arched doorway into the next room. Cass and Jethro were on my heels.

Pike was right. The large room had been intended as a dining room. At least I came to that conclusion because of the long dining table that had been pushed against the wall, or what I could see of the dining table. It was covered with binders, papers, and cords—so many cords. They were like piles of tangled snakes. Seeing all those cords tangled together made me think of how Rocky had died. Without thinking I touched my own throat.

Jethro buried his nose in one of the piles of wires and sniffed. I had read once that a pig's sense of smell was even better than a dog's, so maybe he was searching for something? In Jethro's case, I would assume that it was something to eat. The well-fed little pig always seemed to be on the lookout for his next meal.

The rest of the room was jam-packed with equipment. Black boxes from sound, video, and lighting. I wasn't sure what everything did, but I was certain that it was all very expensive.

"Where's Linc?" Cass asked.

I was just about to ask the same thing.

There was a lot of equipment in the room, but the producer wasn't anywhere to be seen. Just when I was about to leave to track down Pike and ask him where else the producer might be, there was an oink from Jethro, followed by a loud bang from under the mostly buried dining room table, followed by a string of swear words.

Jethro peeled out from under the table and hid behind my legs.

Chapter 16

I bent over and picked up the pig.

"Geez," Cass said. "I haven't heard phrases like that since I graduated from culinary school."

"Shh," I said.

Linc Baggins crawled out from under the dining room table on all fours. As he did, his left foot got caught in a black cord. He kicked it away and added another swear word to the mix.

"Sounds like a charmer," Cass muttered.

Finally after some more grunts, Linc was on his feet. He wore loafers with no socks, even though it was December in Ohio. He had on a blue button-down shirt with no tie and open at the collar, and I was certain that his pressed slacks cost more than what Swissmen Sweets made in a day. If I was type-casting the role of television producer, he would have been a shoo-in for the part. He glared at Jethro. "What is that farm animal doing inside?"

I held Jethro to my chest. "You should watch what you say around this little pig. He's going to be the next big star."

"Or breakfast sausage," Linc muttered.

Cass reached over and covered Jethro's ears. "He's very sensitive."

Linc's eyes narrowed, but then he plastered an artificial smile on his face. "Bailey, it's so good to see you. Did you come here to talk about your part in the show?"

Cass stared at me. "What? You are going to be in Eric's show?"

I made a face. "I don't know yet."

Linc laughed as if I had said the funniest thing he'd ever heard. "How don't you know? What is there to decide? It would be great exposure for your shop and for you personally."

"I need to hear more about this," Cass whispered to me. "Eric might be a rat, but there is no reason you shouldn't take advantage of this opportunity."

Linc narrowed his eyes. "Who are you?" he asked.

"Cassandra Calbera," Cass said. "I'm Bailey's manager. Anything about the show has to go through me. I'm the pig's talent agent too."

I did my best not to roll my eyes.

Linc blinked and then turned back to me. "Rocky never told me that you had a manager. I didn't know about this complication."

"I wouldn't call it a complication," Cass said. "I just arrived from New York. Flew private, of course."

Linc's eyes went wide when Cass said that. I knew my best friend was having fun getting a rise out of the producer, but it wasn't helping us get Jethro a spot on the show or helping us to find out who killed Rocky Rivers.

"You can't expect an executive producer to share every detail with you, can you?" Cass asked.

Linc gritted his teeth. "It would have been helpful if she had shared at least a few details about Eric's show with me. It was my idea, after all."

"Your idea?" I asked.

"Yes. I was the one who found Eric first. I knew of his pastry shops and of his reputation in New York. I knew he was just what the network was looking for to bolster ratings. The only mistake I made was telling Rocky about it. I thought she could be my producer on the project, but she one-upped me. She spoke with Eric and Gourmet Television before I ever got a chance. There is a proper way to do these things. I wanted my pitch to be flawless. I wrote up a perfect proposal for the network. I was just fine-tuning it when she skipped over me and went directly to the network. I never should have trusted her."

"Sounds to me like you fell asleep on the job," Cass said. "You wasted a lot of time putting the perfect proposal together. You can't blame Rocky for beating you to the punch."

Linc glared at Cass before turning back to me. "As you can imagine, this has been a trying experience for everyone on the crew. I had a very long and difficult conversation with network executives about the next steps."

"And what are those next steps?" I asked.

He straightened his shoulders. "The network, as I do, thinks that the best way to honor Rocky would be to go on with the production." He paused. "They named me executive producer."

Cass elbowed me when he said that. She might as well have shouted, "We have a suspect."

He took a deep breath as if he was trying to center himself. "We should be able to begin filming later today if I can track down the rest of the crew." He frowned.

"Pike let us inside the house, so he must be around here somewhere."

Linc nodded. "Maybe he can find the cable that I was looking for under all this mess." He lightly kicked one of the table legs. "Let's get out of this room. I can't think in here. All of this should have been moved to the production van, but we haven't had a chance with everything that has happened. As soon as I find Pike, I will get him on that. He's the one who should be doing grunt work, not me."

"I'm sure you will be able to get the crew back together and keep everything on schedule. I didn't know Rocky long, but I could tell that she cared about this project. She would have liked it to continue," I said.

He scrunched his black brows together and squinted at me. "Are you one of those glass-is-half-full kind of people?" he asked.

"I guess I am."

He snorted. "That's never done any good for me." He shook his head. "There's a small table in the kitchen. We can talk in there."

Cass, Jethro, and I followed Linc into the kitchen, which was twice the size of the dining room and free of clutter. All the counters and the table were clear. However, the walls were papered with a busy Amish buggy pattern that gave me a slight headache when

I looked at it for too long. When the buggies appeared to be moving, I had to look away.

Linc sat on one of the kitchen chairs and looked at Cass. "I assume you are here for the negotiations."

"Negotiations?" I sat across from him on a chair cushion printed with even more Amish buggies. The tablecloth had buggies on it too. I was sensing a theme.

Cass held up her hand. "Let me handle this, Bailey. Yes, I'm here to talk about the show. First of all, how do I know that my client will be safe if she is involved in this shoot?"

Linc moved the napkin dispenser away from the middle of the table so he had a clear view of Cass. I suspected he wanted a good look at his opponent. "Safe?"

"Yes, her safety is of the utmost importance." She nodded to Jethro in her lap. "The pig's safety too, but we will get to that. What's your plan for Bailey's part in the show?"

Linc cleared his throat. "Bailey is Eric's connection to this little village. She's the reason we are here, so of course we must have her as part of the show. She provides the 'personal' connection. Rocky had wanted it to be a rekindled romance. We would like to shoot a scene in Swissmen Sweets. It will make the perfect set."

I started to say that there would be no scene filmed at Swissmen Sweets if my grandmother's district elders didn't give their blessing, but Cass held up her hand. "We aren't doing the rekindled love angle."

"And I never agreed to have Swissmen Sweets as

the set for your show. The shop is small. There is hardly enough room in there for more than a handful of customers at a time. I don't know how you think a production crew plus Eric and I will fit in my kitchen. Besides, Swissmen Sweets is open, and Christmas is one of busiest times of the year for us. We can't close up shop to help you. But most important, it is my grandmother's candy shop, and she is Amish. We can't film there without the permission of her church bishop."

Linc blinked at me. "What are you talking about?"

I leaned back. "It's how the Amish run their lives. They rely on their church leaders to tell them when they can and cannot do things, especially when related to technology. One of their edicts is to live simply. No one could argue that being on television is living simply in the Amish way."

"That's ridiculous," he snapped.

A tiny part of me agreed with him, but I wasn't going to say anything that would belittle my grandmother's culture. It might not be my way to live, but it had been working well for the Amish for hundreds of years, so who was I to say it was wrong?

"We will make it well worth your while," he said.

"It's not my choice," I said. "It really is not."

Cass leaned forward. "How much worth her while?"

I shot Cass a look and asked, "Was it Rocky's plan to shoot in Swissmen Sweets?"

He shook his head. "No, she wanted most of the shots outside at the Christmas Market. She was obsessed with getting the perfect holiday shot of the village. We had already shot Eric's Amish recipes at a soundstage back in New York, so she didn't see the need to do any more interior cooking shots, but I disagreed. If your appearance is to be a main fixture of the program, we should see what you are able to do."

Cass shook her finger. "I don't know that that's going to work for us."

He held up his hand before I could speak. "I'm not asking you to marry Eric, but we do want to capture some of your chemistry on the screen. The rekindling the romance angle was Rocky's idea. Viewers like intrigue, especially about celebrities like Eric. She wanted to capitalize on that, and thought it would soften his image. Rocky was right about that. We may have signed him initially because he is a volatile chef, but just in the last year, what the television audience wants has changed. Yelling and screaming chefs are out and sweet, wholesome Amish girls are in."

"I'm not Amish," I said in a deadpan voice.

"Details." He waved his hand as if it meant nothing. "You will help him bridge the gap."

"At my expense," I said.

"Rocky was a bulldog, and she was a shrewd businesswoman. She would do anything at anyone's expense if it furthered her career and the network. She lived and died by ratings."

"Don't most television producers?" Cass asked. "It has been my experience as a talent manager."

I inwardly groaned, wondering how far Cass would take this manager thing. I wouldn't be the least bit surprised if she didn't start sending me out on auditions.

"Perhaps. Rocky was an idea person, and the network loved her for that. But she wasn't good with the practical part of producing. That's why I got tagged to this assignment." He balled his hands into fists on the tabletop. "You can't imagine how difficult it was for me to be second chair on this project when it was my idea."

His fists were clenched so tightly, I could easily imagine him having the strength to strangle Rocky.

"Let's focus on my client's safety. Should she be worried about anyone else on the production team?" Cass asked.

"What do you mean?" Linc countered.

Cass leaned on her elbows on the table with the the pig still on her lap. "A woman has died. I want to know if you think anyone on your team could have done it, and if so, is my client at risk?"

"You think someone from the production team killed Rocky?" He blinked at her as if the idea had never crossed his mind before that moment.

I smiled to myself. I knew what Cass was doing; she was trying to get information about the murder suspects while pretending to negotiate my television opportunity. She was so small and compact; it was easy to underestimate her.

"How well do you know Roden and Pike?" I asked.

Linc frowned. "I don't know why this matters, but Pike is a new hire. He's fresh out of film school and very green. I have worked with Roden for years and so had Rocky. In fact, he was on most of her shoots. He was her favorite cameraman."

"Favorite how?" Cass asked. "Like romantically?"

Linc laughed at that. "No, that's the most ridiculous idea I've ever heard. A pretty boy like Eric was much more her speed. She would never date someone like Roden, but they had a great working relationship, much better than Rocky and I had."

I wondered if he made this comment about whom Rocky would date from personal rejection. That would strengthen his motive for killing her. From where I was sitting, it seemed to me that Linc Baggins had the best motive for murder out of any of them so far. I glanced at his left hand. He was wearing a wedding ring, but unfortunately that might not mean much if he'd wanted Rocky to be his mistress and she'd turned him down.

"What about Josie?" I asked.

He blinked. "Josie? The makeup girl? What about her?"

"I heard that she and Rocky had an argument last night."

He waved away my comment. "They may have had a little spat, but it was nothing to worry about."

That was not how Eric had described it. He said it was so bad that he painted it as Josie's reason to kill the television producer. Again, I wondered why Eric had gone off somewhere with someone like that.

"Pike mentioned that Josie left not that long ago with Eric."

He shrugged. "The pair of them are dating, so I'm not surprised."

"Eric said you told Rocky that, which caused the argument between the two women."

He frowned. "I supposed Rocky had a right to know if we were shooting this special to clean up Eric's image. He couldn't be seen running around New York with Josie when he was supposed to get back together with you, his Amish love."

"We *aren't* doing the romance angle between Eric and Bailey," Cass said. "End of story."

"You've made that point loud and clear." He folded his arms. "But I didn't know that when I told Rocky about Josie."

"But is Josie still part of the crew? I had heard that Rocky fired her last night."

"You seem to have a lot of information about the production," Linc said. "But Josie is still with us. I need someone to do Eric's hair and makeup for the shoot. Where am I going to find someone in Amish Country to do that for me?"

Rocky was dead, and Josie was able to keep her job? Sounded like a motive to me, especially if what Eric had told me was true, that Rocky had threatened to ruin Josie's career in television.

He waved his hands. "I know what you are thinking, but you've got it all wrong. The girl can't be more than five feet tall and ninety pounds soaking wet. There is no way she could have strangled a woman as tall as Rocky. That's just not possible."

"What if Rocky was caught unawares?" I asked. "If she wasn't paying attention or was distracted by something else, anyone could have gotten the jump on her."

He scowled and studied me. "It seems to me you've thought about this a little too much for a candy maker."

My cheeks grew hot at his comment, and I realized my mistake.

Chapter 17

By asking the production crew so many questions, I was painting a target on my back as a troublemaker and possibly as a potential threat who might have to be dealt with by the killer at some point. I had put myself in this tight spot before and barely made it out with my life.

Cass laughed away his comment. "Bailey is worried for her safety. This girl will be putting makeup on her. After the murder, it's only natural for her to be a little leery of anyone in the village she doesn't know well."

I cleared my throat. "The police will want to talk to Josie."

He shrugged. "They can if they want as long as they don't impact my shooting schedule. It's afternoon now, so we've already lost most of today. I can't afford to lose any more time. They can talk to her when she isn't working on hair and makeup."

I knew Linc had a job to do, but I flinched at his callousness. Rocky hadn't even been dead for twenty-four hours yet, and it seemed that all he wanted to do was get back to work.

My conclusions about him were proven right when he said, "So, are you in?"

Was I going to have to explain for a second time that the shop belonged to my grandmother? It seemed he wouldn't take no for an answer.

Cass leaned back in her chair and folded her arms. "Considering the danger that Bailey might face by just being part of the show, we are going to need something a little extra due to the extra risk."

"Extra?" Linc asked. "Extra like what?"

Cass leaned farther back in her chair, and the two front legs lifted off the floor. "Make us an offer, and we will consider it."

Linc licked his lips and then snapped his fingers so loudly, Jethro jerked awake in Cass's lap.

"I have another idea," Linc said.

Cass made a gimme sign with her hand.

Linc ignored her and spoke to me. "How would you feel about having your own show? We would call it "Bailey's Amish Sweets." I think it could be a real hit. The Christmas special will be your lead into your very own show. It might even be bigger than Eric's."

I blinked at him. Of all the things the producer might have said to induce me to be part of the Christmas special, that was the very last thing I'd expected. "You want to offer me my own show on your network? Just like that?" He had to be crazy.

Cass rubbed her hands together. "Now we're talking!" She flattened her hands on the table. "What would the merchandising opportunities be? A line of cookware?"

He continued to ignore Cass. "You would have to come back to New York for two to three months to shoot in the studio kitchen. It's just more cost-effective that way, but we would make the set to your specifications. We could make it as Amish as you like. Of course, that would be after we do a screen test and shoot the pilot to figure out if you have the necessary star power on camera. Some people can be positively charming in real life but fall flat on camera, or they could be wonderful on camera and a complete train wreck in real life. Your Eric Sharp is a good example of the latter."

I scowled. "He's not my Eric Sharp."

"So you say," he said. "If we get the green light after the bigwigs in the network see your screen test, I want you to fly out to New York right after the New Year. We can shoot the pilot in a day, two tops. I feel confident you would be picked up as long as you aren't one of those people who chokes on camera." He squinted at me. "You're not, are you?"

"I . . . I don't know. I've never been on camera before."

"She won't choke," Cass said, grinning from ear to ear.

I stared at my best friend. "But my life is here in Harvest now."

She squeezed my hand. "It still can be."

"Leave Harvest? Leave my grandmother?"

"It's not forever," Linc argued.

My head was spinning. "I've never been on television before. How do you know that I would work in front of the camera?"

He looked me up and down. "You are pretty enough to be on television."

I scowled at him again.

"Bai," Cass said. "Wouldn't it be great to have the best of both worlds, to have Harvest and New York?"

It sounded nice when she put it like that.

"I'll have Roden do a test shoot with you at your shop. We'll use the footage for Eric's special anyway. Maybe you and he can make one of your family's recipes together." He ran a hand in front of him, palm out as if wiping a slate clean. "I can see it now. Love and peppermint bark." He raised his eyebrows at me. "You make peppermint bark, don't you?"

"Yes." My head was spinning.

"I like that angle," Cass said. "But not the love thing. There will be no love thing between Bailey and Eric. That has to go."

Linc raised his hand. "Fine, but I still need her in a cooking scene for the pilot. It would be best if it's something *really* Amish."

What's really Amish? I wondered.

"Done," Cass said.

I flattened my hands on the table. "I'm not done. I haven't agreed to this. I have to think it over, and we still don't have permission to film in my family's shop."

"What's to think over?" Linc scribbled on the napkin and slid it across the table to me. "Here. This should convince you."

"Six episodes—fifty thousand dollars." I blinked at the words he'd written.

Cass took the napkin from me and whistled.

That was a lot of money. More than I had made in almost a year at Swissmen Sweets, and I could make that in three months by just shooting six episodes? It was money that I could use to finally break Swissmen Sweets out of debt and pay for all the upgrades I wanted for the shop. It was enough money to get my own place away from the candy shop and to have my own bedroom again. As much as I liked Charlotte, sharing a room with a twenty-one-year-old Amish woman was getting old. *I* was too old for that.

He grabbed the napkin from Cass's hand and folded it. "Let's see how your screen test on the Christmas special goes, shall we? Then we will know if you can earn this. Until then, this is all talk."

It might be all talk, but I was speechless.

"Let's throw in the pig on your program, and Bailey's pilot, and you got yourself a deal." Cass thrust out her hand to Linc to shake.

He stared at the pig.

"The pig is in or no dice," Cass said. "Don't worry. I'm positive both he and Bailey have the star power you're looking for."

Linc shook her hand. "The pig is in."

And for the first time, I truly understood what it felt like to be railroaded. I suspected Linc and Cass were professionals at that art.

Linc got up from his seat. "The production crew will be at your shop bright and early tomorrow morning. It would be a big help if the kitchen were clean and clear of any distractions. My guys will know what to do. They're pros."

He headed for the kitchen door. "We are shooting at the Christmas Market later and the live nativity tonight. We'll stop by your booth to get some footage of that, too. Now that that's settled, I have some work to do. I need to be with camera and sound to make sure we are all on the same page as far as my vision for the program. This is my Christmas special now, as it always should have been, and we are going to shoot it my way." He left the room.

"What just happened?" I asked.

"You wildest dreams just came true. That's what happened." Cass grinned and brushed her purple bangs out of her face.

"I don't think these were my wildest dreams. I think I got hit by a bus," I said.

"Maybe," Cass agreed. "But it was a rich bus full of opportunities."

"I don't know that I want to do this. This TV thing. It's nothing I've ever wanted to do. Eric was the one who wanted to be a star."

"You might not know, so I will decide for you. Bai, think of what a great opportunity this is for you and Swissmen Sweets." She lifted up Jethro and held him in my face. "And don't forget about this guy. Think of how great it would be for him. Do you know how much more Juliet would love you if you made Jethro the star of your television series? She will want you to marry Aiden today."

"She already wants that," I said. "I think she's going around the village telling people that we are already engaged."

"She's a visionary and says what she wants," Cass said, setting Jethro on the floor. "I can respect that. Also, I did a great job at the manager thing. There are a few particulars I want to go over with him prior to finalizing the contract. . . ."

"Contract?" I squeaked.

"Of course. There is always a contract."

"I thought we came here to solve a murder. I think I am much better at solving murders than being a television star."

"You haven't given the TV thing the old scouts try yet."

I groaned.

Across the kitchen, Jethro had his snout buried in the dirt surrounding a potted plant. "Jethro!" I called.

The pig lifted his head from the pot with dirt on his black and white nose. I sighed and grabbed several napkins from the dispenser on the table. I knelt in front of the pig and cleaned his nose. He seemed perfectly content to let me do it.

"See," Cass said. "You and Jethro have chemistry together. Gourmet Television's audience will love it, and Juliet will be over the moon."

As I cleaned his nose, I said, "I don't know what Aiden will think of it though."

Jethro looked up at me with a bemused expression on his face as if to say, "Oh, you silly human girl."

"I agree with the pig." Cass got out of her chair. "It all will be well. We just have to catch a killer, get the bishop or whoever to give your grandma permission to shoot in the candy shop, and launch your new career. Easy."

"So easy," I muttered.

I stood up. "At least Juliet will be pleased that Jethro might become a television star. I came through on that."

Cass shook her head. "Technically, I came through

on that, but I will let you take this one because of Aiden."

"Gee, thanks." I looked down at the pig. "The question is, Do you want to be a star?"

Jethro stood up as if he was ready to get to work.

"He definitely has star power," Cass said.

I had to agree.

The pig ducked his head as if embarrassed. I knew he was nothing of the kind. Jethro had to be the most self-confident pig in the world with the number of compliments Juliet bestowed on him on a daily basis.

"Now what?" Cass asked.

"Well," I said. "We are in the guest house where Rocky was staying, and no one is around."

"True."

"Her room must be in here somewhere . . ." I trailed off.

Cass smoothed her purple hair back over her right eye. "Ahh, I see, and you want to search it."

"Not search. Just check it out." I tucked the kitchen chair back under the table. I would be happy just to get out of this buggy-happy kitchen. I love Amish buggies as much as the next person, but it is all a little much to digest en masse."

She laughed. "Search, check it out, I'm game. Let's go find some clues, shall we?"

"We shall," I said.

Chapter 18

I picked the pig up, tucked him under my arm, and walked out of the kitchen. Cass and I went back through the dining room with the boxes of equipment and miles of cords. The staircase to the second floor was right next to the front door. I half expected to see Pike in the living room where we had met him less than an hour ago, but he was gone.

"If anyone asks us what we're doing," I said, "just say we are looking for Eric."

"That's true," Cass said as we reached the foot of the stairs. "Because I *am* looking for Eric. I want to give him a piece of my mind."

I shot her a look as I went up the first step with Jethro still in my arms.

The wooden stairs creaked and whined with my every step. They were plain, polished wood, which made me think that even if this wasn't an Amish house, it had been Amish made. On the second-floor landing, the floor was lined with doorways on either side. There had to be six rooms on the second floor. All the doors were closed.

Jethro was a small pig, but he was dense. He grew heavy in my arms, so I set him on the hardwood floor when I reached the second floor.

"How can we know which room was hers?" I asked. "We can't try every single one. What if someone is inside their room? We can't barge in on them."

"Sure we can," Cass said. "If someone is on the other side of the door, we say we are housekeeping and book it."

"I don't think the guest house has housekeeping."

"They should." She brushed her hair out of her eye. "We really should have thought this through more."

"What do you mean?" I asked.

Jethro pressed his snout on the floor and sniffed. He snuffled down the hallway behind us.

"Well," she began, "if we'd thought this through a bit better, we could have borrowed some plain dresses from your grandmother and looked like Amish housekeepers. We really need to start packing multiple disguises if we are going to keep doing the crime-solving thing."

I sighed. "Cass, you would never pass for an Amish woman, even in a plain dress."

"It's the hair, isn't it?" She touched a black piece of her hair. "It's too much."

"The hair is part of it," I admitted. "Let's get this over with." I started to reach for the closest door-knob when a large Amish man stepped out of a bedroom farther down the hallway. He turned to make his way toward the stairs. When he spotted Cass, Jethro, and me standing in the middle of the hallway, he pulled up short.

In the time that the man stood there frozen in

place, I got a good look at him. I would say that he was about fifty and had a dark-but-turning-to-gray beard. His eyes were narrowed, so I couldn't make out the color, but I got the feeling they might be dark. I recognized him from somewhere, but I couldn't place him.

At the same time, I could feel him sizing me up. "We're looking for Eric Sharp," I said.

The man didn't utter a word, but my speech must have spurred him into action because as soon as I spoke, he began to move again. He ran toward us.

Cass and I jumped out of the way, but as he hurried down the hallway, Jethro stepped in front of him. The man stumbled over the pig, falling to the floor.

Jethro squealed.

I scooped up the pig, hoping he wasn't hurt. If Jethro was injured on my watch, I wasn't sure if Juliet would ever forgive me, no matter how big a star I made him. She might be excited about the idea of her son marrying me, but her pig was really number one in her life.

I stared at the man on the hardwood floor, holding Jethro to my chest. "Are you all right?"

He scrambled to his feet without a word.

"Are you hurt?" I asked.

He didn't even bother to look over his shoulder at me but ran toward the stairs. As he ran away, something fell from his coat pocket and clattered to the floor just before the top step. He didn't slow down to see what he had dropped. He just kept running.

Still with Jethro in my arms, I hurried to the edge of the stairs and watched as the front door slammed

closed after the Amish man. I looked to the floor to
see what had fallen. Something had rolled up against
the wall. First, I set Jethro on the floor, then I picked
up a small wooden baby rattle.

It was clearly a toy for an Amish child. It was made
of plain wood that had not been painted or adorned.
I shook it, and the beads or dried beans inside clattered together. I stared at it.

"What have you got?" Cass asked.

I showed her. "It's a baby rattle."

Cass took the rattle from my hand and shook it.

"Why would an Amish man, who clearly was somewhere he shouldn't have been, be running around
with a baby rattle in his pocket?" I asked. "Does he
have a baby and keep the rattle just in case? It seems
like an oddly shaped and noisy item to carry around
in your coat unless you have a baby with you."

"I didn't see a baby," Cass said, handing the rattle
back to me.

"Neither did I." I turned back and faced the hallway. Holding the Amish rattle, I walked up to the
doorway from which the man had come. Could it be
Rocky's room? Before the Amish man had tripped
in the hallway, I had been all ready to give up my
plan of searching her room, but that had been because I didn't know which room had been hers, and
now I just might know.

Jethro stood next to me, pressing his warm body
into my leg as if he needed the comfort or perhaps
trying to encourage me to open the door. The latter
seemed more in keeping with the adventurous pig.

"You think that's Rocky's room, don't you?" Cass stood on the other side of Jethro.

For a moment, I wondered what kind of picture we made. Two women standing on either side of a black and white polka-dotted potbellied pig. We made quite the trio.

"I could be wrong," I said. "It might not be Rocky's room, but we need to check. If it is, the Amish man running away needs to be reported to Aiden."

Cass nodded. "For sure, and it would be better if we had all of our facts straight before we took this information to Hot Cop."

I sighed. "Please stop calling him that."

She shook her head as she reached for the doorknob. "That's not going to happen. It's the perfect name for him. Very descriptive."

"It's probably locked," I said.

She turned the knob with no trouble. "Nope. Not locked."

Jethro pressed his snout against the wooden door and pushed in.

I couldn't help but laugh. "Okay, okay, I guess we all are curious about that room."

Cass pushed the door open the rest of the way, and the three of us stepped inside. Waning sunlight streamed in through the window. A lacy curtain covered half of the window and blew in the breeze. The chill air in the room made it twenty degrees colder than the rest of the house. I shivered.

It was December. Why would the window be open? It was freezing outside. I looked back at the bedroom door that Cass had left half open. The window and the door were the only two ways into the room.

I walked over to the window and was careful not to touch anything as I peered outside. Just to the left of the window there was latticework with some sort of vine growing up it. It was the perfect way to climb up the side of the house and enter without being seen.

I stepped back. There was a clear boot mark on the windowsill. This must have been the way the Amish man had gotten into the room. It made me wonder why he hadn't gone out that way too. Why risk walking through the house where he could be seen, which he had . . . by Cass and me, and Jethro, too, I supposed.

Cass joined me at the window. "You have something there, Sherlock?"

"I think so. I think this is how that man got inside."

I knew I should call Aiden, but I didn't think we were in any immediate danger. The man was long gone by now. If I wanted to take a look around the room, now was the time.

I stepped back from the window, taking care not to touch anything. Cass did the same. "What are we looking for?" she said.

"I'm not sure. Whatever that man was looking for, I guess."

"Not super helpful, Bai."

I shrugged. The bedroom was clearly a woman's room. There was a pair of earrings on the dresser, as well as hair spray and a bottle of expensive-looking lotion. Now that I thought about it, the hair spray was expensive too. I recognized the name brand. A pair of black three-inch-high heels stood at the foot of the bed. I walked over to the closet. The door was open.

Form-fitting dresses and ladies' suits hung in the closet. I didn't know where she'd planned to wear those outfits in Holmes County, or the high heels for that matter. Neither were common attire in Harvest. She would have stuck out like a sore thumb at the Christmas Market.

My conscience was nagging me to call Aiden, so I knew I needed to search the room before I chickened out completely. I put on my gloves, which I had handy because it was below freezing outside, and opened the desk drawer. There was nothing inside it other than a notepad and a Gideon Bible. On top of the notepad there was a business card. I picked up the card. The card read Rocky Rivers Productions. The tagline read, "Where reality becomes television." I frowned. Rocky must have owned her own production company in conjunction with Gourmet Television. Or perhaps it was completely separate. In any case, I knew it was something Aiden must be aware of by now. I was certain he'd looked into Rocky's financials since her death, or at least someone in the department had and reported back to him.

After I put the card back, I noticed there was a laptop cord plugged into the outlet but no computer. Had the Amish man been carrying a computer, I would have noticed it, especially when he fell. I realized that the police must have already been in this room and taken Rocky's computer, her phone, and anything else that might give them a clue as to who might have killed her.

The nightstand drawer had a flashlight in it; that was all. I moved on to the bathroom. Makeup and bottles and tubes of creams and lotions lined the counter. Even though there was a lot there, it was all displayed in a neat row with the labels pointed out. It looked nothing like the counter in my apartment back in NYC, which had been strewn with makeup and hair products that I'd slapped onto my face and hair before I ran out the door. Since moving in with my grandmother, I had streamlined my morning routine considerably and wondered why I'd ever felt I needed all those products in the first place.

Most of Rocky's skin treatments and makeup said "anti-aging" or "look younger" on them. She had been a beautiful woman, and apparently she had been bound and determined to stay that way. Maybe by dating a younger man like Eric, she'd put extra pressure on herself to stay and look young.

I couldn't see why a male Amish intruder would have any interest in anything on the bathroom counter. I almost left the bathroom, but at the last second I picked up her makeup case and peered inside. It had all the things I would have expected in it: makeup brushes, mascara, blush, and foundation. I was about to set it back down on the counter when I realized that there was a tiny tear in the lining.

I heard Cass rummaging around in the bedroom.

I bit my lower lip. Should I investigate the tear? If I did, what would I say when Aiden saw it, as I knew he would. I had to report the break-in to the police. We should never have come into the room, should have reported the Amish intruder right away. That's what an upstanding citizen would have done.

Before I could change my mind, I wiggled my pinkie finger into the lining. It touched something smooth like paper. It was hard to tell exactly what it was with my gloves on. In any case, I knew it wasn't part of the lining.

I pulled back with my finger, and it came away easily from the side. I saw that the lining was held in place with a thin piece of Velcro. Inside was a glossy piece of paper. I removed it and set the case back on the counter exactly where I'd found it.

The piece of paper had been torn from a magazine. As I unfolded the glossy slip, it was slippery in my gloved hands, but I didn't dare take the gloves off and risk leaving my fingerprints on what I thought must be an important bit of evidence.

The glossy was an advertisement for Keim Christmas Tree Farm right here on Tree Road, just half a mile away. Cass and I had passed it on our way to the guest house.

The professional photograph in the ad showed a picture of fir trees with an Amish buggy positioned on the side. The ad read "Authentic Amish trees!" As far as I knew, there wasn't any difference between an Amish tree and an English tree. A tree was a tree, but it was an interesting marketing tactic, since for some people buying Amish-made or in this case Amish-grown things seemed to be more authentic and real than those bought at a big-box American store.

Keim Christmas Tree Farm was the farm that was selling Christmas trees at the Christmas Market on the square. Had Rocky planned to buy a Christmas tree from them? How could she get it back to New York, I wondered, but I suppose a woman with her money would find a way to do it. Or maybe she'd wanted to buy a Christmas tree or use the farm for a scene in Eric's Christmas special. That made much more sense, but if that was true, why would she take such care to hide the ad in her makeup case lining? The Velcro clearly had not been part of the makeup case's original design, so that meant Rocky had tampered with the lining in order to hide things there, important things that she didn't want to be found.

I stared at the piece of paper in my gloved hand. That meant this was an important detail, a clue even. I could be holding the very reason why she was killed. Where I had seen the Amish man before came back to me all in a rush. It was at the Christmas Market. He was selling the Christmas trees at the market for Keim Christmas Tree Farm, the same one in the glossy ad in my hand. That couldn't be coincidence, could it?

He'd broken into Rocky's room looking for this because it tied him to her somehow. But how? What relationship could Rocky have had with an Amish Christmas tree farmer? Maybe that was for Aiden and the police to sort out.

I removed my cell phone from the back pocket of my jeans and took a picture of both sides of the piece of paper and several of the makeup bag and its secret pocket in the lining.

There was a knock on the door to the bedroom. "Is someone in here?"

My heart jumped into my throat because I immediately recognized the voice.

"Bai, we have company," Cass whispered from the bedroom.

Chapter 19

As carefully as I could, I tucked the glossy magazine clipping back into the makeup pouch and set it back on the counter right where it had been before. I removed my gloves and shoved them into the pockets of my coat.

"This is the sheriff's department," an official voice said.

"Don't shoot," I heard Cass say on the other side of the door.

"What are you doing here? Where's Bailey? I know she's here if you are."

I opened the door to find Aiden with his gun drawn but pointed at the floor. Cass was standing in the middle of the room with her arms folded over her chest. Deputy Little stood just behind Aiden. His eyes were the size of dinner plates.

Aiden, who I suspected never swore unless under extreme duress, cursed. He took a deep breath. "Bailey, what are you doing here? Do you realize that I could have shot you, or you, Cass? That this is a murder victim's room, and the killer could have come back here? What on earth were you thinking?"

It was time to distract Aiden. I reached into my coat pocket and removed the plain wooden rattle.

"What is that?" Aiden asked.

"It's an Amish baby rattle, or at least that's my best guess. I came here to talk to Linc about Eric's television show," I began.

"And about Jethro," Cass interjected.

I gave her a look. "While I was leaving"—I hadn't been technically leaving at the time, but Aiden didn't need to know that—"an Amish man ran down the stairs and dropped this, kind of like when Cinderella dropped her slipper."

Aiden made a face at my analogy.

"Anyway, I saw that he came out of this room, and I was just curious."

"I thought you said you were downstairs," Aiden said in a tone that told me he was trying to catch me in a lie.

"Well, I did come upstairs to see which room he was running away from," I admitted, fudging the order of events just a bit to lessen Aiden's annoyance with me, or at least I hoped it would.

Jethro wandered out from around the bed. He had one of Rocky's heels in his mouth. It looked as if he had been gnawing on the heel. He dropped it at Aiden's feet like a cat offering up a dead mouse.

"And why is he here?" He pointed at the pig.

"Your mom wanted me to talk to Linc about making Jethro a television star."

"We got him cast, by the way," Cass said proudly. "Your mom will be very happy with Bailey. I'm giving her all the credit. She has more potentially on the line than I do."

Aiden looked at the ceiling as if he were appealing to the heavens for help. The thin curtains ruffled in the breeze, catching his attention. "Did you open the window?" Aiden asked.

"No," I said. "It was open when we got here. I think that's how the Amish perp got in."

"Amish perp?" Aiden tried hard to suppress his smile but failed.

Good. I needed Aiden to be in a good mood. I wasn't sure how I was going to tell him about the clipping featuring the Christmas tree farm hidden in Rocky's makeup bag.

I knew Aiden would find out I had searched the room if I admitted that I had found the advertisement.

"Did your officers search this room?" I asked.

Aiden scowled. "Of course, and I searched it myself. We took all pertinent evidence with us."

"Then why are you back here?" Cass asked. "If you had already searched the place, why come back?"

Aiden holstered his gun at his hip. "I'm investigating a murder. It's not unusual to visit a scene several times. To make sure nothing was missed."

Well, something was missed, I thought, thinking of the advertisement in the bathroom.

"That makes sense," Cass said graciously.

I felt my best friend watching me. Cass knew me better than just about anyone. She knew when I was holding something back.

"Little," Aiden said. "Take photos of the footprint for us, and call the crime scene techs to come in and see if they can lift the print." Aiden studied me. "After you are done taking the photos, I want you to give the room a thorough search again. From top to bottom. Be creative. Think of every possible place someone could hide something. There had to be a reason someone broke into this room. He was looking for something."

The younger deputy did everything but salute his superior. His hero worship of Aiden was out on full display. He removed a large SLR camera from the equipment bag. "Right away, Deputy Brody."

"We will be in the hall," Aiden said. He walked to the door and raised his eyebrow at me when I didn't immediately follow him. "Bailey? Cass?"

I picked up Jethro and carried him out the door. Cass trailed behind me. The hallway was quiet, just as it had been when Cass and I had first entered the room.

"I think you need to be a little more honest with me, Bailey, as to why you were in Rocky's room."

"I told you about the Amish man. In fact, why aren't you out looking for him now? He's most likely the killer."

Aiden opened his mouth as if he were about to reply to the question when Little came through the open door. "Deputy Brody, I think I found something."

Little was wearing latex gloves and held the glossy ad about the Christmas tree farm out to Aiden. He held it by the corner, so everyone had a clear view of the ad. I gave a sigh of relief. Now I wouldn't have to point Aiden in the direction of the Christmas tree farm ad.

Cass saw the ad too. I could feel her watching me. I gave a slight shake of my head, hoping that she would understand that meant for her to ask me later.

Aiden removed a leather glove from the pocket of his department-issued bomber jacket and put it on. He took the ad from Little's hand. "Where was it?" Aiden asked, seeming surprised that the deputy had actually found something.

Deputy Little puffed out his chest with pride. "It was in the lining of her makeup bag. Very well concealed. That's the only reason I can think that we might have missed it before."

"That's the same Christmas tree farm that is selling trees at the Christmas Market on the square," I said as if this were a new discovery for me as well. "I wonder why Rocky would have the ad, and if she did, why she would hide it in her makeup bag? Must be important."

Aiden eyed me as if he wanted to say something but was holding it back. I'm guessing that was because Little and maybe Cass were there. "Must be." He turned his attention back to the young deputy. "Bag it. We'll take it into evidence. It seems that I need to have a little chat with Thad."

"Thad?" I asked.

"Thaddeus Keim. He owns the Christmas tree farm in question. But I thought you might already have known that." His voice was suggesting that I was holding other bits of information back.

I wasn't about to rise to the bait. "Nope, no clue about that." I wondered if Thad was the Amish man Cass and I had seen running away from Rocky's room.

Aiden scowled as if he'd let something slip. It wasn't

like I wouldn't find out who owned the Christmas tree farm as soon as I got back to the square.

I bent over to pick up Jethro. "I had better take him back to your mom. She will be wondering about him. She's at the church helping organize the live nativity."

Aiden made a face.

I raised one eyebrow in surprise. "I thought you would be bitten by the Christmas spirit. Your mother told me you love Christmas."

"I do love Christmas," Aiden said. "I'm not excited about the live nativity is all."

"What about it?" Cass asked. "It sounds like it will be nice, and a great way to keep tourists in Harvest after the Christmas Market today."

"I don't doubt that it will, but it is a little more complicated than you might think. Margot is in charge of it."

"Oh." I took that as some kind of warning. Usually when Margot was in charge of some sort of village function, it did become complicated, but I couldn't see how this would be. Juliet had told me the plans. There would be a manger scene on the other side of the square across from the Christmas Market. Members of the church would play the characters. I'd seen the list of names. It seemed to me that Margot had all her ducks, or actors in this case, in a row, and I had to admit it would be a great addition to Eric's Christmas special. I believed the plan was for him to walk through the manger scene talking about the tranquility of Amish town life. The funny thing was, there would not actually be any Amish in the scene. Acting wasn't an Amish activity.

"Is there anything else you need me for here?" I asked.

He studied me.

"No, Bailey, you can leave, but remember next time you see someone running away from a crime scene, do not investigate on your own. Please." He turned to my best friend, who was holding Jethro. "That goes for you too, Cass."

Cass saluted him. "You got it, Hot—"

I yanked on her arm and pulled her down the hallway before she could finish calling Aiden "Hot Cop" to his face. "Thank you," I called over my shoulder to Aiden.

I felt Aiden's eyes on my back all the way down the steps.

Chapter 20

While we had been inside the house, it had begun to snow harder. Large, white flakes fell on our hair and on Jethro's snout. Cass peppered me with questions as we made our way through the snow, but I refused to answer any of them until we were safely in the car.

Cass slammed the passenger-side door after her and Jethro. "Now, tell me what is going on. Why did you drag me out of the house so fast? And what is the deal with that piece of paper the young deputy found? I could tell it meant something to you." She took a breath.

"I found it first, before Deputy Little did, when I was searching the bathroom," I admitted. "I think it must be what the Amish man, who almost ran us over in the hallway, was after. I bet his name is Thaddeus, too."

Cass nodded. "Okay, that makes sense, but why would an Amish Christmas tree farmer have any connection to a woman like Rocky?"

I shook my head. "That I don't know, but we are going to find out."

"How are we going to do that?" she asked.

I glanced at the large, white frame house. How long would Aiden be occupied by the break-in? Did I dare try to beat him to the Christmas tree farm? Maybe he wouldn't even go to the farm because he'd said Thad was selling his trees at the Christmas Market. Maybe he would go there first? But with the farm being so close to the guest house, I guessed he would stop in or ask one of his deputies to do so. My best hope was that he would send Little and not go himself.

I started the car. "I think we are in the market for an authentic Amish Christmas tree, don't you?"

She grinned. "'Tis the season!"

I backed the car up on the road. Despite driving snow that caused close to whiteout conditions, we made it to the Christmas tree farm in less than three minutes. It took me a moment to see where I could park the car. Finally, I shifted into park behind a fence post, hoping that I hadn't torn up the yard with my tires.

Cass pulled on her gloves. "Let's do this."

"Right, but let's leave Jethro in the car," I said.

"But Jethro is number three in our Three Musketeers. We need him," Cass protested.

"We don't know what kind of animals are here," I said. "It's best if he stays in the car."

"Good point," she agreed, and pushed Jethro into the backseat of my car. "Sorry, buddy. You should take a pig nap while we're gone."

"Pig nap?" I asked.

"I didn't think it was appropriate to advise him to take a catnap."

"Let's go. We're running out of time."

Cass and I climbed out of the car. Outside, I pulled a stocking cap out of my coat pocket and put it on my head, pulling it way down over my ears. Cass might not do hats, but I didn't have the same qualms. More than that, I hated to be cold.

We were about to make our way to the house when an elderly Amish woman came out of the barn. She wore the longest winter coat I had ever seen. It was so long that it dragged behind her. I guess that on me it would hit somewhere around my calves, but on the small woman it hit the ground.

She smiled at us. She was missing a few teeth. "If you are looking for a tree, it would do you best to buy it from my grandson Thad at the Christmas Market. That's where all the best already-cut trees are. Unless you brought a saw and an axe to cut the tree down yourself." She looked me up and down. "You look sturdy for *Englisch* girls."

I found myself squinting. I wasn't sure that sturdy was a compliment from this woman.

"We are looking for Thaddeus Keim," I said.

She nodded. "Because you are looking for a tree. Everyone comes to look for my grandson when they need a tree. He grows the very best trees, or has since he came here to take over his grandfather's business."

"Oh, I moved to Holmes County to help my grandmother with her business after my grandfather died, so I can relate to what your grandson has done."

"Who might your grandfather be?" She squinted at me through the falling snow.

"Jebidiah King."

She placed a hand on her heart. "Oh, you are Clara's granddaughter. I'm Leah, but everyone calls me Grandma Leah because I'm so old. I'm the oldest woman in the church district," she said with pride. "Because of that I'm a grandmother, of sorts, to all, although Thad is technically my only grandchild."

I was surprised to hear that. Most Amish came from very large families, but then again, my grandparents had only one son and I was my father's only child, so it was not unheard of.

"I heard that Clara's *Englisch* granddaughter moved to the village to help with the candy shop. I don't move as well as I used to, so I don't get into town often. My old bones are not up to all that walking, and there is nothing there that I haven't already seen a dozen times before. Where did you move here from? I heard it was a big city."

"The biggest," I said. "I came here from New York. And where did Thad move from?"

"Indiana. His mother's family lived in an Amish community in the western part of that state, but when I needed help with the tree farm he came here. That was about twenty years ago, and things were such for my grandson that he needed a change. It was a good move for all of us. Thad works just as hard as his grandfather ever did in his prime. I know it is not godly to boast, but I am quite proud of the man he's become, especially after everything he's . . ." She waved her hand. "But you didn't come here to listen to any of that. You are here about a tree. There might be an axe in the barn if you want to cut one down."

"I'd like to try," Cass said. "I've never used an axe before."

I glanced at her from the corner of my eye. "That's probably for the best."

"Thad may have taken the axe to the village though. Sometimes *Englischers* are very particular and want a certain tree even if it's too large for their home, and Thad or Daniel has to trim it down."

"Daniel?" I asked.

"My great-grandson. He's a *gut* boy, a very *gut* boy. He is with his father at the Christmas Market. It's a wonder how *gut* he really is."

I raised my eyebrows at that, wondering what she meant by calling Daniel's goodness a wonder. Was it surprising that an Amish person was well behaved?

"He's already been baptized into the church," she said with even more pride. "He made the decision when he was only fourteen. He had barely a moment of *rumspringa.* He just wanted to get on to the work that *Gott* had chosen him for, and that was to run this Christmas tree farm someday when his father is gone, even though Thad is one of the healthiest men you might ever know. He might even live as long as I have. I am older than dirt itself." Grandma Leah laughed.

"Do you know the guest house up the road? I just came from there."

She nodded. "That's the old Boyce place. They were an *Englisch* family. They left and live in another state now. I think it might be Virginia or one of the Carolinas. In any case, instead of selling the house, they decided to rent it out to vacationers. Thad does the maintenance on the property for the Boyces for a small fee." She took a breath.

"He would know the property well, then," I mused. He would know about the trellis below Rocky's bedroom even before he got there, but wouldn't he have a key to the property since he did the maintenance? Why come in through the window unless he was afraid of being seen? I kept those thoughts to myself.

She nodded. "He knows it very well. I would say that he knows it better than the Boyce family ever did. They weren't the sort to do their own chores, and country life didn't suit them. I think they were more in love with the idea of the country than actually living here."

"Do you have a key to the house?" Cass asked.

She frowned. "Are you interested in buying it? I don't think the Boyce family is selling, but they might for the right price."

"Umm, I am looking for a place, and it is a lovely home," I said. Both of these facts were true even though the guest house was far too big for just me. But the real reason I was feigning interest in the house was to find out if Thad's key was missing.

"Right," Cass agreed. "And as her manager, I need to approve wherever she lives."

I groaned. Cass wasn't going to give up on this manager thing. I would be hearing about it for a week if not months.

Chapter 21

"Well, you both look like nice girls." She cocked her head as she studied Cass. "Even if your hair is *different*. If you are willing to wait, I can go fetch the key so you can see that house. I really only know when *Englishers* are staying there. Thad and I rarely talk about it. You can wait on the front porch if you like. To get out from under the snow."

Cass and I thanked Grandma Leah and followed her across the snow-covered grass to the large porch on the front of the farmhouse. Cass and I perched on white wooden chairs while Grandma Leah went inside. "Don't you think it's odd that she is so willing just to hand over the key to the Boyce house to us?" I whispered.

Cass shrugged. "Maybe, but she said we looked trustworthy."

I frowned. "A lot of people can look trustworthy and not actually be such."

Cass touched her purple bangs. "Do you think her saying my hair is different was intended to be an insult?"

"Cass, she's an Amish woman in her nineties. To her, your hair is very different."

Cass made an irritated sound, and Grandma Leah reappeared from the house. She walked back out to us leaning heavily on her cane. "The key is gone. Thad must have taken it. I just remembered that he got a call from the Boyce family to go over and check on the guests staying there. I heard it was a bunch of TV people. I'm sure the Boyce family is having them pay a little extra because they can afford it, so they might be a demanding bunch."

Demanding bunch was one way to describe the production team.

"I'll talk to Thad about it when I go to the Christmas Market," I said. "Swissmen Sweets has a table there."

"I would expect you would. Your grandfather made the very best candies. Why don't you girls take a look at the trees here? You might find something you like."

"We should really get back to the village," I said. "My grandmother will be wondering what became of us."

Grandma Leah nodded.

I was about to thank her and head back to the car when Cass said, "Bailey, I think we should take a peek at those trees. They might be important."

I frowned. "How?"

"The advertisement," she whispered just loud enough for me to hear. "Maybe the trees will give us a clue as to why Rocky had that ad."

I didn't know how they could, but I was willing to

give it a shot to get to the bottom of this baffling piece of evidence.

"We'd like to see the trees after all," I said to Grandma Leah.

Grandma Leah smiled. "*Gut.* Follow me." She walked us to the edge of the trees. "This is where I will leave you to it, then. I don't go into the trees any longer. It's far too easy to lose your way."

I stared at the dense rows of trees as she said that.

"And stick to the path when you are out there. My grandson likes to catch rabbits, so he has some snares set among the trees," Grandma Leah added. "You wouldn't want to be caught in one of those."

"Great," Cass muttered.

"If you pick a tree, let me know before you go, and I will make sure we save that one for you. I will let my grandson know. He's a good man." Grandma Leah turned to go.

"Grandma Leah," I said, stopping her. "Can I ask you one more question about the guest house down the street? You said that some TV people were staying there."

She nodded.

"Does the name Rocky Rivers mean anything to you?"

She cocked her head. "Rocky Rivers? Is that a place?"

I shook my head. "No, it's a person who was staying at the guest house."

"Was staying?" Grandma Leah asked. "So, she's not staying there any longer?"

I swallowed. "No, she isn't."

She shook her head. "I don't know that name. Must be an *Englischer* with a name like that. My grandson, Thad, might know of her. As I said, he helps with the guest house."

I had a feeling Thad might know Rocky very well, but their connection was still unknown.

"Now, if that is all, I will leave you girls to pick your trees." She continued on her way.

Cass and I stood at the edge of the trees after Grandma Leah shuffled back to the house.

"You know," Cass said. "If I was going to hide a dead body . . ."

"Don't even say it. We aren't finding any more dead bodies today. I've reached my quota for the week."

"I'm just sayin' . . ."

"I know."

The pine trees grew in what felt like endless rows. One row was barely three feet from the next. I could hold out my arms and touch the trees on either side of me. "What could be Rocky's connection to this place?"

Cass shook her head. "No idea. Grandma Leah didn't seem to have a clue, and she seemed as sharp as a tack."

I nodded.

The pine needles rustled. I told myself that it was just the wind. Maybe a winter storm was coming on. The temperature seemed to have dropped by ten degrees since we'd met Grandma Leah. I had to admit that I liked the old woman, and I prayed for her sake that neither her grandson nor her great-grandson were involved in this murder, but I knew they just might be. The only way to be sure was to find Thad Keim and confirm that he was the man we'd seen running away from Rocky's room.

I followed Cass through the rows of trees. The bristly branches on either side of me caught at my sleeves and the sides of my coat. They felt like fingers poking and prodding me. I shivered. It wasn't a pleasant image. "Where are we going?" I asked Cass.

She looked back at me. Snow dusted the top of her black hair. "Grandma Leah seemed keen on our finding a Christmas tree, so I figured we should at least take a look. Could be a good one here for the shop."

"What about this one?" she called. She was about twenty feet away from me, standing in a clearing in the middle of the rows of trees. She shook the branch of the tree.

It was a perfectly shaped Christmas tree, and I could see it in the front window of the candy shop covered in gumdrops and candy canes. "It's beauti-ful," I said. Then the wind picked up, and gusts blew all the snow clinging to the tree's branches onto Cass.

"Ahhh!" she screamed.

I stifled a laugh as she shook the snow out of her hair and brushed it off her designer coat.

"I can tell you want to laugh," Cass said. "Are you ready to go?"

"More than ready," I said.

She nodded. "Even though the tree attacked me, I'll stop by the house and tell Grandma Leah we want it for the candy shop."

Again, I didn't tell Cass I couldn't have a shop tree.

* * *

On the ride back to the village, Jethro sat on Cass's lap. He had his hooves pressed up against the dashboard, and he stared intently out the windshield.

"This is one intense pig," Cass said. "He really might have a chance to make it in the big time."

I didn't answer. I was too deep in thought. My brain whirled over thoughts of Rocky, the murder, Grandma Leah, Eric, and Aiden. For some reason, Aiden was on my mind most of all.

It wasn't a long drive back to the village, maybe twenty minutes on a normal day, but this wasn't a normal day. The closer I got to Harvest, the worse the traffic became. Traffic was known to be bad in Berlin on Route 39 at the height of tourist season, but never in Harvest. There were no major roads that came into the village, which was one reason why Margot was so determined to have events like the Christmas Market, to convince tourists to come off the beaten path to Sugarcreek and Berlin and visit our village.

I drove up Apple Street and parked behind a buggy. Getting into the spot was tricky because there were so many buggies and cars backed up on Main Street, which ran perpendicular to Apple.

"I guess the Christmas Market is a big deal around here," Cass mused.

"I don't know if this is just the Christmas Market. The Amish Confectionary Competition this fall brought over two thousand people to Harvest, and the traffic wasn't this bad."

Cass and I climbed out of my car. Jethro was in her arms. I could tell Cass and the little pig were bonding. The sidewalk was crammed with pedestrians, standing and staring. Cass led the way. "Excuse us, excuse us, pig coming through."

English and Amish tourists jumped out of her way. I followed in her wake.

"I really can't figure out what all the commotion is," I said in Cass's ear.

She stopped on the corner. "You will."

"What do you mean?" I asked as I came up behind her.

She pointed to our left, and that's when I saw the camel standing in the middle of Main Street.

Chapter 22

"I don't know much about camels," Cass said, "but I don't believe they are native to Ohio."

"I think this is Margot's big surprise," I said.

The camel stopped in the middle of the street and chewed. His long, crooked teeth clicked back and forth across one another. I didn't know much about camels either, but it looked like a big one to me. It had one hump, and a red, orange, and yellow woven blanket was over its back. Falling snow gathered on the blanket. Just like a horse, it had a bit connected to a lead in its mouth. Abel Esh yanked on the lead, but to no avail. The camel wasn't having it.

All the camel did in response was blink its long lashes.

"Abel doesn't seem to be having any luck with that camel." Cass laughed.

The camel spat at Abel and hit him in the side of the face. The crowd gave a collective "Yuck!"

I grimaced. "I would say that's an understatement."

Abel removed a handkerchief from his back pocket and wiped it down the side of his face.

Margot Rawlings ran out into the street. It was the first time I had seen her since all the talk about Eric's show and the Christmas Market had begun. Her short curls bounced on her head as she rushed over to Abel. "Now, take care of Melchior," she said. "He's on loan from a friend."

"Margot has friends who lend out camels?" Cass asked out of the side of her mouth. "Why don't I have friends like that? You don't own a camel I don't know about, do you?"

I didn't bother to answer.

Abel said something in Pennsylvania Dutch. I didn't understand the words, but from his hand gestures I guessed it wasn't a compliment to Margot or to Melchior, the camel. He threw down the lead and stomped across the street.

Margot watched him go. "Abel! Come back! I don't know how to take care of a camel! I hired you to do it!"

Abel threw one arm up in the air and kept going.

Margot listlessly picked up the rope and looked around at the crowd. "Can someone help me with the camel? He really is a sweet animal."

No one moved. I believe that we all were collectively recalling the camel spittle that hit Abel in the face.

"Anyone?" Margot asked in plaintive voice.

I sighed and pushed through the crowd.

"Oh, come on," Cass said, but she followed me, still carrying Jethro.

Margot beamed. "Bailey. I knew someone as kind as you would come to my rescue. Could you help me

get Melchior over to the manger scene?" She pointed
to the square. To the right of the gazebo where
Rocky had died was the Christmas Market. It was in
full swing now, and shoppers moved through the
booths carrying fresh-made holiday wreaths and
cups of steaming hot chocolate. To the left of the
gazebo was the nativity scene. Members of the big
white church milled around in biblical robes and
head coverings. Would-be shepherds carried staffs,
and two of the three wise men shared a laugh. A
donkey chewed on one of the snow-covered bushes
on the green.

A car honked. The camel was backing up traffic
for at least a mile.

Margot held out Melchior's lead to me. I sighed
and took it from her hand. Looking Melchior in the
eye, I whispered, "Please move. And don't spit on
me, please! The last couple of days have been a little
rough for me."

The camel blinked one long-lashed eyelid.

I pulled on the lead, and he took a step forward,
then another, then one after the other until we were
standing on the green.

Traffic resumed.

Cass stared at me in awe. "When were you going
to tell me that you're a camel whisperer? I think this
was something I should have known."

"It was an untapped talent until now," I confessed.

Margot clasped her hands in front of her chest.
"That was amazing, Bailey, and it's just so perfect. It
makes sense for what we need."

I didn't like the sound of that. "For what we need?"

"This might be a case where it's better not to ask

too many questions," Cass whispered into my ear. "I suggest a hasty retreat." She handed Jethro to me. "Or you can use the little oinker as a pig shield."

The camel leaned down. I winced, certain I was going to be camel slobbered. Instead the large animal bumped noses with Jethro. The pig wiggled in my arms, kicking his little hooved feet. I didn't know if that meant he was excited or terrified. In any case, Jethro's presence seemed to be just what the camel needed.

Margot smiled. "They want to be friends," she cooed.

"Retreat! Retreat!" Cass whispered harshly in my ear.

"Bailey, thank goodness you got the camel under control," Margot said breathlessly. "I'm so glad that we were able to snag Melchior for the live nativity. There were lots of animals at the first Christmas. We had to have animals! How can it be a real live nativity without animals? We have a donkey, sheep, and a goose, of course, but I knew we needed more, and that's when I called in a favor and got Melchior."

"You have connections where you can call in a favor and get a camel lined up?" Cass asked.

"Doesn't everyone?" She sounded surprised.

"No," Cass said. "Everyone does not."

"I've had the most wonderful idea," Margot said.

"I think you missed your opportunity to get away," Cass said to me.

"Mary is in the hospital!" Margot exclaimed.

"Geez! I didn't even know they had a hospital in Bethlehem back then," Cass said.

"You are not helping," I muttered out of the side of my mouth.

"And I need a new Mary. You would make a perfect Mary. You have the long dark hair. The soulful blue eyes."

I frowned. I had never viewed my eyes as soulful, and since Mary had been Middle Eastern, I highly doubted she had blue eyes.

"What happened to Mary? Is she okay?"

"She's fine. She's just in the hospital having her baby two weeks early." She threw up her hands. "Can you believe that she would have her baby early when we need her to play the part of the Blessed Virgin?"

"I'm sure she didn't plan to ruin your nativity," I said.

"I thought the point of the nativity was that baby Jesus was already born," Cass said with a laugh. "If she's pregnant, how was that going to work?"

Margot sighed. "We were hoping to do a before-and-after thing. We planned to put her behind Joseph or the donkey to hide her baby bump after the miraculous birth."

I took a step back. Cass was right. I should have retreated a long time ago. "I'm so very sorry that the nativity isn't going the way you would like, but I'm sure you will find a replacement. There are so many ladies who attend your church. Surely one of them will help you out."

Margot shook her head. "No! Not a one would agree to do it. You're my last hope for a Mary. I asked four other young women before I asked you, and you know the Amish won't do it."

"You're a fifth-string Mary," Cass said.

"Margot," I said as calmly as possible. "I'm not pregnant for starters, so I can't do that before-and-after thing you want."

Margot waved away my concern. "We aren't asking you to do that. It's too late to figure out how to make it work. All you have to do is sit on a donkey, look pretty, and hold the baby Jesus. Is that really too much to ask?"

It kind of was. "Swissmen Sweets has a table at the Christmas Market. There's only an hour left before the market closes. I should be helping Charlotte," I said aloud, and then I thought to myself, *I have a murder to solve.*

"Charlotte can handle it. She told me that she could. I checked with her before speaking to you."

I scowled.

She patted the curls that wove around her puffy pink earmuffs. The earmuffs were huge, twice the size of my fist. It was a wonder that she could hear anything. Her hearing must have been top-notch. "I have something to show you." She stepped into the manger and came out a second later with a life-sized baby doll.

Cass grimaced. "Dolls that look like real babies creep me out."

"Shh," I said to Cass. "Really." I waved my hands as if to fend off the doll. "I can't. I have so much going on at the store with the Christmas sale and the Christmas Market, and Eric and his production team are in town." I eyed her. "It would have been nice to know about it before his arrival."

"Surprises are always nice," Margot said brightly.

Not all surprises.

"Aiden Brody will be playing Joseph." She waggled her eyebrows. "It just seems fitting in this case that you should be Mary."

"I—"

"She'll do it," Cass interrupted. "She would love to."

My mouth fell open as I stared at Cass.

"Brilliant!" Margot shouted. "Oh, and Bailey, I heard that you were here this morning when that unfortunate discovery was made."

I grimaced as I remembered the scene. "I was."

"Did you happen to see a shepherd's hook lying about? It seems one the shepherds had left his hook in the stable overnight and now it's missing. It is a tall hooked staff and has been used in the Harvest village nativity scene for years. It belonged to my father originally and has his initials on it—JR. It would be an absolute shame to lose it. Did you see it?"

"I didn't," I said.

She sighed. "What a pity!" She closed her eyes for a moment. "You'll dress at the church. All the costumes are there, and the parade will leave from there too." She flounced away.

"Parade?" I asked.

She wiggled her fingers at me and walked away, leaving me holding the baby Jesus and Jethro in my arms. When had my life taken such a strange turn?

Chapter 23

I stood outside the manger scene with Melchior looming over me and handed Cass the doll and the pig. It was a little after three, and the Christmas Market was humming. Shoppers bought Amish-made scarves, quilts, cheese, honey, maple syrup, and our candy from Swissmen Sweets. Others staked out prime spots along the parade route. I hadn't known about the parade, and it made me nervous that people were already claiming spots two hours before the parade was to begin. How extravagant was it? I dreaded the parade.

"Whoa, I'll take Jethro, but I don't want that doll," Cass said.

"Just hold on to it while I secure the camel," I said, and tethered Melchior's lead to a tree.

"I never thought I'd hear you say that."

"You wouldn't believe the things I have said since moving to Amish Country that I never would have believed would come out of my mouth." After Melchior was secure, I took the doll from Cass and tucked it back in the manger. The goose that was nestled in a pile of straw inside honked at me. I adjusted baby Jesus in place and ran out.

"Bailey!" Juliet's high-pitched voice floated across the square to me. "There you are! I was getting worried about Jethro."

I noted that she was more worried about the pig than she had been about me, but that was to be expected where Juliet was concerned. I expected her son, Aiden, was in the same boat as I was.

Juliet took Jethro from Cass's arms and tucked him under her chin. The pig cuddled back. No one could question the bond between woman and pig, that was for sure.

I had to hand it to Juliet. She didn't even bat an eyelash at Melchior, who was leaning over her shoulder to get a better look at the pig. Which made me think that Margot had had it wrong. I wasn't the camel whisperer at all. Jethro was.

"How did he do? Does he have a part in Eric's show?" Her eyes were so full of hope.

"He will. It's a very small part, but a lot of the big stars in Hollywood get their starts that way," I said, knowing nothing of the kind. "You really have Cass to thank for it. She pushed hard for Linc to include Jethro."

Juliet wrapped her free arm around Cass. "Oh, thank you so much! You don't know what this means to Jethro and me!"

"Jethro will be starting out small," Cass said sagely. "But I think he has real potential."

"Oh—" She nodded. "I understand. Jethro is new

to the business and has to pay his dues. That makes perfect sense to me. You did a wonderful job, Cass."

"I even got him a part on Bailey's new sh—"

"Well, I'm so glad you're here to collect Jethro," I interrupted Cass. I didn't want anyone to know about Linc's offer to give me a show yet, especially Aiden's mother, who would spread the news all over the village and to Aiden before I could even speak to my grandmother about it. "But can you bring Jethro back tonight during the live nativity? The TV crew will be shooting that . . ."

Juliet clapped her hands. "And you and Aiden will be Mary and Joseph. I was the one who suggested it to Margot. I cannot imagine a more perfect couple to fill the roles."

Cass tilted her head. "I think it's nice of Aiden to jump in and help, but isn't he busy with the murder thing?"

"He might have to leave if a call comes in, but I thought it was better for Bailey that he be her Joseph rather than anyone else, don't you?"

"Definitely," Cass agreed.

Juliet hugged her little pig a bit tighter. "Jethro will be a smash hit in the nativity. I'm going to take him home first and give him a bath to make sure he's ready for his big debut, and we will have to find his best bow tie." Juliet blew us each a kiss; she even blew one to the camel and went on her way.

I doubted the animals at the first Christmas wore accessories that night, but it wasn't my battle to fight. That was something Juliet would have to take up with Margot.

"Have you ever wondered how anyone can be that happy all the time?" Cass asked.

"Daily. Let's get away from the nativity before you are drafted into being an angel."

Cass snorted. "No one would *ever* give me that part."

Cass followed me through the holiday tourists to the other side of the square and the Swissmen Sweets table.

Charlotte set a white candy box into the waiting hands of an English woman. "Thanks so much for stopping by. You also might want to visit our store. We have even more candies there. It's just across the street."

The English woman thanked Charlotte for the tip and went on her way.

"Great marketing," Cass said. "I should hire you for JP Chocolates."

"Marketing?" Charlotte asked, sounding confused.

I shook my head. "Cass just thinks you are doing a good job promoting Swissmen Sweets, and so do I."

"I do," Cass said. "Hey, I'm going to take a loop and check out the other booths." With that she left our table.

The Amish girl blushed. "*Danki.* Bailey, while you were gone both Eric and Aiden came looking for you." Her face turned a slight shade of red. "I know they are both *gut* friends of yours."

I frowned.

"I do hope you will pick Aiden in the end," she said all in a rush. "The whole village would be heart-broken if you broke Aiden's heart. He is such a kind man. He's one of the few in the sheriff's department who really cares for the Amish. We don't want anything bad to happen to him."

"I know that," I said as patiently as I could. "But Aiden and I aren't in a position that breaking hearts is at risk for either of us."

She wrinkled her nose as if she wasn't so sure that was true. I wished that the village inhabitants wouldn't try so hard playing matchmaker. They were only making it more difficult for Aiden and me to get past anything more than a tense friendship. I didn't know yet what I wanted our relationship to be, but I did want Aiden and me to be the ones who decided what it would become.

"All right," she said, shaking her head as if to get rid of unpleasant thoughts. "The Christmas Market has been very busy. The peppermint treats have been a hit. I had to run over to Swissmen Sweets to get more peppermint bark. We thought we had made too much, but what we made most definitely won't last the entire Christmas Market. Clara is making some more now. She said after the Christmas Market tonight that she and I could make more peppermint candies. She's going to teach me how to make peppermint divinity, which is my favorite."

The green-eyed monster reared its ugly head again in my mind. It wasn't the first time I'd thought that Charlotte was better suited to be my grandmother's granddaughter than I was. She was the Amish granddaughter my grandmother must have wanted. I could never be that. Maybe it wouldn't be a bad thing if I took Linc up on his offer and was away from Harvest for a few months. *Maami* and Charlotte would be fine without me. I wondered why the thought upset me so much.

"And was that a camel in the middle of the road?" she asked.

I nodded, happy for the change of subject. "Yes, his name is Melchior."

She shook her head. "Harvest grows stranger by the day."

"Tell me about it." I looked around the Christmas Market. All the shops in the village were represented in the square as well as a select few from other parts of the county, but there were no other candy shops. The only out-of-town shops Margot had allowed into the market were not in direct competition with any of the village's businesses.

Esh Family Pretzels' table was right next to ours. As Emily packed up her pretzels, I waved at her. "Hi, Emily."

She pretended not to hear me as she shuffled her already perfectly lined-up pretzels in the battery-operated warmer at her table. I sighed and pressed my lips together. This had to stop. It was so typical of the Amish way of dealing with things to ignore and pretend nothing had ever happened. It reminded me that I would have been a terrible Amish person even if my father had stayed in the faith. I hated to brush things under the rug. I wanted to talk about what was wrong and what was going on. I wanted to make amends.

"Is Esther holding down the shop?" I asked, making at least an attempt at a conversation.

She didn't reply.

"I saw your brother earlier helping with the live nativity. It looks like Margot is putting on quite a production again." I didn't add that Abel had quit helping with the live nativity because of Melchior. Chances were she already knew.

Still nothing.

"If you need anything, Charlotte and I are happy to lend a hand."

"I can help too," Cass said.

Emily looked at me then and whispered, *"Danki."*

It was more than I had gotten from her in weeks, so I would take it.

Charlotte watched Emily with a worried look on her face. She might not know exactly why Emily was upset, but she had probably guessed that it had something to do with her, since Emily paid even less attention to Charlotte than she did to me.

I couldn't worry about Emily at the moment. I had too many other problems to contend with. Just then, I noticed a teenaged boy and an Amish man standing in front of the Christmas trees at the Keim Christmas Tree Farm.

The young man—I would guess he was almost twenty—had black hair from what I could see of it sticking out from under his black stocking cap. He was clean shaven and wore wire-rimmed glasses. He continually glanced over at the pretzel stand at Emily. Emily blushed when she looked up and caught the boy staring at her.

The man with the boy smacked him lightly on the back of the boy's head as if to get his attention. He pointed at a tree and at an English family who had presumably chosen to take that tree home.

When the man turned around I gasped. I knew that face. I was looking into the face of the man I had seen running away from the guest house. I was looking into the face of Thaddeus Keim.

Chapter 24

Thad and I stared at each other for a long moment until he spun around and melted into the crowd.

"I'll be right back," I said, and hurried after the Amish man. I didn't wait for Charlotte or Cass to respond.

When I made it to the other side of the Christmas trees, I realized what an impossible task it was to find Thad. Now that the Christmas market was closing, there was a crush of people on the square making last-minute purchases before the parade started. All were eager to get a jump on their holiday shopping with unique gifts from Amish Country.

The Amish teenager appeared at my side. "Do you need help finding a tree, miss?" he asked.

I grew very still. His eyes were a smoky shade of gray. I had seen eyes that color only one other time. The image of the baby rattle, which had fallen from Thad's pocket at the guest house, came back to me. The image of Rocky's body and her eyes came back to me. No. I couldn't be right. It was impossible that this farfetched idea was true. I was jumping to conclusions and searching for connections that weren't there.

"Umm, no, I . . . I mean—" I couldn't find the words. What I wanted to ask was "Is Rocky your mother?"

He smiled. "I know for some *Englischers* picking the perfect tree is a challenge, but I can assure you, you can't go wrong with any of our trees. They are organically grown and cared for like members of the family."

I shook the unlikely conclusion from my head. "I . . . I might need a tree soon, but not right now. Who was that man who was with you earlier?"

"Man?" the boy asked.

"Yes, he was here a little while ago."

"Oh, you must mean my *daed*." His expression cleared. "He was just here. I don't know where he went, but he should be back soon. Did you want to talk to him about a tree? I can help you just as well. I've been working at the tree farm since before I could walk. I can answer any questions that you have about the trees. What about a Douglas fir? They are a favorite of mine." He shook the tree. "They are sturdy, grow straight with soft needles. You don't have to worry about this tree toppling over, miss."

"What's your name?" I interrupted him.

He blinked at me. "I'm sorry. I should have told you earlier. I'm Daniel Keim."

"Does your mother work at the Christmas tree farm too?" I asked.

His face flashed red. "Do you want a tree, miss? I'm here to sell trees." His whole demeanor had changed; no longer was I faced with the friendly Amish salesperson.

I shook my head, feeling awful for the blunt question. "I'm sorry. I didn't mean to pry."

"No tree, then?" he asked.

I shook my head. "No tree," I said, realizing that I might just have blown my chance to talk to Daniel Keim, who might very well be Rocky's son.

He turned away from me and walked back into the pen of trees, smacking his yardstick against the piney branches as he went.

"What was that all about?" Cass said, her arms full with packages wrapped in brown paper.

I pointed at her arm. "What's all that?"

"Holiday presents for everyone back in the city. No one is going to have gifts like this. I got Amish honey, Amish cheese—you know how I love the Amish cheese."

I did know. The last time Cass was in Harvest, she had almost bought all the cheese in the cheese shop on the opposite side of Swissmen Sweets from Esh Family Pretzels.

"I got a couple quilted pillows, too," she went on to say. "I thought Jean Pierre would like those. He loves things that are quaint." She adjusted the packages in her arms. "Now, why did you run away from your table like your tail was on fire?"

"I saw Thad Keim," I whispered. "And he is the man we ran into at the guest house."

"He is?" she shouted. "Where is he?"

"Shh, keep your voice down. I don't know where he went. He ran away from me when he saw me."

"Because he's guilty."

"Guilty of what? Dropping a rattle?"

"Or murder," Cass said.

Or murder, I silently agreed.

"Where's your dad?" I heard a voice ask behind me. I turned to find Aiden standing with Daniel by the Douglas fir he'd tried to sell me.

"I don't know," Daniel said, much more defensively than when I had asked him the same question just a moment ago.

"I need to talk to him," Aiden said.

"I'm sure he will be back soon," Daniel said.

"I think we are onto something here," Cass whispered.

Aiden's head snapped in our direction, and he scowled at Cass and me. My best friend really had to work on her stage whisper.

Aiden nodded and walked over to me. "Bailey, shouldn't you be in your booth selling candy?"

Cass smiled. "Charlotte has it covered. The market is closing anyway."

Aiden's gaze slid in her direction.

"Aiden, there's something I need to talk to you about," I said.

He raised his eyebrows at my serious tone. "Did you break and enter into another crime scene and want to come clean about it?"

I frowned.

"Aiden," Cass said. "You shouldn't just assume that Bailey is up to no good."

He smiled, and the dimple in his cheek popped out. "When you are with her, the likelihood of her being up to *something* jumps tenfold."

Cass grinned. "I'm glad that I make a difference around here."

Over Cass's shoulder, I found Daniel watching us with those haunting gray eyes.

"Aiden," I said. "I really do need to speak with you in private. It won't take long."

Cass looked from Aiden to me and back again. "I'll leave Mary and Joseph to it." She held up her packages. "I need to get these to the candy shop, and I can help Charlotte at the booth."

"Mary and Joseph? What is she talking about?" Aiden asked as Cass returned to the Swissmen Sweets booth.

I shook my head. Aiden didn't seem to know that he was playing the lead as Joseph in the live nativity, and I wasn't going to be the one to tell him when I had far more important information to share with him.

I walked away from the Christmas trees and closer to the gazebo.

Aiden glanced to the side of the gazebo. "Is that a camel?"

I sighed. "Margot."

He shook his head.

"His name is Melchior. You might want to talk to Margot about the nativity."

"What about it?"

"Umm, you should take that up with her." I nodded. "It would be much better if it came from her."

He folded his arms. "Is that what you want to tell me?"

I shook my head. "I wanted to talk to you about Daniel and Thad. Thad was definitely the man Cass and I saw coming out of Rocky's room at the guest house."

"You're sure?"

I nodded. "And it makes sense because it was the tree farm advertisement hidden in her makeup case. I think she is connected to the Keim family."

Aiden was quiet for a moment. "How?"

"I think Rocky might be Daniel's mother," I blurted out.

Aiden blinked at me. "What on earth are you talking about? How could Rocky be Daniel's mother? She's not Amish."

"Maybe she was Amish? Maybe she gave her baby up to the Amish?"

Aiden looked at me as if I'd just said aliens had landed their UFO in the middle of the Harvest village square.

"It makes sense. The baby rattle, why Thaddeus would want to break into her room—he must have been looking for any connection to Daniel so that he could destroy it, and why he ran away right when he saw me. He recognized me. I know he did. That's why he ran away from the Christmas Market. As soon as he saw me, he ran away. He knew that I saw him at the guest house."

"It's still quite a leap to jump to the conclusion that Rocky was his mother. We have no evidence of that."

"We might not have evidence, but have you seen the boy's eyes? They are the same unusual shade of gray Rocky's were. I had never seen eyes that color, and I remember thinking that when I first met her, and . . ." I couldn't finish the thought. I couldn't say that I had seen the same color of eyes staring at me after I had found Rocky's lifeless body in the gazebo with Eric standing over her dead body.

Aiden touched my arm as if he knew what I was thinking. Maybe he even had the same image in his mind, of those staring gray eyes. I hoped that one day I would forget them. I wondered how many equally gruesome images Aiden had seen as a police officer and wished he could forget someday. Had he been able to forget any at all?

Aiden's frown deepened. "I'm not saying what you think is impossible; it's just quite a stretch on a lot of circumstantial evidence. You can't look at someone's eyes and know they are related to someone else. I will look into it though."

"Thanks," I said. It was the most I could ask for, but I knew in my bones that I was right. "I'm not crazy."

His mouth lifted in the corner and one of his dimples popped on display. "You might be a little crazy, but a lot of the time you are also right. I won't discount that."

His response was more than I deserved.

Chapter 25

"Christmas in Amish Country is like none other," Eric said as he walked across the square with the collar on his wool coat popped up and his hair perfectly in place. "Living in New York City, I don't have much time to enjoy the simpler things in life. I have always respected the way people in this fascinating culture have been able to live in a simpler way."

I stifled a snort as I stood with Cass and Charlotte at Swissmen Sweets' candy booth. The Christmas Market would close in fifteen minutes, which was a good thing because we were almost completely sold out of candy. I had a feeling the first time Eric had even thought about Amish Country was when he found out that's where I had gone after I left New York. I'm guessing it was Rocky who really new about the Amish.

A group of Amish children ran by Eric as he continued to walk and speak in front of the camera. Eric waved at the kids, who waved back. Roden followed the children with his camera. Pike held his boom high to catch every sound.

"Cut!" Linc cried when the children were out of the shot.

Roden and Pike lowered their equipment.

"This is the perfect shot!" Linc's booming voice broke through the other chatter on the green.

"I think we need to run through it again," Eric said. "I think I can do better."

"The shot was perfect. Those kids running through, we couldn't have timed it better. That's our shot. I will say when we need retakes."

Eric frowned. He wasn't used to someone dismissing his opinion.

Linc panned his hand in front of himself as if he were the one holding the camera. "Roden, we need to capture as much of this as possible. We might not use it all, but it's better to leave footage on the editing room floor than to miss a shot."

Roden stood a few feet behind him holding the camera awkwardly on his shoulder. He look tired.

"Hold the camera still," Linc snapped at the camera man.

Roden's jaw twitched as if he was barely keeping back whatever it was he wanted to say.

"We only have one chance to get this shot. Don't screw it up." Linc's voice was sharp. "I can't have any other screwups on this shoot."

Was that how he saw Rocky's death? As just another screwup? I was liking Linc less and less the more I learned about him. He also went up a couple of notches on my suspect list, and he already had the number one spot.

Pike had lowered his boom and straightened. I bet he didn't want to be in Linc's line of fire.

"Linc!" Margot called as she bustled across the square. She pushed tourists aside as she went. "It's so good to see you."

I hid behind Charlotte, hoping that Margot wouldn't see me. Between Margot and Linc, I was more afraid of Margot. In the span of a few minutes she'd put me in charge of moving a camel and made me Mother Mary. It was best I disappeared before she gave me another assignment. I made a hasty retreat back to Swissmen Sweets' table, but not before I looked back at the Christmas trees. Daniel was no longer there. I wondered if the Keims had decided to close up early for the day.

Charlotte and Cass were busy with a line of customers. I was happy to see that our peppermint-themed table was such a hit.

"You will love these mint meltaways," Cass told a young woman with a toddler in her arms. "They are great bribery tools for kids too."

The young mother laughed and accepted the candy.

When she was gone, Cass asked, "What's going on over there?"

I turned and saw Margot talking to Eric and Linc. She pointed at different spots on the square. "I really don't want to know."

Then Margot turned and pointed at me.

"Busted," Cass said.

Eric and the crew pivoted to see what she was pointing to, and Linc headed our way.

"There's our star!" Linc pointed at me.

I pointed at myself as if to ask, "Who me?"

"Of course, this will be the perfect scene of you

and Eric walking together. That way we can capture everything that is happening around you but be focused on your relationship."

"I thought we weren't going with the relationship angle," I said.

Eric wrapped his arm around my shoulders. "Don't worry, I won't bite. All you have to do is walk and smile pretty for the camera."

Cass glared at him. Eric noticed and dropped his arm. At least someone intimidated Eric.

"I have candy to sell," I said. "I thought this show was about the candy."

Linc smoothed his mustache, which looked like a wooly bear caterpillar on his upper lip. It wasn't a good look. "Okay, forget the other shot. What about this? We shoot you selling candy, maybe you can tell us how the candies you sell relate to your Amish culture. Then later we will shoot in your kitchen, getting footage of you and, we hope, your Amish grandmother, making the candies. I know that the footage sounds out of sequence, but that is what editing is for."

"I haven't had time to ask my grandmother about all this yet. Besides, she might not want to be on camera. Not many Amish do."

"She will have the time of her life," Linc said. "Here." He backed away. "Just act natural."

"Natural?" I slipped behind the table. Charlotte was standing next to me with wide eyes.

"Just do it," Cass whispered. "Pretend no one else is here."

That was easy for her to say. She didn't have a camera pointed at her face. Suddenly I didn't know what to do with my hands. Out of desperation, I picked up a box of fudge.

"Okay. Eric, stand across from her at the table. Remember to look friendly!"

Eric stood across from me and picked up a bag of peppermint taffy.

"The scene is set," Linc said. "Let's start filming, and Bailey tell us about the candies."

"The candies?" My mind went completely blank. I couldn't remember my middle name. How was I supposed to remember how these candies related to Amish culture?

While my brain searched for something interesting to say, Linc looked around. "Roden, Pike, what are you doing? We are in the middle of a shoot."

The two men stood off to the side with Josie.

"Josie, Bailey could use a little touch-up," Linc said. Touch-up.

The girl came over with her makeup kit, holding a makeup brush like a sword.

I winced.

"Trust me. You want to look good on camera." She ran the brush over my cheeks. "You need a little color. You are awfully pale." She applied another brush to my eyelids. "There, much better. Now you won't like a corpse on the screen."

"Umm . . . thanks."

Roden and Pike were in their spots to the right of Eric and me so they could capture our conversation from the side. Roden lift his camera onto his right shoulder. He panned the camera back and forth across the square. Even in the cold and snow, beads of sweat popped up on his forehead.

"Roden, stop messing around and get a wide-angle shot and then zoom in on Eric as he walks this way from the gazebo. Pike, for the love of God, you get your head in the game too. Eric, you walk in with the intro again."

Pike held his boom out as far as he could without getting it into the shot of the camera, and Roden panned the square, taking in everything from the merchants at the Christmas Market to the preparation for that evening's live nativity.

"Good, good," Linc said. "Eric, go!"

Eric walked toward the camera. "We are here in Harvest, Ohio, in the middle of Amish Country for a real Amish Christmas. As all of you know, there is nothing I love better than simple ingredients in my award-winning recipes."

Eric's cooking style was anything but simple. The man used dry ice in at least a third of his recipes.

"I'm here in Amish Country to meet up with my dear friend, Bailey King, of Swissmen Sweets, an Amish candy shop right here in Harvest. Bailey has told me so many nice things about this place. I knew I had to come check it out this holiday season."

Another lie. Eric didn't find out about my connection to Amish Country until the media broke it because I was caught up in a murder investigation.

"And here is my friend Bailey now. Hi, Bailey," Eric said with so much forced cheer that he made my teeth ache.

I took a breath and smiled. "It's good to see you,

Eric." And then I went into a description of the candies on my table.

Ten minutes later, Linc clapped his hands. "Cut!"

I blinked. I had completely lost track of time while talking about the candies. In fact, I had completely forgotten that the camera was even there.

Roden lowered the camera from his shoulder with a slight wince and heavy sigh.

"Beautiful, Bailey. You are a natural," Linc said.

"How did I do?" Eric asked.

"You did fine."

Eric scowled. He didn't like to be outshone.

"We can use that for your screen test. The network will love you." He grinned.

"Screen test?" Eric asked. "What screen test?

"You are a natural," Cass exclaimed. "We are definitely going to ask for a raise when your show is picked up."

"Her show?" Eric asked. "What show? I'm the one with the show."

Cass narrowed her eyes at Eric. "This doesn't involve you."

"Cass," Eric said.

"Jerk," Cass replied.

"Cass," I said.

She glanced at me. "I'm just calling it like I see it."

I felt a headache coming on.

Chapter 26

Linc and the rest of the film crew moved to the side to discuss the next shot while Cass and Eric had a standoff right in front of my table.

Eric laughed. "I appreciate your honesty, Cass. It's one of your best qualities. Unfortunately, it also gets you into trouble."

She narrowed her eyes. "I'm not the one in trouble here."

"What *are* you doing here?" he asked.

"I'm visiting my best friend." Cass linked her arm with mine. "And it would serve you well to remember that I have her back."

Eric waved his hands. "I don't have any intention of making trouble for Bailey."

"What about the dead ex-girlfriend slash executive producer?" she wanted to know. "Don't you think that made some trouble for Bailey?"

"That wasn't my fault. I would never have done anything like that."

"If it served your goals, you just might."

Eric scowled, which marred his handsome features.

"Guys, guys, please. I have to play Mary in an hour. I could use some serenity so I can get into character."

"Enough," Linc said. "We got the shot at the candy table that we wanted with Bailey. Now we need to get a few more shots of the market in general and reset for the live nativity."

My stomach dropped when I realized that I would be the Mary in the live nativity on Eric's show.

I worried over being Mary as Melchior walked by my booth, his long lead trailing behind him through the snow. The crowd divided to let the camel through. No one attempted to stop him or grab his lead.

"Go on, camel whisperer. It's your time," Cass whispered.

I straightened my shoulders and walked out to the camel. "Hey there, Melchior. Let's get you back to the manger scene, okay?"

He blinked his long lashes at me.

I leaned over to pick up his lead, and he bared his teeth. The rope was frayed. I eyed the camel, wondering if he had chewed through it. If that was the case, there was no hope of keeping the camel in place. An alarming thought.

"Easy there," I said. "I'm just going to help you back across the square. It's much quieter over there, and I think you would be happier on the side away from the commotion." I held my breath and picked up the lead. I was certain that I was about to get slapped on the side of the face with camel spit at any moment. That would be the icing on the cake of the awful day I'd had. I tugged lightly on the lead, and much to my surprise Melchior followed me with no further protests. The crowd clapped. Maybe Cass was right and I was the camel whisperer.

"Roden, are you getting this?" Linc asked in a harsh whisper.

Roden slowly lifted the camera onto his shoulder.

Margot met me at the manger. "Thank goodness you brought him back." She made a move to pet the camel, and Melchior showed his teeth again. She retracted her hand. "Oh, all right, you beastie. I'm beginning to wonder if bringing the camel here was a good idea. He is turning into much more work than I thought he would be. My friend insisted that he was a calm animal." Her face cleared. "As long as you are here, we will be fine. It's clear that he has taken a shine to you."

I tethered Melchior back to the tree. This time I tied him there with a double knot. I wasn't sure I would be able to untie the knot when the time came, but I would deal with that later. Of course, if Melchior chewed through the rope, it wouldn't matter how tightly I tied it. I turned away from the tree and found Pike and Roden right behind me. I jumped.

Roden lowered his camera. "We can edit out the jumping."

"For sure," Pike agreed.

"Bailey!" Margot shouted. "Thank heavens you are here! We still can't find the shepherd's staff that was left at the manger scene last night. I can't believe the gall of the person who would have stolen it. From the nativity of all places. Are you sure you didn't see it when you were here early this morning?"

"I didn't," I said for the second time. I didn't add

that I had been a little too distracted by the dead body in the middle of the gazebo to notice a missing shepherd's hook.

"Well, you do have a camel," Cass said, "so I don't think many people are going to be looking at the shepherds or their props."

"It's just not acceptable," Margot disagreed. "We need this live nativity to be perfect. It's going to be on television." She pointed at Roden and Pike just in case I wasn't aware that they were there.

"I'm sure the staff will turn up. Could it be in the church? Aren't all the props and costumes for the live nativity stored in the church? Perhaps Juliet knows where it is."

"I've already had her look," Margot moaned.

I patted her arm. "I'm sure it will turn up."

Pike untied Melchior's lead.

"What are you doing?" I asked.

The camel ducked his head, and Pike scratched him on the nose. "Do you want to go for a walk, old boy? I know you must not like to be tied up that way."

The camel nuzzled Pike's hand. The rest of us stared at him openmouthed.

"What?" Pike asked in his surfer dude voice. "I worked at a zoo when I was in college. I took care of the animals. I loved being around the creatures, but it wasn't the right job for me. There was just too much s—"

"Maybe it would help Melchior if you would take him for a walk," I interrupted Pike. I could see where his sentence was going, and Charlotte had been exposed to enough since she'd moved into

Swissmen Sweets. She didn't need any more shocking revelations.

Eric, Josie, and Linc joined us at that point.

"We could use some stills of Eric with the camel. It could be good for promotion."

Eric fussed with his scarf until it looked like he didn't care, and he threw it on. I knew he cared and the laissez-faire scarf wearing was for effect.

"Powder!" Josie rushed at him with her makeup brush. She swiped the bristles across his face and then stepped back and nodded. "Much better. There will be no shine on my watch." She pointed at me. "You could use another coat."

I waved my hand. "I'm fine."

She held her brush at the ready. "If I don't do this, you will look awful on camera. Your shine is terrible. In fact, I could give you a full makeover. I think that it would do so much for you. A little eyeliner goes a long way."

"Bai, I think a makeover would do you some good," Cass agreed.

I frowned at her. "How?"

"Excuse us just for a moment." Cass pulled me away from the nativity and Josie. "You want to talk to Josie about the murder, don't you? She is a main suspect."

"Oh!" Some questions answered for the price of a makeover.

"Right."

We returned to the nativity, and Margot was back. "Bailey, it's time for wardrobe. You need to head over to the church to dress for your role."

"Umm, Margot, about that. Are you really sure

that no one else at the church wants to play the part? I would hate to take it away from someone else."

"Don't you worry about that at all."

"I'll go with you for moral support, and Josie will come too," Cass suggested.

Margot squinted. "Why does the makeup girl need to go?"

"To do her makeup and make Bailey appear more virginal. I think it would really sell her as Mary, don't you?" Cass responded.

"Oh yes." Margot clapped. "That is a lovely idea! We want our Mary to be the very best."

Cass grinned. She knew she'd won.

"Hurry, we don't have much time before the live nativity parade."

"What's the parade route?" I asked, praying it was short.

Margot smiled. "It goes right through the center of the village. The tourists love it every year. You get to ride a donkey."

Cass wrapped her arm around my shoulder. "Come on. Let's go to the church. We will swing by Swissmen Sweets and grab some candy. I can always tell when you need some fudge."

Before we left the square, I felt eyes on the back of my head. I turned and found Pike walking Melchior around the square, watching me with a scowl. Perhaps I had misjudged the young sound guy. Maybe I shouldn't have eliminated him from my list of suspects so quickly. A shiver ran down my spine.

Chapter 27

Even though I wasn't a member of the church on the square, I had been there many times since I had moved to Holmes County. Juliet was an active member of the church and had managed to pull me into many activities there. Aiden was also a member of the church. His mother reminded me that he was "a good Christian man" as often as she could.

The double front doors of the church were bright purple and could be seen all the way across the square outside of the candy shop, where I had fortified myself with fudge. At that moment, they were open and the lovely melodies of Christmas carols floated out.

Juliet had mentioned that there would be choir practice that evening. She was a member of the choir, of course. Actually, I couldn't think of any group in the church that she wasn't involved with somehow. She was certainly Reverend Brook's number one volunteer.

"I love Christmas carols," Josie said, and walked past me into the church.

"Huh," Cass said. "She didn't strike me as a Christmas carol kind of girl."

Cass and I followed Josie. There was a narrow entry and then another set of double doors that opened into the sanctuary. The choir stood at the front of the sanctuary and sang.

"The First Noel" rang through the entire church.

Josie watched in rapt attention. Tears rolled down her cheeks.

"Josie," I said. "Are you all right?"

She shook her head and slipped into the very last pew. "How can I be all right when Rocky is dead?"

"I didn't know you cared about Rocky." I slid into the pew next to her.

"I didn't. She was a terrible woman who wanted to ruin my career just because Eric chose me over her, but she didn't deserve to be killed. I didn't want that to happen to her." She took a breath. "And it's my fault she's dead. That's something I'm going to have to live with."

"You killed her?" Cass asked.

"Kill her? I would never kill anyone!"

"Then why are you responsible?" I asked.

"If she and I hadn't gotten into that stupid fight about Eric, she never would have left the guesthouse last night, and she would still be alive." She held on to the back of the pew in front of her. "She wasn't the nicest person in the world, but I respected her. I was sorry to hear she was dead. It's so hard to believe. Rocky is the last person you would ever think of dying. She just seemed like someone who would fight death with everything she had."

Her comment gave me pause and made me wonder

if there had been any signs of a struggle at the crime scene. Maybe she *had* tried to fight off her attacker. She wasn't a small woman. I would have to ask Aiden. I just wasn't sure he would tell me.

"Have you ever fought with Rocky over anything other than Eric?" I asked.

She looked up. "Sure I have. We were both strong women, and I have worked a lot of shows on her network. Rocky ran a tight production, and we didn't always agree. But we both cared about our jobs more than anything. Our careers came first. I respected that about her. I've worked with her on quite a few projects. Sometimes we didn't agree about how a celebrity's hair should look. I can't tell you how many times we fought over hair on the female chefs. The men, for the most part, are easier. There isn't much you can do to most men's hair. Rocky had a certain vision, and she wanted what she wanted. I was the same way. I have things that I want to achieve, and Rocky and I butted heads when we had different visions."

If Josie was a career girl, she was a good fit for Eric.

Josie leaned back in the pew and stared straight ahead at the choir at the front of the church. They weren't singing at the moment. Instead, the choir director was giving them direction. I spotted Juliet front and center in the middle of the choir. With a red bow tied around his pudgy neck, Jethro was at her feet.

"Because I knew she cared so much about her work," Josie said, "I was surprised when she went off the handle over my dating Eric."

"How did she find out?"

"I don't know exactly. Eric wanted to be very secretive about the relationship. He said he couldn't do anything that might hurt his image, and I felt the same way. I didn't want people to think that I got work at Gourmet Television because I was dating one of its stars. The truth is, I was working for the network long before Eric was. I doubted the media would have paid much attention to that little detail though."

Having had my own story in the media, I could almost guarantee to her that she was right.

"We did little more than smile at each other when we were around other people. My only guess is that someone figured it out and told Rocky, or she recognized the signs because she had been in a relationship with Eric herself. All I can say is that we never were anywhere close to each other when she was around unless I was doing Eric's hair and makeup at the time, and that was strictly professional."

"How did the fight start?" Cass asked.

"I arrived late yesterday evening at the guest house; by the time I got there, Rocky must have already known. I didn't so much as walk through the door before she jumped down my throat. I had never seen her that angry, not even at Linc, and she yelled at him constantly. I really don't know how he's put up with it all these years." She took a pencil from the back of the pew and flipped it over in her hand. "Eric must have been upstairs when she started yelling, because he came downstairs and tried to defend me. I think it only made Rocky angrier. As soon as he came into the picture, she told me to turn around and head back to New York because I was fired."

"Was she angry at Eric, too?" I asked. "If she felt betrayed in any way, Eric was really the person who'd betrayed her."

She shrugged. "I guess she was, but she wasn't going to fire Eric. There was no show without Eric. If she wanted to exact revenge, I was expendable. She could find a makeup artist like me anywhere, or so she told me."

"What did you do after she told you that you were fired?"

"I went up to my room for the night. It was too late to go anywhere else. Eric was able to convince her to at least let me stay the night. I was supposed to find and catch a flight back to New York today, but you know what happened."

I shifted uncomfortably. "Were you alone in your room?"

She scowled at me. "Yes, I was alone."

"You didn't see Eric the rest of the night."

"No. I didn't see anyone the rest of the night. I ate the cereal bar I had in my purse for dinner and went to sleep. I woke up this morning to learn that Rocky was dead."

"Who told you?" Cass asked.

"A sheriff's deputy. A young one. Deputy Little, I think he said his name was. Pike and I were in the kitchen. Pike was eating and getting ready for a day of shooting. I was wondering how I would make it to the airport for my flight. There aren't a lot of taxi or Uber options out here."

I nodded. She was right away about that. "When Little arrived, what did he say?"

"The deputy told us what had happened. As you can imagine, we were shocked. I don't know if I have ever been so shocked in my life." Tears sprang to her eyes. "Rocky was a hard woman, but I respected her. I wouldn't have wanted something like this to happen to her. I wouldn't want this to happen to anyone, really."

"After you had that fight with her, do you know where she went?" I asked.

"I assume the gazebo where she was killed."

"Why would she go there?"

Josie sniffled. "How would I know that? It wasn't like we were friends. I didn't like her, but I didn't want anything like this to happen to her." Her hands shook. "I wish I could have a cigarette. I'm probably not allowed to smoke in here."

"That would be my guess," Cass said as the choir broke out into "The Little Drummer Boy."

"I shouldn't light up anyway. I promised Eric that I would quit smoking and just haven't been able to cut the habit yet. He doesn't like it. He says it ruins your taste buds. He won't be around me when I smoke."

It was the perfect opening. "How long have you been dating him?"

She nodded and turned the pencil in her hands. "For a couple of months. He's so interesting and exciting. I've never dated anyone like him before."

I bit the inside of my cheek when she said that. I remembered what it had been like to date Eric early on. Everything had been thrilling and exciting. He would whisk me away to the Hamptons or Vermont for the weekend. We never stayed together in the city, because we couldn't be seen with each other for the sake of both our careers. Part of me wanted to warn Josie that the honeymoon stage would soon pass or he would find someone else more interesting, but it wasn't my place. If someone had warned me, I knew I would have dug in my heels even more. I guessed that's what Josie would do too.

"It must have been hard working with Rocky, considering . . ." Cass trailed off.

"Considering that he used to date her?" she asked. "Not really. Eric told me that he and Rocky weren't together very long and it didn't work out. No hard feelings."

"But Rocky didn't feel the same way about the breakup?" I asked.

"I guess not. Eric and I have kept a low profile, but honestly I thought she already knew about us. I was wrong. She found out yesterday when we arrived at the guest house, and she lost it." She shook her head. "If I had known she'd be so upset about it, I never would have taken this job. I have no trouble booking jobs, and there are always plenty of hair and makeup gigs this close to the holidays. I came along only because Eric said he wanted me here. I did it for him."

"That was sweet of you," Cass said. Her voice implied that she didn't really mean it.

Josie removed a crumpled tissue from her pocket and rubbed the tip of her nose with it. "Eric told me about you too. You're the Amish girl he dated."

"I'm not Amish. My grandmother is Amish, but I have never been Amish."

She shrugged as if that was only a minor detail. "You are the one that got away."

"Got away from what?" I asked.

She put the pencil into its place in the back of the pew. "Eric."

"I moved to a different state, and neither one of us wanted to do that long-distance thing. It was a natural decision to break up."

She shook her head. "That's not how the tabloids told it."

"I'm sure it was not, but don't believe everything you read."

"I don't, but I do enjoy reading the glossies." She studied me a little too long to be comfortable. "I can see why he felt that way. You are very pretty. I bet with the right hair and makeup, you could be stunning."

I counted to ten in Pennsylvania Dutch in my head. Those numbers were some of the few words I knew in the language, and they were coming in handy at the moment. "Maybe we should find out where everyone is getting ready for the live nativity now."

She cocked her head. "You might not believe it," she went on as if she hadn't even heard me, "but Eric talks about you all the time, even when he doesn't mean to talk about you. He was in love with you, you know. He might be still. I'm hoping he will love me as much."

I winced. "Eric was never in love with me."

"Then why do you think he's here in Ohio?"

"To film the Christmas special for his show."

She shook her head as if she felt sorry for me.

"No, it's because you're here. You would have to be completely dense not to see that. I came because Eric wanted me to, but I also came because I wanted to meet you. I wanted to meet the girl who captured his heart. I wanted to know what it was about you that he found so captivating, and I wanted to know if you still felt the same way about him."

Cass was sitting in the pew in front of us and now she turned to face us. "And what did you find out?"

Josie frowned. "I can see why Eric is in love with you. You are a kind person. I have been watching you, and I notice how everyone naturally gravitates to you to solve their problems. Isn't that what Eric did? I think he misses that about you."

Cass nodded. "I agree with that. Bailey is dependable."

"But," Josie added, "I am glad I came, because the question I really wanted an answer to has been answered."

I swallowed. "And what was that?"

She looked me in the eye. "Eric might still be in love with you, but you don't feel the same way. You're over him."

"I am," I said.

"Hallelujah," Cass said just as the choir began the "Hallelujah Chorus."

Chapter 28

Cass, Josie, and I finally found the rest of the nativity scene in the church's fellowship hall. Shepherds, angels, and wise men milled about. Just inside the door, the angel Gabriel was talking on his cell about the latest football scores.

"I have entered a parallel universe," Cass said.

"You and me both," I replied.

"Look at how pasty everyone looks under these yellow lights." Josie whipped out her makeup brush. "I have to take care of this. I couldn't live with myself if I didn't!" With her makeup brush in front of her she left us to accost a wise man.

"I know I don't have any way to prove this, but I don't think anyone was worried about their skin tone the night of the first Christmas," Cass said.

"I may not be able to stay the entire time," a familiar male voice said.

Instinctively, I turned to the voice to find Aiden in a long robe, dressed like Joseph. One of the volunteers covered the top of his head with a cloth and tied a braided band around it to hold it in place.

Margot stood in front of him with a clipboard. "Understood, but we need you for the parade and the filming by Gourmet Television. If you need to leave after that, we can get one of the other men to take your place."

"Is it wrong to say Joseph is cute?" Cass asked. "Will I be struck by lightning or something?"

"Don't ask me," I replied. "I don't know the rules."

Margot must have heard us, because she pivoted around. "Thanks heavens! There's my Mary. I was afraid you might have gotten lost!"

My face turned bright red as every shepherd, angel, wise man, and Joseph stared at me while I hovered in the doorway to the fellowship hall. I had an overwhelming urge to retreat. Cass gave me a little shove, and I stumbled into the room. "Go get 'em, Mary."

There was a rolling rack of costumes to Margot's right, and she plucked one of the robes off it. "I'm glad you're here. We haven't much time—put this on."

The robe, if I could even call it that, wasn't more than a smock, but it was a large smock, which meant I could wear it over my coat. I was grateful for that. It was freezing outside, and the temperature was dropping the closer we came to sunset.

"I'll help you put it on." Cass took the smock from my hand.

"Traitor," I muttered, but she only smiled in return.

I slipped the blue smock over my head, and Cass pulled it all the way down to my knees. Then she took the bit of rope that Margot gave her and tied a makeshift belt around my waist. "How do I look?" I asked Cass.

Cass clicked her tongue. "Well, with that bulky winter coat on, you look more like the about-to-pop version of Mary than the just-had-a-baby version. Is that what you were going for?"

I scowled. "I don't think so."

Margot clapped her hands. "Perfect. We need to find just the right head covering. There is a box on the table."

"I can help you pick it out." Cass followed Margot over to the table, leaving Aiden and me alone.

Aiden smiled at me. He really did make a cute Joseph, but I didn't say it aloud just in case Cass's lightning theory was true.

"Cass is having way too much fun with this."

He smiled. "I'm guessing this is not a normal Friday night in New York."

"Not even close." I scanned the room.

Aiden grinned at me. "You look very angelic."

"You're funny. I feel like a bloated blueberry in this robe."

His dimple was out in full force. 'You're a very cute blueberry."

I thought it best to ignore that comment. Josie was on the other side of the room doing an angel's makeup.

"I saw that you came in with Josie," Aiden said.

"She wanted to help with the makeup, so I said she could come along."

"That's the only reason you said she could come along."

I didn't reply.

"Bailey," Aiden said.

"Do you know about the argument between her and Rocky the night before Rocky died?"

He nodded. "I do. Every member of the production team mentioned it."

I frowned. "Even Eric?"

He nodded.

"I've been thinking about that fight," I said.

He nodded, and the cloth of his head covering moved. It was a little difficult to take him seriously as a cop dressed in that getup, but I tried to focus on the case.

"Josie said she didn't know how Rocky found out about her and Eric. They were very careful to keep their relationship secret from the rest of the crew."

"Rocky may have just noticed something between them and taken a stab in the dark."

I thought about this for a moment. "That's possible, but what if someone else in the group knew and told her?"

"That's possible too." He shrugged. "Do you think this person told her with the hope of stirring up trouble?"

I shook my head. "I don't know. It's possible."

"It would have to be someone on the production team, wouldn't it? No one else in town knew Rocky or Josie."

I gave him a look.

"I know what you're thinking. We are still looking for Thad. When we find him, I have a whole slew of questions I would like him to answer."

"I'd like to hear the answers to those questions too. Talking to Thad is important, but I think if anyone told

Rocky, it had to be someone from the production team who knew her. Maybe this person wanted to create some infighting."

"To what purpose?"

"I have no idea," I admitted.

"Okay, assuming that Rocky was told, and it was someone on the production team, what does that mean?" Aiden asked.

It was a logical question. Unfortunately, I didn't have a logical answer. "I don't know."

He sighed. "Please leave the detective work to me. I'm worried you might get hurt," he said in a lower voice, and then in a normal tone again he said, "Concentrate on your shop."

"And your show," Margot said as she and Cass returned. Cass held a large piece of navy cloth. I guessed it was supposed to be Mary's shawl.

Aiden frowned. "You mean Eric's Christmas special?"

"No, the show Bailey will be doing."

"How did you hear about it?" Cass asked.

"Linc told me," Margot said. "I'm already thinking how Harvest could be involved in future episodes. He said that most of the filming would have to be done in New York, but they would want to come back here from time to time to film and get some exterior shots as well as shots of Bailey in Swissmen Sweets." She beamed at me. "I knew good things were going to come from your moving here, but I never expected anything like this. You are the best thing to happen to the village in a long time."

"Most of the filming will have to be done in New York?" Aiden asked.

"Right." Margot took the piece of fabric from Cass's hands. "Let me do that. I have more experience with these."

Cass backed up. "I'm guessing that you do."

Margot shook out the piece of fabric and laid it over my head.

"What about the filming in New York?" Aiden asked.

Margot had the fabric covering my face now. I couldn't see, but fortunately the fabric was thin cotton so I could breathe.

"It's so exciting!" Margot said. Her voice sounded muffled to me as she wound the piece of fabric deftly around my head and ears. "Bailey will be in New York City for three to four months to film her candy-making show. Isn't that wonderful?"

I took a deep breath. I was becoming a tad claustrophobic behind the fabric.

"Three to four months?" Aiden said.

Finally, the cloth was lifted off of my face, and my breath became more even. As soon as my vision was clear, I wished I could cover my eyes again because Aiden was standing there looking stunned and, dare I say, disappointed by the news.

"Have you told your grandmother this?" he asked.

"I haven't gotten a chance to tell anyone."

"You say that like you're going to do it."

"Of course she's going to do it," Cass said. "She aced her screen test at the Christmas Market this afternoon. She's a natural."

"But," Aiden said as if Margot and Cass weren't even there, "what about your grandmother? You moved here to take care of her. You are just going to leave her like that?"

Aiden was stating all my own concerns, which I kept trying unsuccessfully to push aside. "She has Charlotte," I said. "She's a huge help at the shop, and they enjoy working together."

"Charlotte is a great girl," Aiden said. "But she's not you. Your grandmother needs you here, especially after losing your grandfather."

"If I do this, I can invest in the candy shop. My grandmother would never have to worry about money again."

"Money isn't the most important thing. Your family is."

"I know that."

"Then why would you consider this?"

I stared at him, unable to think of an adequate response.

Margot walked to the double door that led into the fellowship hallway. "Everyone!" she shouted into a bullhorn. "It's time to line up. I want the angels first, then shepherds, wise men, and finally the holy family bringing up the rear."

"Who in the world would give that woman a bullhorn?" Cass whispered in my ear.

"I think it was a gift she gave herself. I doubt anyone would be so stupid as to buy her one."

"I hope you're right about that," Cass said.

Josie appeared in front of me with her makeup kit. "Thanks goodness I caught up with you before you marched out. Sit, sit, let me put on your face."

Aiden stood a couple of feet away, shifting from foot to foot as Josie expertly applied makeup. "You are stunning now," Josie said. "I went for Mary, but with a more modern edge." She stepped back to admire her work.

I was afraid to ask what Mary with a modern edge looked like.

"Just think Mary if she had access to Sephora and shimmering powder," Cass said. "You definitely have an angelic glow about you now."

I wasn't sure if that was the look Margot had envisioned for the live nativity, but it was far too late to change it now.

Chapter 29

"Everyone," Margot said into the bullhorn. "We are leaving now. Out the door and line up again in the church parking lot. The procession will go around the square twice. Remember, we have a TV crew in the village here from Gourmet Television. Stay in character and make a good impression. If all goes well, they will be back and put our little village on the map. All thanks to our Bailey King, who will have her very own television show on the network!"

All the shepherds, angels, and wise men looked back at me. I closed my eyes for a moment. Why on earth had Linc told Margot about the television show? The woman had a personal bullhorn, for crying out loud. She would have been the very last person I would have told.

Cass squeezed my arm. "I'm going outside with Josie so we can get good spots to watch the parade." Her eyes slid in Aiden's direction. "You okay?"

"I'm fine, Cass." I stood up from the folding chair where Josie had done my makeup.

"Okay, I'll see you in a bit." She hugged me. "You are the prettiest Mary I've ever seen."

I smiled.

"Let's go!" Margot shouted into the bullhorn.

The line of nativity players started to move. I shuffled to the very end of the line. We had almost reached the outside door when Aiden turned back to me. "Bailey, I'm sorry for what I said. It was uncalled for. I know—"

"Please, Aiden," I said as we emerged into the parking lot. I was grateful for how dimly lit it was so he couldn't see my face. "Let's just get through this parade with no more talk about murder, television shows, or New York."

"I am sorry," Aiden whispered.

"Bailey!" Margot hurried over to me holding something in her arms. She handed me the life-sized baby doll she had showed me before. "Here's baby Jesus. Originally, I had a real baby lined up, but the mother dropped out when the camel came on board, and none of the other church members with newborns would agree to it." She clicked her tongue. "Can you believe that?"

"Shocking." I eyed Melchior. He seemed to wink his long lashes at me.

An Amish girl I didn't know led a donkey over to us.

"Thank you, Bea," Margot said. "Get on, Bailey."

The donkey flicked his ears and stamped his rear hooves.

"Umm," I said, holding the doll to my chest. "Can I just walk?"

"No!" Margot cried. "We need to wow the television

people, which means you have to be on the donkey's back."

"I'm not sure how to climb on him. I'm not the most graceful person in the world."

Aiden walked over to me and plucked me off the ground as if I weighed no more than the doll in my arms. He set me sidesaddle on the donkey's back.

I had my right arm wrapped around the doll and my left hand gripping the donkey's blanket for dear life.

Aiden looked me in the eye. "Do you have your balance?"

I swallowed. When he looked at me so intently like that, I definitely did not have my balance.

I adjusted my grasp on the blanket. "I think so," I told him.

He squeezed my side and then let go.

"Margot!" Juliet ran down the steps of the church with Jethro in her arms. "Jethro is here in time for the parade."

Margot waved her arms. "No, no, no. I told you he can't be in the live nativity. He's an unclean animal. He wouldn't have been at the first Christmas."

Juliet gasped and covered the little pig's ears with her hand. "How can you say such a thing? Reverend Brook said it was perfectly fine to include him. He said the live nativity wouldn't be the same without him."

Margot scowled. "Of course Reverend Brook would say that to *you*."

"What's that supposed to mean?" Juliet asked, clearly confused.

"Margot," I said from my perch on the donkey's back, "just let Jethro come. Aiden can walk him."

"But, but, we need this to be perfect."

"Please," I said. "The parade was supposed to start ten minutes ago. Do you want to make so many visitors wait longer?"

Margot threw up her hands. "Fine." She pointed at Jethro. "But that bow has to go."

"Of course," Juliet said. "We want to be authentic."

I had the urge to roll my eyes. I suspected authentic went out the window a long time ago as far as the live nativity was concerned.

Juliet removed the red bow from around Jethro's neck and clipped a leash to his collar. She handed the end of the leash to her son. "Be sure to keep an eye on him. You know how he likes to slip away."

"I know, Mom," Aiden said.

Jethro stamped his little hooves as if he was ready to march. At least someone was excited about this activity.

"Listen up!" Margot cried into the bullhorn. "We are starting now. Angels, lead the way!"

I rubbed my ear. She was dangerous with that thing.

"Remember to smile!" Margot cried.

The line began to move out of the parking lot, and after a couple of tugs on the lead by Aiden, the donkey, with me on his back, joined the parade.

We walked out of the parking lot into the streets around the square, which had been closed to traffic, and I wondered how my life had taken such an odd turn. If someone had told me last year this was where I would be this close to Christmas, I would have laughed in that person's face.

I sat sidesaddle on the back of the donkey with the doll in my arms and the camel behind me. Aiden walked in front of me. In one hand he held the donkey's lead, and in the other he held Jethro's leash. We walked around the square twice. The crowd waved and cheered. After I felt more secure on my seat, I began to wave back with my left hand. My right arm was wrapped tightly around the doll. It wouldn't do if I dropped the doll; that was my worst fear. Maybe second. Falling off the donkey was my real worst fear.

When we were on our second pass around the square, I saw my grandmother and Charlotte standing outside of Swissmen Sweets. They both smiled and waved at me. I waved wildly back at them. I finally was feeling comfortable in my spot. As we turned onto the square to stop at the manger, I saw Eric and the entire film crew. Linc was shouting directions I couldn't hear, and Roden and Pike were filming and recording the parade. I almost waved to them too when I saw someone who stopped me.

Just over Eric's shoulder was an Amish man. It was Thad Keim, and he was pointing at me. My heart skipped a beat, and I dropped my hand back to the donkey's blanket. The ride from the paved road onto the frozen grass of the square was bumpy.

We reached the manger, and Margot waited there. She barked orders as to where she wanted the characters to be. I wasn't paying attention. All I could think of was Thad's angry face and his hand pointed at me. Why would he point at me like that?

Finally, the donkey stopped just outside the manger. Aiden handed Jethro's leash to one of the shepherds.

I leaned over the donkey's neck. "Aiden! Aiden!"

He turned to me. "What's wrong? You are as white as a sheet."

"I saw Thad Keim when we turned and came onto the grass."

"Where?" Aiden asked.

"He was behind the film crew, on the other side of the pretzel shop. He pointed at me."

Aiden put his hands on my waist again and lifted me off of the donkey's back. When my feet were on the ground, he removed his head covering.

"Aiden!" Margot cried. "What are you doing? Don't take off your costume."

"I have a police call I need to handle." Aiden draped his head covering over the donkey's back.

"But you can't leave right in the middle of the live nativity. The film crew is here. We need you for the scene." As she said this, Eric and the film crew walked up to the manger.

"I have to go. You will have to find another person to play Joseph. Police business has to come first." Aiden's tone left no room for argument.

"I'll play Bailey's Joseph," said Eric, who was standing to the side with the crew.

"That's a great idea," Linc seconded. "It will add some humor to the special."

Margot sighed. "That will have to do. We have a lot of visitors in the village right now, and we don't have any time to waste."

Aiden scowled, and I thought for a moment that

he would argue. But then he tore off his robe and handed it to Eric. As he did, he looked at me. His expression was so strange, I couldn't tell if he was upset to give up his job as Joseph or happy for the excuse to leave.

Eric put on the robe and smiled at me. "I guess this means we're married," he whispered to me. "If only for this one night."

I groaned. "Stay on your side of the stable."

Eric laughed.

Chapter 30

The live nativity seemed to last forever. As the night passed my toes, fingers, and even my nose grew numb. I could no longer feel my face. I never did drop the baby Jesus doll, because I think it had frozen to my body. At some point, Cass told me that she was frozen solid and abandoned her position in the first row of spectators for the warmth of Swissmen Sweets. Before she went, she eyed Eric. "Don't try anything, Buster."

"How could I?" Eric asked. "I'm an ice cube from the cold."

"Keep it that way," Cass advised before leaving.

I glanced at Eric. My eyes seemed to be the only part of me that I could move easily in the cold. "You said that you and Rocky dated for a few months."

He turned toward me and pretended he was looking at the baby. The camera and smartphone flashes almost blinded me. "Let's not talk about her anymore."

"If you want me to solve this case, we have to talk about her."

He sighed and straightened up.

"Did you know that Rocky had her own production company?"

Eric shook his head. "Rocky almost had a production company, but in the end she didn't go through with it."

I turned my head even though it was in the direction of the freezing wind. I wanted to see Eric's face when I asked the question. "Why not?"

"Gourmet Television gave her a great opportunity when she was hired. They offered her a boatload of money and a promotion, but they also included a noncompete clause in her contract. She would have been in breach of contract if she'd started her own company."

I thought about this. "Was she planning to open the company on her own?"

"I think so, but you can't do anything on your own really, can you? Not in New York at least. I know she must have had partners. I don't know who they might have been though."

"Don't you think her partners were upset she didn't go through with the company?"

"Sure." Eric raised his eyebrow at me. "Wouldn't you be?"

I would, but not enough to kill someone over it.

"I doubt Rocky gave it that much thought. She was looking out for number one. She and I were the same in that way." He sounded wistful.

And that was how Eric and I were different.

Margot finally let the live nativity break up at seven. I hurried over to the church to remove my costume and return Jethro to Juliet before I made a beeline to Swissmen Sweets. It had been an impossibly long day, and I needed a break from ex-boyfriends, camels, potbellied pigs, and most especially murder.

Nutmeg meowed at me when I stepped into the shop and then closed and locked the door behind me. The front of the shop was empty, but I heard murmuring coming from the kitchen. The door was propped open with a bag of sugar. I peered inside to see my grandmother standing in the middle of the kitchen. Ruth Yoder and her elderly husband, who was my grandmother's district deacon, sat on backless stools, looking like a jury about to give a verdict.

"I'm sorry, Clara," Ruth said. "But this is the district's decision. You knew when you allowed your *Englisch* granddaughter to come here to stay, there was bound to be conflict."

"Bailey is a *gut* girl," my grandmother said. "She does not do anything without checking with me first."

I winced, thinking that wasn't completely true. I had let Linc and his team film me at the Swissmen Sweets table at the Christmas Market before I knew whether the district would approve. By the looks of things in the kitchen, they did not.

Ruth started to get up. "I warned you that there might be trouble from her presence here." She glanced at her husband. "But if the district elders are not against your having an *Englischer* under your roof, I am not one to question them."

She sounded like she was one to question them, and she sounded like she wanted to question quite a lot.

I stepped through the door. "Hello, Deacon and Mrs. Yoder," I said, doing my best to be polite.

My grandmother smiled at me. "Hello, my dear. The deacon was just telling me the district's decision on the television show."

My face fell. I could tell it was a "no." I was surprised to find that I felt disappointed. Maybe I had wanted my own show, or maybe I had wanted just to be on TV. Both of these possibilities had been as unexpected as my reaction to losing them.

"We respect your wishes," my grandmother said.

The deacon nodded. "I hope you will do so in all your filming."

I blinked at him. This wasn't what I had expected him to say. "In all our filming? You will let us film?"

The deacon looked at me. "You can film in Swissmen Sweets, but no Amish member of my district may be on camera. I cannot stop *you* from being on camera."

My mouth fell open.

"The building may be used," he said. "But I do not believe it is *Gotte's* will for any member of our district to appear on this television show."

Ruth sniffed. "The bishop spoke with my husband about this for a long time before deciding. This was not an easy decision, and the elders' permission should not be abused. Even if the Amish do not appear in the program, we trust that you will present our culture in a favorable light."

"Of course," I said.

Ruth looked me up and down as if to gauge whether I might be lying. She picked her bonnet up off the island and set it on her head, leaving the ribbons untied. "We should be getting home, husband. Dinner will be late as it is."

He nodded and stood up much more slowly. I backed away as they and my grandmother walked into the front of the shop. Nutmeg was waiting by the entrance, ready to make a break for it as soon as the door was opened. I scooped up the little orange cat.

Maami held the front door as the elderly deacon shuffled through. Ruth paused and tied her bonnet ribbons under her chin. "Clara, don't make my husband regret his decision by bringing shame on the district or the Amish community."

My grandmother frowned.

Ruth looked at me. "The same goes for you. I would hate for you to jeopardize your grandmother's good standing in the district." With that she went out the door, and to me, her parting words sounded like a threat.

The next morning, I woke up on the floor. I had slept on the floor an awful lot since moving to Holmes County, and it was really starting to get old. The night before, I had let Charlotte sleep on her cot as usual and had given up my bed to Cass. I really had to get my own place.

I sat up, and unsurprising, Charlotte's cot was empty. She was an early riser, and I knew that she would be helping my grandmother make sweets for the day. They would have to make twice as many as usual. The shoppers at yesterday's Christmas Market had all but wiped us out. The peppermint table had been a hit. More surprising, the bed was empty too. Cass woke up early every morning as the head chocolatier at JP Chocolates, but I didn't expect her to be up before me when she was away from home.

I needed to get moving, but I flung my arm over my eyes and lay back down. The day before had been one of the most confusing of my life. Could it be that I had only found Rocky's body in the gazebo twenty-four hours ago?

Cass walked into the room with a hair dryer in her hand. As usual, she was dressed head to toe in black, and her purple and black hair was perfectly styled. "You know," she said, "it's super inconvenient to have to go downstairs to dry my hair. Would it really be so bad to put an outlet or two up here?"

I sat up and pulled my knees into my chest. "If my grandmother did that, she would be breaking her district's rules. They can have electricity in their businesses but not in their homes."

"Am I the only one who sees how ridiculous that is?" She dropped her hair dryer back in her suitcase, the contents of which were spilling out all over the floor.

I sat upright. "Oh no!"

She stared at me. "Oh no, what?"

"What time is it?"

Cass checked her cell phone. "Almost seven. Why?"

I jumped off the floor. "I forgot to tell *Maami* the filming would start this morning. Eric and the crew will be here any minute!" I rushed around the room, looking for something to wear. "I have to get down there before they arrive."

"Bailey?" Charlotte stood at the door. "Clara sent me to fetch you. Eric and the TV people are here."

"Too late," Cass said.

It seemed that I was running into *too late* a lot recently.

"Tell them I will be downstairs in twenty minutes," I said. I turned to Cass. "I don't know what to wear."

"Already handled." Cass pointed at the bed, where the perfect outfit was laid out.

"When did you do that?"

"While you were whirling around the room like your tail was on fire."

I hugged her.

Chapter 31

Twenty minutes later, I hurried down the stairs from the upstairs apartment to the main room of the shop. The shop wasn't open yet for the day, so the front room was dark and empty. Voices floated into the room from the back kitchen through the open swinging door. As I came around the counter on my way to the kitchen, I saw that someone had propped the door open with a huge jar of molasses.

I stepped into the kitchen, and even though it was a large industrial space, it felt cramped. *Maami*, Charlotte, Cass, the members of the crew, and Eric were all there. Adding myself to the mix made eight people. Not to mention all the filming gear.

"There is our star," Linc said in a booming voice.

Eric beamed at me too.

I waved. "I just want to speak to my grandmother for a moment, and then I will be right back."

Linc looked as if he wanted to protest, but I didn't give him the time to do it.

I pulled my grandmother aside through the swinging kitchen door.

When we were in the main part of the shop, my grandmother blinked at me. "Bailey, dear, what is going on?"

"I should have told you that I agreed for Eric to film here today."

"And Linc said that he is doing this for when you go to New York. Are you going back to New York? Are you moving there?" There was hurt in her voice.

That was another thing I hadn't told her. The conversation with the deacon and his wife the night before had been so tense, I hadn't wanted to upset her any more by telling her about my chance to have my own show, a show that would keep me in New York for at least three months of the year. That had been a mistake.

"I have an opportunity. It would be good for the shop," I said. "It's just a chance. Nothing might come of it. I'm so, so sorry that I didn't tell you about it before now."

She looked back through the door at the crew setting up in her kitchen. Roden was putting up large lights that pointed at the island where we did most of our candy making. Pike was setting up microphones.

"This opportunity will take you to New York?"

"Yes, but—"

"Bailey, we need you for makeup." Josie popped through the door and walked to the other side of the counter. She held a makeup case in her arms. She set all of her tools out on one of the café tables in the middle of the room.

"You should do what you agreed to," *Maami* said.

Charlotte came through the kitchen door.

My grandmother took Charlotte's hand. "They won't be very long, I hope, in the kitchen. Charlotte and I will go upstairs and wait until they have gone. It is what the elders have told us to do. We have many candies to make today."

"Bailey." Josie waved her makeup brush at me. "I'm ready."

Linc poked his head through the kitchen door. "Let's go. We are burning daylight here."

I looked from Linc to my grandmother. I had thoroughly messed this up.

Maami shuffled to the narrow hallway that led to the stairs to the second floor. She took Charlotte's arm, and the pair of them walked up the stairs.

I stared at her. Everything in me wanted to go after her so that I could explain that I would only leave Holmes County to make her life easier, so she wouldn't have to work so hard in the future. I was doing it for her and the shop. A small voice in my head reminded me that I was doing it for myself as well.

"Bailey," Linc said. "We don't have all day."

I bit my lip and sat in the paddle back chair that Josie had pulled out.

"Thank goodness I have a battery-operated curling iron," Josie said, "for when I'm on set. It's not easy finding outlets around here."

While Josie did my hair and makeup, Linc told me about what the shoot would be. "The scene is this: You and Eric will be making peppermint bark together. Be friendly and approachable. For goodness' sake, act like you and Eric are at least friends. I want you to teach Eric how to make the candy, and I want you to be in the moment."

"I don't have script?" I asked.

"You're a natural. You will know what to say. A script would feel too stilted, and I don't want you looking at cue cards when you should be looking at the camera. Just think of the camera as your best friend."

Cass was leaning against the counter. "So just think that the camera is me. You'll be great!"

I sighed as Josie fluffed my hair.

"We're going for casual waves," Josie said.

Cass nodded. "I love that look."

"You have five minutes more in hair and makeup, and then we are rolling," Linc said as he went back into the kitchen.

I looked at Cass, and she must have recognized the worry in my eyes. She walked over to me and squeezed my hand. "Don't worry. I know you're upset that you didn't get a chance to warn your grandmother about this, and I'm sure it was a bit of a shock for her to find out this morning, but she'll come around. You and I both know that. She only wants what's best for you."

I wasn't so sure of that.

Josie finished my makeup, and I went into the kitchen. I blinked. Bright light made the room look as if it was a kitchen in a hospital.

Linc clapped his hands to get everyone's attention. "Let's roll." He paused. "Where's your grandmother? I'd like her in this scene."

I shook my head. "She doesn't want to be a part of it. Her bishop was against her and Charlotte being on camera."

"That's ridiculous. Can't you talk to her?" he asked.

"No. That's the Amish way," I said, leaving no room for argument. "Her church district won't allow it. Just be happy that we are able to film here."

Linc frowned. "Since we're running out of time, we'll just have to go on without her, but it would be helpful if you could get her on board for your show. Having actual Amish people in the program will be one of my selling points to the network." He clapped his hands again. "Enough of that. Let's get rolling."

"We're just about ready," Pike said. "Should we have some tribute to Rocky at the beginning? Or we could put it at the end. It might be nice if Eric said something about her."

Eric winced.

"Why would he want to do that?" Roden asked. "We will put an *in memoriam* line in the credits. Why should we do more than that?"

Pike's eyes went wide. "I just thought it would be a nice gesture. None of us would be here without Rocky. This show was her idea. I thought it would be appropriate to acknowledge her, that's all. She did a lot for each of us by giving us this job."

"You think Rocky hired you for who you are?" Roden asked. "She didn't care about you. She didn't care about anyone but herself."

"Aww, man, I think that might be a little harsh," Pike said. "Rocky was always cool with me."

"I knew her for fifteen years; you didn't."

"Please," Linc said. "Let's drop it. I agree with Roden that the credits are enough." He waved me over. "Bailey, we're ready."

I nodded and went to stand by Eric. He squeezed my elbow. "It's just like old times."

"The old times are long over, Eric," I whispered out of the side of my mouth.

"We'll just have to make new ones then."

Before I could correct him, Linc shouted, "Action."

Chapter 32

Two hours later the filming was complete. Roden and Pike had finished packing up the gear and carried it out to the production van parked in front of Swissmen Sweets. Linc stood in the front room of the shop appearing very pleased. "You were a natural, Bailey. There aren't many people who have so much ease in front of the camera right from the start." He shook my hand. "We're going to shoot a few more exterior scenes here in the village, but I believe that when we add in what was already filmed in New York, we now have enough footage for Eric's special. I am certain after seeing this, the network will give you a shot. It will be a pleasure to be your producer." He went out the door.

Eric, who was the last one to leave, stood by the door. "He's right, you know. You could be a star, if that's what you want." He turned and walked through the door.

I closed the door behind him and locked it. "I'm glad that's over."

Cass flopped onto one of the café chairs in the

front of the shop. "Me too. Being your manager is a lot of work."

"I have an idea."

"Why don't I like the sound of that?" Cass asked.

"Charlotte and *Maami* will be busy the rest of the morning making more candies for the shop, and we have two hours before the Christmas Market begins again this afternoon."

"Oh-kay. I still have a sense of foreboding here."

"I think we should go back to the Christmas tree farm and talk to Grandma Leah. There must be a connection between Thad and Rocky. Maybe she doesn't know exactly what is going on, but there might be something she can tell us to point us in the right direction."

"Is there a chance that Thad would be there?" Cass asked.

I had told her the night before everything that I had learned from Aiden and about seeing Thad in the crowd during the parade. "Possibly, but I'm sure he wouldn't try anything. He has to know by now that the police are looking for him. He could be hiding with anyone in the district."

"The Amish would hide a murderer?"

"I don't think they see Thad as a possible murderer. He's just another member of their community who is being mistreated by the police. The Amish in this county don't trust the police. A lot of that is because of the sheriff's poor attitude toward them. They would hide one of their own from the police." I stood up.

"I don't think Aiden would like it if he knew that you were going back out to the Christmas tree farm."

"I'm sure that he wouldn't."

"What about your grandmother?" Cass asked. "Don't you want to talk to her about the show in New York before we go?"

I shook my head. "I think I need to really make up my mind about it before I talk to her."

"That's fair. As for the Christmas tree farm, I think if we're going to keep bothering Grandma Leah, we should really buy a tree this time."

"I agree."

Ten minutes later, Cass and I were back in my car and headed to Tree Road. Overnight a blanket of fresh snow had fallen over the county, making it appear that a giant white sheet had been spread out over the pastures and open fields. As we turned onto Tree Road, a red-tailed hawk perched on the street sign. His feathers were fluffed out to protect him from the cold. As I turned the car into the long driveway that led to the tree farm, crystalized snow glistened on the trees' thin needles.

I parked, and Cass and I got out of the car. We walked to the front door of the house, and I noticed animal tracks in the snow. I saw deer, rabbit, and maybe even the tracks of a fox.

I knocked on the door. There was no answer.

"Maybe they aren't home," Cass said.

"Or maybe they just aren't answering the door," I said.

"Hello there!" Grandma Leah called from across the snow-covered yard. "Come on over. We're in the barn."

Cass raised her eyebrows at me. "I wonder who's with her."

"I hope not Thad."

"Me too," she said, and removed her cell phone from the pocket of her black coat. "I'll be ready in case we have to call the cops."

"Let's hope that won't be necessary."

Cass and I made our way across the snowy yard. Our boots left deep prints in the snow.

Grandma Leah stood at the barn door. She wore a long down coat over her Amish dress. The hem of her skirt was encrusted with snow and dirt. "You just caught us as we were finishing up the chores."

I was about to ask who was with her when Daniel popped his head out of the barn. I gave a sigh of relief, but it didn't appear that Daniel was as happy to see me as I was to see him. In fact, Daniel looked as if he felt trapped by our arrival.

Grandma Leah smiled widely. "Have you girls returned for your tree? I had a feeling that you would be back. I can always tell when a person finds just the right tree for Christmas." She beamed. "After selling so many trees over the years, I just have a sense of it."

"We would love to look at the tree again," Cass said. "Do you think it would fit on the roof of Bailey's car?"

Grandma Leah peeked out of the barn door. "That is a small car, but Daniel can make it work. It is a short ride to the village. If you just go slowly, you should be fine." She turned to her great-grandson. "Daniel, can you help these girls cut down and tie up their tree?"

He nodded with his shovel in hand.

"Before you do that," I said, "I wondered if I could ask you both about Rocky."

Daniel let go of the shovel handle, and it thudded against the barn wall. The cow in the back of the barn mooed in response.

"Rocky? Is that the woman staying at the guest house down the street whom you asked me about earlier?"

I nodded. "I think she knew you, Daniel."

The boy stared at the top of his boots.

Grandma Leah rubbed the bottom of her chin. "Maybe she knew him because Daniel helps his father to care for the guest house."

I shook my head. "I think she knows him better than that. Daniel, can you tell me about Rocky?"

He continued to stare at his feet.

When he refused to say anything, I decided to press a little harder. "Daniel, where is your mother? What was her name?"

"Rachel, his mother, is dead," Grandma Leah said. "She died when Daniel was just a baby. It was such a tragedy for both Thad and Daniel. My husband died close to the same time, so I invited my grandson to move here from Indiana to take care of the tree farm with me. I'm so grateful that he did. I would have had to sell this place many years ago if he hadn't arrived."

I turned my attention back to Grandma Leah. "Who told you that Rachel had died?"

"My grandson told me, of course." Her brow wrinkled.

"Was there a funeral? Did you go?" I asked.

"They lived in Indiana. Even though I was younger then, I would not have made such a journey alone, and as I said, my own husband had just passed. It wasn't possible for me to travel. Why are you asking about Rachel?"

"I think Daniel knows why," I said.

The young Amish man looked trapped. Cass stood in the barn doorway, blocking his exit.

Grandma Leah turned to her grandson. "Daniel?"

The boy dropped his head and sat down on a bale of hay. He covered his face.

Grandma Leah hurried over to him. "What's wrong, my boy?"

"*Daed* lied to both of us." His voice was muffled through his gloved hands.

"What do you mean?"

"My mother didn't die. She ran away." He looked up at her with tears in his eyes. "Rocky, the person she was asking you about, that was my mother. She told me so."

Grandma Leah stumbled backward. I hurried forward and steadied her with my hand so she wouldn't fall over. "That can't be. She must have lied to you."

"She didn't. She knew too much about *Daed* and me and about this farm. She told me all of this in our language. She never would have been able to speak so well if she was an *Englischer*."

"You met with her?" I asked.

He nodded. "The first night she was here. I met with her at the gazebo. She looked so *Englisch*, but she told me everything she knew about us in our language. She could describe the farm down to the smallest detail."

Grandma Leah pressed the back of her hand to

her own forehead as if she were checking her temperature.

"Did your father know she was here?" I asked.

He stared at his hands. "I told him when I got back to the tree farm. I wanted to know why he had lied to me. Why did he tell me that my mother was dead instead of the truth, that she ran away for the *Englisch* life?"

"What did he do when you told him?" I asked in a low voice.

Daniel still wouldn't look me in the eye. "He said he wanted to talk to her. He left and didn't come home for a long while. I didn't see him until the next morning, and then when we went to the square to set up for the market, we heard . . . we heard that she had been murdered." He started to cry in earnest now.

My heart broke for him because I believed he was thinking what the rest of us were: that his father, Thaddeus Keim, had killed his mother.

"Get off of my farm!" A booming voice shook the barn rafters. There stood Thaddeus Keim with a pitchfork in his hands. And the business end of it was pointed at me.

Cass took two giant steps back from the very angry-looking man. "Watch where you point that thing," she said.

"Mr. Keim . . ." I started to say.

"Don't call me, Mr. Keim, *Englischer*. You need to leave."

Grandma Leah took a step forward. "Thad, my

grandson, is what this girl says true? Was this Rocky woman your Rachel?"

Thad clenched his teeth and pointed at Cass and me. "Leave. I want you off of my land. You have no right to be here."

Cass tapped on the screen of her phone. "Gladly."

I wasn't ready to go just yet. "You lied to your son about his mother. Rocky was his mom, and you didn't want him to know that."

"Rocky!" He spat the name. "She is no one to my son. She should have kept her promise and stayed away. The best thing she ever did was leave. She wanted the *Englisch* life, and so I let her go. But we agreed she would never return. She had no reason to come back. Her coming back has ruined everything."

"She only wanted to see her son," I said. "Maybe she was ready to make amends for what she did."

"Daniel is not her son. He is my son, and she made her decision to give him up years ago. She cannot go back on it now." He lifted the pitchfork in his hand a little bit higher, but I ignored his threat.

"Then after she died, you broke into her room at the guest house to search for anything she might have left behind that would reveal the connection between you and her. You wanted to destroy any evidence."

"You don't know what you are talking about."

By the way his glance shot to his son, I knew I was right. "The police have the baby rattle."

Thad paled. "Get off my farm."

I opened my mouth to argue with him some more, but Cass pulled on my sleeve. "I suggest that we leave unless we want to meet the pitchfork up close and personal." In a lower voice, she added, "I called the police."

I held up my hands. "We will leave, but you have to move away from the door so that we can go."

Thad stood there for a long moment as if he were considering this. Maybe he thought it would be best not to let us go. If he'd really killed Rocky, would it work to his advantage to let us go? We were two witnesses who knew about his connection to Rocky. We were the two witnesses who'd seen him run away from her room in the guest house and drop that rattle. A rattle that I was certain had been Daniel's when he was a baby. Rocky—or rather, Rachel—must have taken it with her when she left her Amish life as a memento of her baby son. There would be no photographs of the baby to take. The Amish do not take pictures of one another. It is against their teachings.

Thad stepped out of the way. When Cass and I were safely on the other side of him, I said, "I am sorry. I didn't mean to upset you."

"That is the *Englisch* way, to say sorry after they do something wrong. The *Englisch* never *mean* to do anything and can always make excuses for their actions. That is where you differ from the Amish. We do what we say and mean what we do. It would serve you well to follow your grandparents' example in that way."

Cass yanked on my arm and whispered in my ear, "Bai, come on, it's time to go. The chance to convince this man to talk to you in a civil manner has come and gone."

I nodded and let her pull me away from the Amish farmer.

We had reached my car when Aiden's departmental

car, followed by two cruisers, pulled into the Keim yard. Aiden and the other officers jumped out of their vehicles.

I spun around to see Thad's reaction. He didn't move. Maybe he was done with running.

Aiden slowed his pace as he saw how calm Thad was being.

"Mr. Keim," Aiden said in his cop voice. "I need to talk to you about Rocky Rivers."

"You want to talk to me about my wife," Thad replied.

Aiden didn't appear the least bit surprised by this revelation. Perhaps he had been listening to me when I'd told him my suspicions about Keim's relationship to Rocky.

"Please put the pitchfork down." Aiden held out his hands. They were in front of him. Nowhere near his duty belt and gun.

Thad looked at the pitchfork and then unceremoniously dropped it on the ground as if he had no use for it at all. Grandma Leah stood in the doorway of the barn with her hands pressed palm to palm in prayer.

Behind the police cars, an Amish buggy turned into the driveway. A young woman climbed out of the driver's seat. Daniel ran by his father, Cass and me, and the police. He gave the girl a hug, and the pair of them climbed back into the buggy and drove away. It wasn't until the girl poked her head out of the buggy to look back at us that I realized who it was. Emily Esh had just rescued Daniel Keim, but the question remained, who would rescue Emily?

Chapter 33

Cass and I were uncharacteristically quiet on the ride back to Swissmen Sweets until her phone rang.

"*Bonjour,* Jean Pierre!" she said in a perky voice.

A barrage of French shouting came over the other end of the line.

"Yes, yes, Bailey is fine." She rolled her eyes at me. "He did what? Right. Right. Yes, I appreciate your letting me come here to check on Bailey. Caden clearly can't handle Christmas in the shop." She paused. "Oh, you want me to come back today?" She looked over to me.

I nodded. Rocky's killer had been found. Eric and his crew were wrapping up filming to return home tomorrow. It was time for Cass to go back to her real life, and it was time for me—all over again—to figure out what I wanted to do with mine. If Linc was right and the network wanted me to fly to New York to shoot a pilot, did I want to do that? I'd thought when I moved to Holmes County that I had made my final decision about what I wanted to do with the rest of my life, but an opportunity like this had never even entered my mind as a possibility.

Whatever I decided, I needed to talk to my grand-mother soon. I didn't want her to believe that I would break my promise to my grandfather and abandon her. I loved her more than anyone. If I chose to do the show, it would partly be for her. She had worked her entire life. I wanted her to have time to rest and enjoy herself, but I had to ask myself if that would be something she would want. The Amish way was to work until you were unable to work. In their culture, work was pleasing to God. It was hard for me to imagine my grandmother agreeing to a true retirement, but I would love for her to slow down. The shop was a lot of responsibility even with Charlotte's and my help, and I wanted to expand it and hire more workers, perhaps even Emily.

Thinking of Emily made me wonder what her relationship with Daniel was. Were they courting? How had she known that he needed help right then? Had Daniel been the Amish man I'd seen walking away from Emily in the alley when Nutmeg got loose? Probably, I decided. And I couldn't help but wonder where they had gone. I hope Daniel was okay. He was understandably upset. In the span of a few days, he'd discovered his mother didn't die when he was baby and his mother, whom he'd just met, was murdered by his father, or at least that's what the police believed. Aiden hadn't been very forthcoming with me when he'd arrested Thad at the tree farm. I wondered what evidence he had that proved Thad Keim was the killer.

"Yes, yes," Cass said into the phone. "I'll leave as

soon as I can. It's a short flight, so I should be back in the shop by this evening. I'll fix everything that Caden screwed up." She ended the call.

I glanced at her as we came into town on Apple Street. "You have to go back."

She nodded. "Apparently, Caden had mixed up a bunch of the special orders. He'd sent a box of chocolate Santa Clauses to a Hanukkah party."

I winced.

"Yeah." She rubbed her head. "It's going to take a bit of doing to unruffle those feathers, but I'm sure when we say we will replace their candies for free and throw in some freebies, all will be forgiven."

I parked my car in an open space in front of the yarn shop. "Thank you for coming out here. You were a big help."

She smiled. "Even though I live hundreds of miles away, I will always be your wingwoman, Bai."

I smiled back. "I know."

"And listen," she said in a more serious tone as she looked me in the eye. "As much as I want you to come back to New York for three to four months to shoot a show for Gourmet Television, you have to ask yourself what you want. Don't think about what I want or what your grandmother wants. Think about what you want."

"Okay," I whispered.

"And if you choose to go forward with the show, just remember that I'm your manager. I'll get you the deal!"

I laughed. "I won't forget that."

An hour later, I was helping the taxi driver heft Cass's giant suitcase into the trunk of his car for the drive to the private airport in Canton where Jean Pierre's plane waited for her. Finally, the driver slammed the trunk closed.

"You brought enough to stay here a month, not just one night."

She grinned. "I like to be prepared." She gave me a hug. "Take care of yourself and remember what I said."

I hugged her back. "I will."

Cass moved on and gave *Maami* and Charlotte hugs, too. "The shop looks great. I can't wait to return."

Maami smiled at her. "You are welcome any time."

"I'm counting on that," Cass said. She looked at her phone. "I'd better go. I'm sure Jean Pierre is driving the pilot crazy asking him when we will be back in the city."

I hugged her one more time, and she climbed into the car. *Maami*, Charlotte, and I waved until her taxi disappeared around the corner.

"I am going to miss her," Charlotte said. "She is very . . ." She searched for the right word. "Flamboyant."

I laughed. "That's true." I followed them back into the shop.

"We heard about Thad Keim being arrested for the murder," Charlotte said. "It's so awful to believe that a quiet man from our district could do such a terrible thing, and they say, too, that she was his wife, who ran away from the Amish, and Daniel's mother."

I wasn't the least bit surprised that the details about the arrest had gotten out. The Amish telegraph was better than any gossip magazine in New York that I knew about.

Maami clicked her tongue. "It's best that we not talk about it for fear of spreading more gossip. All we can do is pray for Thad, and for his son and grandmother. I'm sure they are distraught."

The image of Grandma Leah's heartbroken face came back into my mind.

Across the street on the square the Christmas Market was about to open. "We had better set up," I said to Charlotte.

The young Amish woman opened the door to Swissmen Sweets. "I'm hoping for a quiet day at the market."

I followed her and *Maami* inside the shop. "Me too. Good thing I made so much peppermint bark when Eric and I were filming. We should have enough to get us through the market today."

Maami smiled. "And Charlotte and I did the rest while you and Cass were out."

I went into the kitchen and found that Charlotte already had everything packed for the market. "I guess we're ready to go," I said.

Maami touched my arm. "Before you leave, can I have a word with you?"

I bit the inside of my lip. "Of course, *Maami*."

Charlotte looked at us. "Why don't I wheel the cart across the street and get started? Bailey, you can come over when you're done." The swinging door closed behind her.

"Is everything okay, *Maami*?"

She shook head. "Not everything. I need to ask you to forgive me."

I held on to the counter. "Forgive you? For what?" I couldn't think of a single thing that my grandmother had ever done that required my forgiveness.

"For how I behaved this morning. It wasn't right. I know that you didn't purposely omit to tell me that the television people were coming."

"It was just an oversight," I said. "But if anyone should be asking for forgiveness, it's me. I'm the one who messed up and forgot to tell you."

Maami shook her head. "And I didn't handle the fact that you might want to return to New York well. I am sorry for that too."

"*Maami*, you did nothing wrong. I can understand why you wouldn't be happy about my being gone for months at a time; you need my help in the shop."

"It is not that. We have Charlotte now with us, and she is a great help."

I winced. *Maami* didn't know how painful that was for me to hear. It just confirmed my feelings that Charlotte, being Amish, was a better fit for the candy shop and for my grandmother than I could ever hope to be.

"About New York, you have to decide what you want to do. I will support any decision you make." *Maami* didn't know it, but she had repeated Cass's sentiments.

I hugged her. "*Danki*," I said, using the Pennsylvania Dutch word for thank you. "I haven't decided yet, but when I do, I will tell you first."

Chapter 34

A little while later, when I walked back to the square, I cringed to find Margot hurrying toward me. The curls that peeked out from under her winter hat bounced with every step. "Bailey, I have news."

"What kind of news?" I asked.

"It was a false alarm yesterday and our original Mary didn't have her baby, so she's back to take over the role."

"Oh," I said. In my head, I was doing backflips.

"We don't need you to play the Virgin Mary this evening." She held my right hand in both of hers. "I hope you won't be too disappointed."

"I think I'll be able to survive this," I said, unable to hold back my grin.

"We don't need Aiden either, because the original Mary's husband will take the part."

"I think Aiden will survive too."

Speaking of Aiden, I saw him walking across the square and headed in our direction. I pointed at him. "He's right there."

Margot spun around, and I took this as my chance

to make a hasty retreat to the candy shop's table. Charlotte already had everything laid out. She sat in the folding chair behind the table and was flipping through a songbook.

She smiled up at me. "The organist at the church is on vacation this Sunday, and Reverend Brook asked if I could play the organ for Sunday services. I'm trying to pick out the pieces that I know best and enjoy the most. I really want to impress the congregation. I don't think they have had an Amish girl play for them on Sunday morning before."

"I would say you are probably right about that." I stacked one of the peppermint bark boxes on top of another. There really was very little for me to do there. I was debating about going back to the candy shop when Aiden approached the table.

"What were you doing siccing Margot on me like that and running away?" he asked.

"I didn't sic Margot on you," I said.

He rolled his eyes.

"Aiden, can I ask you something about Thad?"

"I'm not sure why you are asking permission when we both know that you will ask anyway."

I smiled. "When you questioned him about breaking into the guest house, did he say why he climbed in through the window and didn't just walk through the door? As the caretaker for the place, he had a key."

"I had been wondering the same thing," Aiden admitted. "When I asked him, he said that he was afraid of running into the TV people. He didn't want anyone seeing him going into Rocky's room."

"But why didn't he go back out the window then?" I asked.

"He said that he tried, but the trellis had become slippery as the snow picked up. He couldn't get a good foothold. He thought he would fall, so he decided the safer route was to take the risk of being seen and go out through the front door."

"Oh."

Aiden smiled. "Any other questions?"

"Not at the moment."

He looked as if he didn't believe me, when his cell phone rang. He unclipped the phone from his duty belt and answered. "Brody here. . . . Yes. Okay. I'm on my way. Yes, I know where that is." He ended the call.

"Something wrong?"

"That was Little. It seemed he finally tracked down Daniel, Emily, and their buggy. I had Little out looking for them because I was worried about those two."

My heart warmed at Aiden's concern for the two young Amish people.

"Little says their buggy is on the side of the road not far from where Daniel lives. Little is out there now. He says he needs some help. He doesn't want to call for backup on the radio because of the sheriff's attitude toward the Amish."

I walked around the side of the table and stood next to him. "I'm going with you."

Aiden shook his head. "You are needed here at your table."

I glanced at Charlotte, who said, "Go. I have everything handled here."

Considering what my grandmother had said about Charlotte, I didn't find that very comforting. It wasn't easy to be replaced, and that's what seemed to be happening.

Aiden looked as if he wanted to protest, but I didn't give him a chance. "Let's go. Someone will have to stand with Emily while you talk to Daniel."

He frowned. "Fine. I don't have time to argue with you." He turned and headed to his departmental car, which was parked along the edge of the square. I was right behind him. He unlocked the car, and I climbed inside.

He climbed in on the driver's side and closed the computer mounted to his dashboard.

"Are you sure they're all right?" I buckled my seat belt.

"Little says that they are. You're right—it might help that you come along, because I think you will make Emily feel a little more comfortable."

I frowned. I wasn't so sure about that, but I wanted to go. I wanted to know what was going on and to see that Emily was okay with my own eyes. I cringed to think of what her brother and sister would do when they heard about this. They already were very strict with their youngest sister. They might lock her in the pretzel shop forever and throw away the key. She'd be the Amish version of Rapunzel.

Aiden was quiet as we drove out of town, but just as soon as we cleared the village proper and were on a country road, he said, "I want to apologize for yesterday." Aiden stared straight through the windshield. Outside the warmth of the car, it started to snow again. Tiny crystalized flakes fell from the sky.

"Aiden . . ."

He took his right hand off the steering wheel and held it up. "Please, just let me get this out. My behavior was unacceptable. I know that you love your grandmother and know that you gave up a lot to be here with her. She knows that too. What I say should have no bearing on your decision to stay or go. It has to be your decision. You need to make up your own mind."

What was it with everyone saying that I had to make up my own mind? I was starting to wonder if my family and friends saw me as indecisive.

"I just hated the idea of you leaving even for just a few months," he went on. "I know that my mother and others have been trying to push us together. I know that can be awkward at times."

I shifted uncomfortably in my seat. This conversation was awkward. I was regretting coming along on this ride.

"But the truth is, I do want to get to know you better, so I was disappointed at the prospect of you going back to New York even for only a part of the year."

I didn't know what to say to that. Thankfully I didn't have to respond, because up ahead I could see the flashing lights of Little's cruiser reflected off the snow. Just in front of the cruiser, the buggy was pulled to the side of the road.

Aiden parked behind the cruiser, and he and I got out.

"I don't know why you are making me do this," a slurred male voice said.

"Just walk the line, Daniel," Little said, sounding more in charge than I had ever heard him.

I came around the buggy and found Deputy Little standing at the side of the road, pointing at the line that ran down the center. It appeared that someone, Little I assumed, had brushed the snow from the white line.

Daniel stared down at the line and pointed. "You want me to walk that line. Why should I?"

"Little," Aiden said.

The younger deputy hurried over to us. "Deputy Brody. I'm glad you're here. The kid is drunk."

"You didn't mention it when you called." Aiden flipped up the collar on his coat against the cold.

"I didn't realize it until he fell out of the buggy."

"The Amish get drunk? I never heard of that." I pulled my stocking hat down farther over my ears. The December wind was biting cold.

Aiden laughed. "Of course the Amish get drunk, and they get high, and they get in barrels of trouble just like every other member of society. There are upstanding Amish just like there are upstanding English, but there are Amish who get in trouble too, just like there are English who get in trouble. There is no cultural escape from trouble."

When I thought about the murder investigations I had been a part of since moving to Amish Country, I knew that trouble could, indeed, be found in Holmes County, too much trouble as far as I was concerned.

"A DWI is a serious offense," Aiden said.

"You can get a DWI in a buggy?" I asked.

"You can get a DWI on a lawn mower," Aiden said. "Did you give him a Breathalyzer test?"

Little shook his head. "He refused to take it, so I just asked him to do the line test. He's refusing to do that, too."

Daniel took a couple of steps along the line and then threw up, after which he promptly toppled into the snow. Aiden sighed. The horse shook his reins, and Emily reached up and grabbed the horse bridle with her small gloved hand.

Aiden walked over to the teen in the snow. "Daniel?" Aiden said.

There was no response

"Is he dead?" Deputy Little asked.

As if he wanted to prove himself far from dead, Daniel moaned and rolled onto his side.

"Maybe we should take him to a hospital," I suggested. "He could have alcohol poisoning."

"We will to be safe, but he's also getting a ticket for DWI, " Aiden said.

"Where did he get the alcohol?"

Little nodded to the buggy. Aiden and I peeked inside. There were seven jugs of clear liquid, and I didn't think it was water. The open bottle smelled like strong liquor. "Moonshine," I said. "Where did he get all that?"

Emily, who stood a little bit away from the buggy, wrapped her arms more tightly around her waist. "It was my brother's. It was inside the buggy. I didn't know it was there until Daniel found it. I told him not to drink it, but he wouldn't listen."

"This is Abel's buggy?" I asked.

She nodded.

"Does he know you borrowed it?"

"*Nee.*" She looked down at the top of her black boots. "Abel is going to be so angry."

I grimaced. Her temperamental brother became angry over the slightest thing. The fact that she had taken her older brother's horse and buggy without his permission, her boyfriend had drunk his moonshine, and the police would probably arrest him for having that moonshine made me believe she was right. Abel threw a fit over far less.

I walked over to her. "Are you hurt?"

The girl shook her head and then looked at Daniel, who was staring at the line as if he didn't know what to do with it. "I should have stayed at the pretzel shop. My sister and brother will be furious. They must have noticed by now that I'm gone and so is the buggy." She shivered.

"You're freezing. Aiden, can we go sit in your car?"

He nodded. I walked Emily to Aiden's SUV and had her climb into the backseat, where I sat beside her. "Tell me what happened from the beginning."

She folded her hands on her lap.

"Please, Emily, I want to help you."

A large tear fell from her eye onto her folded hands. She brushed it away. "I don't know why you want to help me after the way I've treated you these last few weeks. I wouldn't even speak to you."

"I know you were hurt that I couldn't give you a job at Swissmen Sweets after Charlotte came on board, but you have to believe me when I say I wanted to. I would love to expand the business so that you

can work for me. I know what a great worker you
are and what a help you were to me during the
Amish Confectionary Competition. I'm not going
to forget that."

She sniffled. "I've missed talking to you. It's been
very hard. I've missed Nutmeg, too."

I smiled. "He's missed your visits very much. He
goes to the window every morning looking for you,
and he's always trying to escape the shop to see you."

She looked up at me. Tears brimmed in her big
blues eyes. "He does?"

I nodded. "He does. He may be my cat now, but
he was your cat first. We share him."

"That's so nice of you to say."

She looked as if she were about to burst into another bout of tears, so I asked, "Are you and Daniel
courting?"

Her face turned red. "For just a few weeks. He's
so nice to me. He knows . . ." She trailed off. I knew
she had been about to say that he was aware of the
baby she'd had out of wedlock and whom her siblings had forced her to give up for adoption. Illegit-
imate children were still a big no-no in the Amish
world. Having a child in the community under those
circumstances could be very difficult. I knew that it
was one reason why her older siblings were so strict
with her, but Emily was twenty now. She was an adult.
They needed to learn to trust her again.

"Esther and Abel don't know. They are very strict
with anyone who tries to court me. Daniel is from my
church district. I have known him my whole life, but

I wanted to get to know him in this way without my siblings becoming involved."

"I can understand," I said. "How did you end up at the Christmas tree farm with Abel's buggy when the police arrived?"

"I didn't know that the police or you would be there. Daniel had called the pretzel shop from his shed phone and asked me to come. He said there was something important he had to tell me. I was the only one in the shop at the time, but he was so desperate sounding that I felt I had to go. He needed me." She licked her lips. "I had come into town with my brother in his buggy and knew it was out back behind the pretzel shop. Abel was busy getting things ready for the Christmas Market for Margot. She'd hired him to move tables and the like, and Esther had stayed back home on the farm because she has a bad cold. I thought I could get to Daniel's and back before anyone noticed that I was gone." She shook her head. "I saw Daniel's father with the police. I knew that the police thought he had killed that *Englisch* woman from New York."

That English woman from New York? Did that mean Emily didn't know that Rocky was Daniel's mother, Rachel? I wondered if that's what he was so desperate to tell her. It made sense that he would want to talk to her about it. It was clear he couldn't talk to his father, who would have been furious, or Grandma Leah, who'd had no idea of the truth until I had told her.

"But his *daed* didn't kill that woman," she said in hushed tones. "I know this."

I stared at her. "How do you know?"

She chewed on her lower lip.

I grabbed both of her hands in mine. "Emily, how do you know that he didn't kill Rocky?"

She looked me in the eye. "Because I saw the murder."

Chapter 35

I blinked. "You saw the murder?"

She dropped her eyes to her hand again. "I wasn't close enough to the gazebo to see any faces. I was at the pretzel shop. We needed to have plenty of pretzel dough for the Christmas Market, and my sister told me to stay late and make it."

"How late were you there?"

She removed her gloves and twisted them in her hands. "I stayed all night. Abel didn't want to come back with the buggy for me, so I slept on a cot in the front room."

I frowned. "Does that happen very often?"

"Now and again. I don't mind. It's nice to have some time away from my brother and sister. I almost look forward to it."

The more I heard of how Esther and Abel treated their younger sister, the angrier I became. "Emily, if that happens again, come over to Swissmen Sweets. We would love to have you. I hate the idea of you staying alone in your shop all night."

"It is really no burden, but I would like to visit your shop and see Nutmeg."

I squeezed her hand. "Any time. Our door is always open to you."

"Danki."

"Tell me what you saw and when."

"I finished making all the pretzel dough around eleven, so I started to make my cot up in the front room about then. I remember sitting on my cot and looking out the window. It had started to snow. The gazebo and the Christmas lights were so pretty in the snow. I knew that I had a long day ahead of me at the Christmas Market the next day and I should go to sleep, but I just wanted to watch the snow. It was so peaceful. That's when I saw the red-haired woman."

"Rocky?" I asked

She nodded.

"How did she get there?"

"She climbed out of that big white van that was on the square the day the television people arrived. She got out of the van, and then it drove away."

I grew very still. That had to mean that someone from the production team had driven from the guest-house, where she had just had a fight with Josie, to the gazebo. It couldn't be anyone else. In my mind, I wrote Josie off. Why would Rocky get into a van with her after they had had such a terrible fight and she'd fired Josie? I didn't have as strong a reason to do it, but I wrote Eric off for the same reason. Why would Rocky get into the van with him when she was so upset that he was dating Josie? That left Linc, Roden, and Pike.

"Then what happened?" I asked.

She stared at her hands and clasped and unclasped them on her lap.

"Emily, please tell me."

"Daniel came, and she walked with him into the gazebo."

I waited. I knew there was something more she wanted to tell me.

"I couldn't sleep then. I just stared out of the window at the gazebo, waiting for them to come back out. I didn't know that she was his mother then. He told me later. I . . . I thought . . . She's a beautiful woman from New York, and I'm just an average Amish girl."

I shook my head. Emily was far from average. She was one of the most beautiful women I had ever seen. Her features were delicate, and she had blond hair and large blue eyes that gave her an angelic innocence.

"Daniel and Rocky came out of the gazebo twenty minutes later. She hugged him before he left, and I really thought . . . I thought the wrong thing. She hugged him like any mother would hug her child. I just didn't know that at the time. Daniel left, and the woman waited by the road where the van had dropped her earlier. Instead of a van, a horse and buggy drove up. I recognized the buggy as Daniel's father's. He jumped out of the buggy and walked toward Rocky. I couldn't hear what they were saying. She stomped away from him toward the gazebo. It was starting to snow hard then, so it was more difficult to see."

"Did they go into the gazebo?" I asked.

"*Nee,* Thad left in his buggy when she stomped away. She went into the gazebo alone. The snow was much worse at this point. It was almost a whiteout. I couldn't see much of anything, except for the twinkle lights on the gazebo through the snow. I thought I saw someone else on the square, but I couldn't be sure because of the snow."

"You think it was a man you saw on the square," I said.

She shook her head. "I do not know. The snow was too thick then. What I remember most after Thad left was that the lights on the gazebo moved."

I grew still. "What do you mean by moved?"

"Like they were pulled down from around the gazebo."

I swallowed. The image of the Christmas lights wrapped around Rocky's neck came back to me in a rush, as did her staring gray eyes. The same eyes as her son.

"How long did this take to happen? From the moment you saw Daniel until the lights moved?"

She shook head. "I think forty minutes. It wasn't long. I remember looking at the clock on the wall because I thought so much more time had passed. By that point, I was so tired, I couldn't keep my eyes open any longer. I lay down on my cot for just a moment. I must have fallen asleep. The next thing I remember was my sister shaking me awake and telling me to get to work." She looked me in the eye. "All I know for sure was that Rocky was alive when Daniel's father left."

"Did you tell Aiden this?"

She shook her head. "I didn't want to get involved. I knew how angry Esther and Abel would be with me if I got involved in another murder."

"Your brother told me that he saw people coming and going on the square that night."

"He might have. He was there fixing the oven until nine or so, and then he left." She wouldn't look at me. "He said that I was taking too long making the dough for the pretzels and he could not wait for me. He told me that I had to spend the night at the shop."

I wondered if there would ever come a time when Esther and Abel would forgive their sister for the mistake she'd made when she was young. They seemed determined to punish her for it for the rest of her life.

The door on my side of the car opened. "Bailey, can you step out for a second so that I can have a word with you?" Aiden asked.

That was just fine with me. I wanted to have a word with him too. I squeezed Emily's cold hands before I slid out of the car.

She held on to my hand for a moment. "I know you will tell Aiden, and I understand. Thad deserves to be set free."

I nodded and exited the car.

Outside of the car, I looked for Daniel.

Aiden must have known what I was doing, because he said, "Daniel's gone. Little took him to the hospital."

"What's going to happen to the horse and buggy?" I asked.

"Emily can take those back to her brother. I didn't want to cause more trouble for the poor girl by impounding them."

"I'll ride back to the village with her."

He nodded. "I think it would be good for her to have some company. The moonshine," he went on, "I confiscated. And I will have a little chat with Abel when the murder investigation is wrapped up."

"About that, you might be back at square one."

"What do you mean?"

"Thad is innocent," I said.

"Bailey, I know you want to help Daniel, but justice must be served."

"I know. That's why I am telling you that he's innocent. As long as he's in jail, justice is not being served." As quickly as I could, I told him everything that I had learned from Emily.

"Where does that leave us?" Aiden asked.

"Isn't it obvious? That leaves the production crew."

"Including Eric?" he asked.

"I think it is highly unlikely that Eric did this, but if you want to include him on the list of suspects, go ahead. I just know that Thad is innocent."

"If it hadn't snowed so hard that night, we would have been able to pull tracks from the ground around the gazebo," Aiden said.

"And Emily probably could have identified the killer."

He nodded. "Yes, that's unfortunate. I'll have to talk to her before you go. Can you wait in the buggy?"

"Sure."

Aiden walked back to his car and climbed into the

driver's seat. Through the windshield, I saw him pivot and face Emily in the back. I just hoped that she would have the nerve to tell him everything she had said to me.

The front of the buggy was open to the air. In the winter, many Amish inserted clear plastic in their buggies to serve as a window to protect them from the elements. I wasn't surprised to see that Abel, whose mission in life appeared to be acting like a tough guy, had opted not to do that. There was a navy-blue blanket on the floor of the buggy. I opened the buggy door and got in without closing it behind me. As I bent over to pick the blanket up, there was a crack in the frozen air.

My heart froze. I stayed bent over the blanket, but I didn't realize that it was a gunshot until I heard the crack again as the bullet hit the side of the buggy.

"Bailey!" Aiden shouted. He crouched on the ground on the other side of the buggy from where the shots had originated. His gun was drawn.

"I . . . I think someone shot at me."

Aiden straightened. "Are you hit?"

I shook my head. I started to sit up, but Aiden reached for me and pressed his large hand firmly onto my back, pushing down. "No, stay down like this."

"How's Emily?"

"She's fine. I have her lying on the floor in the backseat of my car. I've already called for additional deputies. They should be here in a matter of minutes." He held out his hand. "Let me help you out of the buggy and get you to the car. That will be safer."

I took his hand, but as I did another crack broke through the winter quiet, and Aiden jerked back from me and fell into the snow. I sat bolt upright, no longer caring about whether I might be shot. I jumped out of the buggy. Aiden bled into the snow.

Before another shot could ring out, I covered Aiden with my body and called 911.

Chapter 36

I stood on the side of the road next to the ambulance with a foil blanket wrapped around my shoulders. Aiden lay in the back of the ambulance on a stretcher. EMTs clustered around him. I couldn't see his face. I didn't know if he was alive or dead.

Deputy Little, who had come straight to the scene of the shooting after locking Daniel up, stood next to me. He looked as shocked as I felt.

The activity inside of the ambulance increased, and two EMTs jumped off of the bay. The second man to jump off slammed the doors and smacked them twice. The ambulance sirens came on, and it made its way onto the street. Sirens blared and lights flashed as it took off down the county road.

The EMT who'd closed the ambulance bay noticed Little and me standing there. "He should be fine. The bullet grazed him through the upper arm. It didn't hit any arteries or bones. It's going to hurt like mad for a few days, but he will make a full recovery. I wouldn't be surprised if they release him from the hospital today."

Relief flooded through me, and it took all that I had to remain upright. Aiden was going to be okay. That's all that really mattered.

The news seemed to snap Deputy Little out of his stupor too. "That's good news." He turned to me. "I need to ask you a few questions."

"I've already answered all your questions. No, I didn't see the shooter. I think the gunfire came from the field because of the way the bullets struck the buggy and Aiden."

He frowned. "I know Aiden didn't want to before, but we will have to impound the buggy. There is a bullet lodged in its right side, and we need to collect that for evidence."

I looked back at Emily, who shivered by Aiden's car. As angry as I knew her brother would be with her about the buggy being impounded, I knew there was no point arguing with Little over it. He had to gather the evidence to find out who'd tried to kill both Aiden and me.

That thought brought a question to mind: Who had the shooter been aiming at? Aiden or *me*?

"I can have one of the other deputies take you and Emily back to the village," Little said. "I need to stay here for the investigation." He balled his fists at his sides. "I'll find out who did this."

I raised my eyebrows. I knew Little admired Aiden very much, and this was the most passionately I had heard the young deputy speak about anything.

"Thanks, I think we are both ready to get out of the cold and off of this street, but can the deputy drop me off at the hospital? I want to check on Aiden."

He nodded.

Emily was quiet on the ride to the hospital. When the deputy who was driving us turned in to the emergency room parking lot, I squeezed her hand. "Instead of going to the pretzel shop, why don't you go to Swissmen Sweets? Tell my grandmother what has happened. She will let you stay there as long as you like."

She shook her head. "No, I need to go home and tell my brother and sister what I have done. It will do me no good to delay it." She cleared her throat. "I made a mistake, and now Daniel is in jail and Aiden is in the hospital because of it."

"It's not your fault that Daniel is in jail, and it is certainly not your fault that Aiden is in the hospital."

"It is." She shivered. "What if the person who shot Aiden was really shooting at me because I'm the only person who knows that Thad is innocent?"

She had a point. Or the shooter could have been aiming at me because I was asking too many questions.

I thanked the deputy for the ride and got out of the car. The emergency room was relatively quiet. I had been in the hospital once before when my grandfather died. I tried to focus on the present and not revisit those painful memories. I walked up to the desk. "I'm looking for Deputy Aiden Brody. He was brought in not too long ago by ambulance."

The elderly woman at the desk eyed me. "Are you a relative?"

Behind me the sliding glass doors leading into the emergency room opened. "Where is my son?" Juliet

Brody cried at the top of her voice. Everyone in the emergency room turned and stared at her.

With Jethro tucked under her arm, Juliet flew to the desk where I stood. Reverend Brook followed in her wake. "Where's my son? I want to see my son right now!"

The receptionist stood up. "Ma'am, please calm down. What is the name of your son? I can't help you if I don't have a name."

"It's Deputy Aiden Brody of the Holmes County Sheriff's Department. I was told that . . . that he was shot!" She shouted the last part.

The receptionist looked at me, which caught Juliet's attention. "Bailey, thank heavens you are here. Have you heard any news? How is Aiden? Is he alive?" She started to hyperventilate and crushed me in an embrace, squeezing a wiggling Jethro between us.

"Ma'am," the receptionist said.

Juliet began to cry in earnest.

"Can we have a wheelchair for Ms. Brody, please?" Reverend Brook asked in his quiet voice. I always wondered how the diminutive man could command a congregation so well. Part of me thought he left a lot of the management up to Juliet. But now I saw that he had an air of authority when it was required.

An orderly pushed a wheelchair around the side of the desk and held it in place behind her.

"Juliet," I said as I pulled myself away from her. "Sit down. We got you a chair—please sit."

Juliet fell into the chair with Jethro on her lap.

"Ma'am," the receptionist said.

"I told him not to be a police officer. I told him he would get shot, and it would kill me," Juliet moaned.

"Ma'am," the receptionist tried again. "You can't have a pig in the hospital."

Juliet gasped. "But he goes everywhere with me, and surely Aiden will want to see him. Jethro is a great comfort to everyone."

"He might be," the receptionist said with as much patience as she could muster. "But that doesn't change the fact that pigs are not allowed in the hospital. With have hygiene standards that we have to uphold."

Juliet bristled. "How dare you? Jethro is the cleanest animal you will ever meet, and to suggest that he is dirty is just disgraceful."

Reverend Brook stepped forward, holding out his arms. "Here. I'll take Jethro outside."

Juliet hugged her pig more tightly. "Aiden will want to see him."

"And he can see him when he gets out of the hospital. I'm sure he's looking forward to it," I said. "The hospital won't let you see Aiden as long as you have the pig with you. I think Aiden would much rather see you when he's not feeling well than Jethro."

"I am his mother." Juliet loosened her grasp on the pig, and it was just enough for Reverend Brook to pry Jethro from her arms. Before Juliet could change her mind, he went back out through hospital's sliding glass doors.

Juliet glared at the receptionist. "I want to see my son."

The receptionist nodded. "He's in recovery room fourteen."

Juliet looked at me. "Push me there, Bailey."

The receptionist shook her head. "Only family can visit in recovery."

"They are engaged, so she is family," Juliet snapped.

The receptionist looked back at me. I smiled, not agreeing or disagreeing with Juliet's statement. I knew that not speaking up would haunt me later when Juliet started planning our fictitious wedding, but I wanted to see with my own eyes that Aiden was okay.

The receptionist gave us directions to recovery, and I wheeled Juliet there. I stopped the wheelchair outside of room fourteen. "You go in, Juliet. You and Aiden should have a moment alone." I didn't add that I wanted a moment alone with him, too.

Juliet stood up and went into the room without a word. I could hear her crying and Aiden's low reassuring voice comforting his mother.

Just hearing his voice was enough for me to know that he was okay. I leaned back against the cold, white-titled wall and closed my eyes.

"Are you Bailey?" a voice asked me.

I opened my eyes to see a nurse standing in front of me. "Yes."

"You can go in too. He's been asking for you."

I hesitated.

"It's all right. He'll be moving to a regular room just as soon as one becomes available. He's doing very well."

"He's okay?" I whispered.

She smiled. "He will be fine."

"Thank you," I said, and stepped through the doorway.

Juliet sat in a chair next to Aiden and cried.

"Mom. I'm okay." Aiden held her hand. "Mom, I'm fine. They said I can even go home in a few hours. Please don't cry." There was an IV in the back of his left hand, and his right arm was wound with a bandage. A white sheet covered most of his body, but his upper chest was bare.

I wanted to step back through the doorway I had just entered and not interrupt this moment between mother and son, but before I could, Aiden looked up and saw me. His face broke into the most brilliant smile, and his dimple appeared on his cheek.

"Oh, Bailey," Juliet cried, tears in her eyes. "Aiden is going to be fine."

"I'm glad," I said.

"Here, you sit here." She started to stand up. "I'll leave you two alone."

I waved her back into the chair. "You don't have to leave, Juliet."

She shook her head. "I do. You need to talk, and I should tell Reverend Brook that Aiden is all right and check on Jethro. I'm sure both of them are worried." She stood, kissed her son on the forehead, and hurried out of the room.

I watched her go before perching on the edge of the chair she'd just vacated.

Aiden reached out his hand to me, and I took it in both my own. "I'm glad you're okay," I said, a little choked up.

He eyed me. "Bailey King, are you crying?"

I swallowed. "Nope."

His smile grew wider. "Uh-huh." He squeezed my hand. "I'll be fine. I'm just glad to see you're okay. What happened after I left?"

I gave him a brief summary, but there wasn't much to tell. "We still don't know who the shooter was, but Little is determined to find out. He was very upset you got hurt."

Aiden nodded. "He's a good deputy." He held my hand. "You saved my life. It could have been much worse if you hadn't been there and acted so quickly."

My throat felt tight.

He chuckled, and his chuckle turned into a laugh. "And here I was thinking that it was my job to protect you, not the other way around."

"I'm not a damsel in distress and never will be."

"I know that. I've always known that since the moment I saw you standing behind the counter at Swissmen Sweets months ago. I knew you would be a different kind of woman." He coughed lightly. "And I knew then that I wanted to know everything I could about you."

I blushed.

He laughed. "Even though you aren't a damsel in distress, you sure get embarrassed easily."

"It's my fair skin."

"Ah," he said. "Is that all it is? I will remember that the next time I make you blush."

That made me blush even more.

"I'm so happy you are here, but I'm surprised.

The nurse told me that only family were allowed in the recovery rooms."

"Oh, well, your mom told the hospital that we're engaged."

He laughed. "She might be announcing that a bit prematurely, but we'll get there."

Chapter 37

I stayed another hour at the hospital until Aiden finally convinced me to go home. He said my grandmother would be worried, and I knew he was right.

By the time I made it back to Swissmen Sweets, I was wrung out. All I wanted to do was crawl into my bed and sleep for a year. My head was so jumbled with the murder and with Aiden.

I got lucky and parked my car in one of spaces next to the square. The Christmas Market was still going on for a few more minutes, and Melchior and the live nativity waited for their parade around the square. At least I didn't have to play Mary that evening. That was a small blessing. From what I could see of the nativity through the crowd, they made a nice scene in the falling snow.

Eric sat by himself on a bench under one of the gas street lamps. He wore his stylish wool coat but no hat or gloves. He stood up as I got out of the car. It was as if he had been waiting for me.

I bit the inside of my lip and glanced at Swissmen Sweets. It was just across the street, mere feet away. I could easily run to it before Eric reached me and lock the door behind me for good measure. But I wasn't going to do that. I needed to put an end to whatever this was, or whatever he thought this was.

Eric walked over to me and stopped three feet away in the snow. "I heard about Deputy Brody getting shot." He shoved his bare hands deep into the pockets of his coat. "Is he all right?"

I wasn't surprised that Eric had heard about the shooting. I knew it must be the main topic of conversation in the village if not in all of Holmes County. It was a rare thing for a sheriff's deputy to be shot in Amish Country. Murder was rare, too, but it seemed like that was becoming more common as time went by.

I swallowed. "He's going to be fine. He will make a full recovery. He was lucky."

"I'm glad to hear it."

I studied him.

He smiled. "Are you surprised that I am glad my rival is all right after being shot? What kind of monster do you think I am, Bai?"

"I don't think you're a monster. I have never thought you were a monster." I paused. "That was Cass."

He brushed snow off the sleeve of his coat. "I am well aware Cassandra Calbera will hate me for the rest of my days because of what I did to you. I deserve that."

"I don't know if hate is the right word. I just don't think she would help you up if you slipped on a banana peel or something."

He smiled. "Noted. I'll remember to stay away from bananas when Cass is around."

"Probably smart."

"The crew and I are leaving for New York tomorrow morning."

My heart constricted. That meant the murderer would very likely get away. I didn't believe that Thad was the killer, but with Aiden in the hospital and most likely on medical leave, would the sheriff do anything to stop Eric and the production crew from departing? "When do you go exactly?"

He frowned. "We leave for the airport at seven. Do you want to come along? I know Linc is dying to give you a show."

"Even if he wants it, the network might not," I said. My mind was still preoccupied with the murder. If Thad was innocent, it had to be someone from the crew, didn't it?

"They will," Eric said confidently. "You outshone me on the spot we did at Swissmen Sweets, and you are a natural on camera. Plus, with the Amish angle, you can offer something different. Different is what the network is looking for right now." He laughed. "You look like you don't believe me, but trust me, this is one case where I am right. I've been wrong on so many other things, but I understand business and how to promote myself."

I wasn't going to argue with him about that.

"I've been wrong about you. When I came back here, I think part of me wanted to get your attention again. You may not believe me, but I didn't like how we ended things. I didn't feel we had closure."

I held back the sarcastic retort on the tip of my tongue.

"But when I got here, I saw you had moved on. You have your grandmother, your shop, the support of this entire village. Maybe part of me was disappointed that you were so happy."

I opened my mouth to say something.

But he went on, "For what it is worth and as much as it pains me to say it, you are making the right choice. I have seen you and Deputy Brody together. It's clear that he is a better match for you than I could ever be or ever was." He closed his eyes for a moment. "I didn't appreciate you when I had the chance to, and now that chance has come and gone."

"You have Josie."

He shook his head. "Josie and I broke up earlier today. It was a mutual thing. She gave her resignation to Linc as well. She wants to move on too. It seems that everyone wants to move on without me."

I wanted to ask him whose fault that was, but I stopped myself. Eric made his choices. He had fame and money, and he would find another short-term girlfriend soon enough. He was happy in his way, but it wasn't the type of life I wanted for myself.

Eric kicked at the snow. "Anyway, you've been a good friend to me even when I didn't deserve it."

I smiled. "I would say keeping you from being charged with murder was the act of a good friend. But you've been good for me too. You taught me a lot about myself."

"What you don't want."

I smiled. "Maybe, but it is a good lesson."

"Eric!" Linc called from the square. "Get over here. We are doing stills for a promo."

Linc and Pike stood just in front of the gazebo. I frowned. "You're not taking pictures in the gazebo, are you?"

He shook his head. "I think that photo op is with the camel. Pike has a vision."

"Pike?" I asked. "I thought Roden was the camera guy."

"Roden is back at the guest house. He came down with some type of stomach bug, so Pike had to jump in and finish the shooting. The kid isn't bad at it. I think he has a bright future in television if he's tough enough to stick it out."

"Oh," I said. There was something about hearing that Roden was sick that didn't sit well with me, but I couldn't put my finger on it.

"I have to go," Eric said. "I'd kiss you good-bye, but I think you would slap me."

"You'd be right."

Eric laughed and went over to join the two other men. He was three steps away from me when he turned. "You know how you were asking me about the production company Rocky wanted to set up?"

"Yes," I said.

"I called one of my friends at the network back home who I figured would know about it. It turns out that Roden, of all people, was her partner in the new company. How funny is that? I'm surprised he'd still want to work with her after what she did. I heard he personally lost a bundle of money when she backed out. I know I would be angry."

He walked away, but I stood there in shock.

I jogged across the street to Swissmen Sweets. I almost made it to the door when a voice stopped me. "You have been busy."

I glance to my right and saw Abel leaning against the pretzel shop, smoking his pipe.

"Is there something I can help you with, Abel?"

He looked me up and down. "You can stay away from Emily. I have asked you to do this before, and you haven't listened. Now Emily has paid the price."

"Paid the price? What do you mean by that?"

He didn't answer me.

"Is Emily here?" I asked.

Abel scowled at me. "My younger sister is not here. Esther and I have asked her to leave. We can't accept her misbehavior any longer."

"Misbehavior?"

"She was secretly courting. She cannot do that without our permission."

"She is twenty years old. When are you going to stop treating her like a child?"

"She lost that privilege when she allowed herself to get pregnant."

"That was five years ago."

He shrugged.

"Where did Emily go?"

He shrugged again.

I walked away from him and went into my candy shop. I was more determined than ever to get Emily away from her judgmental siblings.

The shop was filled with customers who had ducked in to get a break from the cold at the Christmas Market. As a result, my grandmother was doing a brisk business. I knew Charlotte was at the market manning our table, but I half expected that Emily would be inside. She was nowhere to be seen.

My grandmother smiled at me and put a bag of licorice into a customer's waiting hand.

"*Maami*, is Emily here?"

She shook her head. "She stopped by and told me what happened to Aiden. I was so sorry to hear it. Is he all right?"

"I just came from the hospital. He's going to be fine."

"Thank the Good Lord for that."

"Did Emily say where she was going? Her brother and sister have turned her out."

"Grandma Leah and Daniel came to pick her up in their buggy. He was released from the hospital once he sobered up and insisted on coming into town to get her."

"I'm going out to the Keims' farm then," I said. "I need to be sure Emily's OK, and I'm going to see if she wants to stay with us."

Chapter 38

Something nagged at the back of my mind as I drove to Keim Christmas Tree Farm. I couldn't sort it out, because the moment I left the village proper the snow started to come down hard.

The weather on the drive to the Christmas tree farm was some of the worst I had ever driven through, and I'd grown up in Connecticut, where the snow at times came in feet. However, I hadn't done much driving in it. I went to New York City when I was eighteen and never moved back. Driving in New York was far too aggravating and expensive for me to own a car. It was on a night like tonight I missed the convenience of public transportation. There was nothing close to resembling a subway in Holmes County, or in Ohio for that matter. The only way to get from point A to point B was by car or buggy.

I patted the dashboard. "You got this, girl." I thought giving the car a little pep talk couldn't hurt, and I was well aware that I was trying to give myself a pep talk at the same time.

The car fishtailed as I turned onto Tree Road,

and I prayed with all my might while turning into the slide. In the blink of an eye, the car came to a stop, and I found myself in the oncoming lane. I was just lucky no one besides myself was stupid enough to be out driving on the remote road on such an awful evening. After my heart rate dropped to semi-normal, I crawled the rest of the way to the tree farm. There was a break in the snowfall, and I saw the farm's barn in my headlights.

The headlights also illuminated the Keims' buggy. I parked by the barn. The horse was no long tethered to it. That was a relief. It was proof to me that Emily had made it there safely.

I jumped out of the car and made a dash for the house. There was a small overhang above the door, but it wasn't enough to protect me from the driving snow. I banged on the door. "Grandma Leah! Emily! Daniel! Is anyone home?"

No one answered.

I tried again and called their names for a second time. Still no one replied. A shiver ran down my spine. I had a bad feeling in the pit of my stomach. I shook it away. Maybe they were in the barn getting the horse settled.

Snow slipped through the gaps in my scarf. I tightened it around my neck. I stepped out from the slight protection of the overhang back into the wind and snow. The storm was fierce, with whiteout conditions all around me. It was very possible if I ventured too far from the house, I might lose my way completely and then I wouldn't be any help to Grandma Leah or anyone. But I had to check the barn, at least, before I gave up.

As I walked to the barn, I thought about Rocky. We still didn't know who'd killed Rocky Rivers, aka Rachel Keim. I knew it had to be someone from the production team, but who was it? Would we know before it was too late? They were leaving tomorrow morning. I doubted the sheriff would allow Aiden to pursue the murder out of state.

I thought about each member of the crew. Eric wouldn't have killed her, because it might ruin his television show. Pike was just a young kid breaking into the business with no motive at all, and both Linc and Josie seemed to be too self-absorbed to kill anyone. Just like Eric, they wouldn't do anything that could potentially ruin their own career or send them to jail and end their futures completely. But Roden, he was most likely bitter over Rocky choosing the network instead of their partnership, and maybe he thought he had nothing to lose. Rocky had been his ticket to realizing his big dream, and she'd snatched that dream away from him when a better offer came along. It was the only solution that made sense. He had a motive, and he'd had the opportunity. It would have been easy for him to return to the gazebo in his rental car after Daniel and Thad had left. Had he planned to kill Rocky all along, or had an argument led to a crime of passion?

Rocky had looked out for herself, and it had cost her. Just as when she'd left the Amish, it had cost her her son. This time it had cost her her life. It didn't make her a bad person, just a selfish one. Unfortunately, her selfishness just might have gotten her killed.

I tried to remember the last time I had seen Roden.

It must have been at the live nativity. He had been there recording it, but with all the commotion over Melchior the camel and Jethro's antics, I'd lost track of him. At the time, I hadn't known it was important to keep track of the cameraman.

I removed my cell phone from my coat pocket. I had to call the police and tell them what I knew. I scrolled through my contacts, looking for Deputy Little's number. I couldn't call Aiden. He was still in the hospital. My fingers cramped from the cold. My thin cotton gloves were no match for this weather.

As I stepped into the barn, I finally found the number. The call went to voicemail. "Little, this is Bailey King. I think you should come out to the Keim Christmas Tree Farm. I know who killed Rocky. It was Roden. He's the only one who makes sense. You need to come out here. I'm looking for Emily. She might be in trouble because she saw the murder."

I ended the call. "Emily! Grandma Leah!"

I turned and saw the shepherd's hook leaning against the barn wall. The one that Margot had said was missing and had been so upset about. How did it get here? Why was it here? Was it really the same hook? There was one way to find out. Margot had said her father's initials had been carved into the wood near the bottom. If this was the missing shepherd's hook, it would have the initials JR carved into the wood.

I picked up the hook and held it in my hands. It was much heavier than I'd expected it to be. If used as a weapon, it could do some damage, but it hadn't been used as a weapon. Rocky had been strangled by another weapon of convenience, Christmas lights.

I shivered as the image of her dead body came back to me. Then what was Margot's father's hook doing in the Keims' barn? I set it back against the barn wall where I'd found it. I wished I could talk everything over with Aiden, but I couldn't do that now. He was in the hospital. If I told him where I was or what I was doing, he would worry. Little would call when he could, or at least that's what I told myself.

A cow mooed at me, and one of the Keims' horses shook his bridle. "Grandma Leah?"

There was no answer. Why would the shepherd's hook be there? I was racking my brain trying to think of a reason that made sense.

I remembered that Margot had said the hook had been left in the gazebo the night before the Christmas Market, the last night that Rocky had been alive. Had the hook somehow been involved in the murder?

I went back out of the barn. Emily and Grandma Leah weren't there. It was snowing too hard for me to drive back to the village just then, but I would feel much safer in my car.

I forced my way through the snow and was almost at the car when there was a gunshot and a scream. The sounds had come from the trees.

As I ran to the trees, I called 911 and told the dispatcher where I was. For half a second, I hesitated at the edge of the trees. The spaces between them were narrow and dark, and I could easily become lost, but another shot rang out.

I ran through the trees in the direction of the shot, and I came upon the clearing where Cass had found her favorite tree. Much to my relief the snow was beginning to slow down. A moment ago it was near whiteout conditions, but as the snow waned, the moon appeared in the night sky, shining bright enough to illuminate the terrifying scene in front of me.

Daniel Keim stood in the middle of the clearing holding a rifle on Roden, who lay on the ground, and Emily stood beside Daniel in tears. Grandma Leah was kneeling a few feet away in the snow in prayer.

I wondered why Roden didn't get up from the frozen ground and try to run away, but then I saw it. His foot was caught in a rabbit snare. The wire bit into his pant leg. Every time he moved, it got just a little tighter. He might have been able to release the snare with his hands, but he didn't dare move as long as Daniel had his gun trained on him.

I stepped out of the trees. Daniel whipped the rifle around and pointed the barrel at me. Maybe making myself known hadn't been the best idea I had ever had. I held up my hands to show him that I didn't have a weapon. "Daniel, don't do this. You could ruin your life."

"My life is already ruined. My mother ruined it when she left."

"I can't know what it was like for you to grow up without a mother, but you had Grandma Leah, and she was like a mother to you, wasn't she?"

He glanced at his great-grandmother. "It's not the same as having your own mother."

"It's not. I'm sure it's not, but how do you know that your mother ruined your life by leaving you with your father? Yes, she made a selfish choice, but

I think she must have also felt that she was making the right decision for you. She wanted to live like the English, and if she had taken you with her, you would have grown up in the English world. You never would have known your father or your friends in the church district. You never would have known Grandma Leah or Emily."

He lowered the gun a little. Now he was pointing at my belly button. I didn't find that particularly comforting.

"Look at Emily; she cares for you," I said. "Don't do this and ruin her life as well as your own. She's already been through too much."

The gun came all the way down when I said that. "I know she has. I want to be a man worthy of her."

I took a few steps forward and took the gun from his hand. The barrel was warm. He held on to it for a moment, but then let it go. "You are worthy of her. You deserve to be happy." I made eye contact with Emily. "And she deserves to be happy too."

I handed the gun to Grandma Leah and glared at Roden. "Did you shoot Deputy Brody?"

"I'm not saying anything," Roden snapped.

I wasn't going to let it go. Aiden was sitting in the hospital right now because of this man. I just knew it. I deserved the truth. "Where did you get the gun?" I asked.

Roden was stone-faced.

"My father's rifle has been missing from the barn for the past day," Daniel said.

I glared at Roden again. "Did you put the shepherd's hook in the barn and steal Thad's gun? Were you trying to make Thad look like a better suspect to the police?"

"I don't have to tell you anything." He glowered at me.

"I know you shot at Aiden. The police will prove it. And they will link the bullet and Thad's missing rifle to you." I shook with anger.

He sneered. "I wasn't aiming at the deputy. I was shooting at you. I knew you wouldn't let this go even after I left town."

I shivered. Somehow his confession was more chilling than my guesses.

"Now will someone let me out of this snare!" Roden bellowed. "It's hurting me."

"You can just sit tight until the police come," I said, standing a foot away from him.

Roden kicked out his one good leg, knocking me to the ground. I fell on top of him. He grabbed me by the throat and held a knife under my chin. "This is what is going to happen. You are going to release my leg. When you do that, we are going to stand up together. If either of you"—he glared at Grandma Leah and Daniel—"make a move, I'll kill her. I would suggest you not do anything with that rifle."

With the knife still at my throat, I knelt and started to work on the snare. I couldn't remove the wire. My cotton glove got caught on the barbs. They tore through my gloves and pricked my skin. It felt like a thousand little cuts. I could concentrate on that. I had to get the snare loose, but then what? Let him use me as a hostage?

A shiver racked my body. I prayed the deputies would show up soon.

"What's taking so long?" Roden demanded.

"I have to remove my gloves or I'm not going to be able to do this."

"Fine," he snapped. "Just make it quick. I need to get out of here, and you are coming with me."

Roden looked away as if he couldn't watch as I removed the barbed snare from his ankle. It struck me that a murderer could be squeamish, though perhaps only when it came to his own pain. The sharp edges of the wire had torn through his gym sock and into his flesh. I knew it must have been painful, but I had little sympathy for him at the moment.

"This would go faster if you'd let me use the knife to cut the wire."

Roden laughed mirthlessly. "I'm not stupid enough to give you the knife."

There was a bang, and the knife went flying from Roden's hand. He screamed and flopped over, holding his right shoulder, the same shoulder that I realized had been hurting him ever since he'd killed Rocky. I knew now that she hadn't gone down without a fight. She had hit him with the shepherd's hook and he had taken it with him in a panic after he'd killed her.

I scrambled away from him, frantically looking for the knife in the snow. The snow was coming down again now, making it even more difficult to see.

Finally, I spotted the knife. I didn't want to touch it, so I just moved to stand next to it.

"Bailey!" A cry came through the trees, and I immediately recognized it as Aiden's voice.

My body went weak with relief at hearing him, but I forced myself to remain upright. "Here! We're here!"

"Where? Keep calling out so we can locate you."

I continued to shout, and after what seemed like a long moment, Aiden and Deputy Little broke through the trees. Aiden's arm was in a sling, and he held it against his body with his good hand.

Aiden took the scene in with a single glance and then was at my side. "Are you hurt?"

"No, but Roden is. He needs medical attention."

As if on cue, Roden groaned and rolled onto his good side on the ground. He was struggling to sit up. Part of me wanted to go over and help him, but I had made that mistake before. He might no longer have the knife, but I wasn't taking any chances that he didn't have something else up his sleeve.

Aiden stared at Roden and then turned to me. "You shot him?"

"I didn't shoot anyone."

"That little girl didn't shoot him. I did," Grandma Leah said.

Aiden turned around and his mouth hung open just a little when he saw Grandma Leah standing there next to Daniel with a shotgun on her arm.

Grandma Leah leaned the gun against her shoulder like a cowboy in the Old West. "My husband, *Gott* rest his soul, taught me how to be a good shot. He said, 'Leah, *Gott* doesn't want you to ever hurt anyone, but I want you to be able to scare someone off if you ever need to when I'm not around.' Being able to scare someone away at times is more difficult than hitting the target."

Aiden looked as if he was pained to hear it. Maybe because he thought he would be forced to arrest the oldest woman in Holmes County.

I touched his arm. "Aiden, Grandma Leah saved my life. To make a long story short, Roden was holding a knife to my throat." I tapped the edge of the knife in the snow with the toe of my boot. "This is the knife."

With his good hand, Aiden removed a cloth from his pocket and bent down to pick up the knife. It was even larger than I remembered, with a serrated side and a razor-sharp side. It could have certainly done some damage.

Reflexively, I rubbed the spot on my throat where the tip of the blade had been, and I realized how close I had come to joining Rocky as one of Roden's victims.

Aiden glared at Roden. Whatever compassion he might have had for the man was gone as soon as I told him what had happened.

Roden bled through his thick coat, and bright red stood out on the snow. Deputy Little removed his coat and pressed it against the wound. "The EMTs are on the way, Deputy Brody," he said to Aiden. The young officer looked more confident than I had ever seen him.

I stared at Aiden. "What are you doing here? You were in the hospital."

"They were letting me go just as your 911 call came in. You saved me earlier, and bad arm or not, I was going to save you." He smiled. "It just seems that Grandma Leah beat me to it." He gave me a big smile, and his dimple appeared.

Epilogue

The next Sunday, my grandmother and Charlotte were at a church meeting, and I was in the front room of Swissmen Sweets decorating the Christmas tree that Grandma Leah had insisted on giving me. It was the same tree she had tried to sell to Cass and me on our first visit to the Christmas tree farm.

The Amish didn't put up Christmas trees, but I was happy that my grandmother was letting me put this one in the front window of the shop. I decorated it entirely in our handmade candies. It was a good marketing tool, too. I was always looking for ways to drum up business.

I had just set the hollow chocolate angel on the very top when there was a *tap tap* on the window. I glanced over my shoulder to see Aiden through the glass. He was out of uniform, and his right arm was in a sling.

I grabbed my coat from the rack by the door and went outside to meet him.

Aiden stood in front of the window. "That's quite a tree."

"A gift from Grandma Leah and the Keims."

He smiled. "Do you have a minute to walk around the square?"

"Of course," I said, and pulled my hat on my head.

Aiden and I walked side by side across the street to the square. We passed by the gazebo where Rocky had died. I thought the worst part of the tragedy was that Daniel hadn't gotten to know his mother, but at least now that he and Emily planned to be married, that would bring him some comfort.

Aiden walked to the middle of the square and stopped. He turned to face me. "Tell me the truth."

"The truth about what?" I asked.

He placed his large hands on my shoulders. "I feel like you are making a choice." Morning sunlight reflected in his dark eyes. At that angle, they didn't look chocolate brown as they normally did. Their color was closer to rich amber.

"A choice?" I managed to ask. For some reason, I was having trouble speaking. My tongue felt too large for my mouth.

"Between New York and Holmes County. Between the television show and Swissmen Sweets."

"But I already picked Swissmen Sweets," I said. "I promised my grandfather that I would stay to be with *Maami*. If I do the television show, it would be for the shop, to help it."

"So, you've already decided."

I nodded.

"You're going?" He didn't sound upset or angry.

I nodded.

With his good hand he pulled a long narrow box out of the inside pocket of his coat. "Since I knew what you would decide, I got you something." He handed the box to me. It looked like a jewelry box.

I stared at it in my hands.

"Go on, open it. Christmas is just a week away. It's close enough."

I was afraid of what jewelry I would find in the box. I opened it and found something even better. A chocolatier's knife. The knife inside was sharp and curved. It was the perfect knife to cut chocolate. I had given my grandfather a knife like this once upon a time as a gift. I knew how much it must have cost. I knew that Aiden didn't make nearly as much money as a sheriff's deputy in Ohio as I had as a chocolatier working in New York or as I would just by shooting a pilot for my own television show.

"Aiden, this must have cost you a fortune," I whispered, and ran my fingers along the broad side of the blade.

He shook his head. "Not a fortune." He grinned, and the dimple appeared in his cheek. "I know I was upset about you going to New York. I just didn't want you to leave. I will miss you, Bailey, but I want you to be happy. I would never hold you back. If your dreams are New York, go. That's what this gift means."

I kissed him. "My dreams can be in both places."

He laughed and kissed me back.

When I pulled away, my face fell. "But I didn't get you a present. I feel awful."

He wrapped his arms around my waist. "This is Christmas present enough for me."

Bailey's Peppermint Bark

Ingredients
- ½ pound of bitter dark chocolate, rough chopped
- ½ pound of semisweet dark chocolate, rough chopped
- 1 pound of white chocolate, rough chopped
- 1 teaspoon of peppermint extract, or to taste
- 20 hard peppermint candies, crushed

Directions
1. Using parchment paper, line a 9 × 13 baking pan.
2. Using a saucepan of steaming water and a glass bowl, create a double boiler. Don't let the bottom of the bowl touch the water in the pan. Stir both types of dark chocolate together continuously in the glass bowl until the chocolate is completely melted.
3. Pour the melted dark chocolate into the baking pan. Let it cool for ten to fifteen minutes.
4. Following the second step, make a second double boiler and melt the white chocolate. As the chocolate melts, add the peppermint extract.

5. Pour the melted white chocolate and extract mixture over the top of the dark chocolate.

6. Using a hammer, crush the peppermint candies. Liberally sprinkle them over the top of the white chocolate while the chocolate is still warm.

7. Stick in the refrigerator to cool for twenty minutes.

8. Remove the peppermint bark and parchment paper from the pan. Cut or break the bark into pieces.

Don't miss the next mystery in
The Amish Candy Shop series,
coming soon!

TOXIC TOFFEE

By Amanda Flower

Chapter 1

Charlotte Weaver stood in the middle of Times Square with her mouth hanging open and the ties of her black bonnet flapping on the hot air pushing its way through the sewer grate where the subway ran below.

"Charlotte!" I took hold of her arm. "Close your mouth. Your Amish is showing."

She snapped her mouth shut.

The truth was that Charlotte's "Amish was showing" the entire time we'd been in NYC. In Holmes County, Ohio, no one would blink an eye at the pretty redheaded young woman in the plain dress, sensible black tennis shoes, and black bonnet, but in New York, she stuck out like a gorilla on the subway. We had been in the city for the last six weeks shooting six episodes for my candy maker television show, *Bailey's Amish Sweets*, which would appear on Gourmet Television in the summer season.

Charlotte was in Manhattan as my kitchen assistant and would also appear on the show, giving it that extra "Amish umph" as my producer Linc Baggins liked to say. Yes, Baggins like the Hobbit. It was best not to mention that when he was around. Charlotte was able to appear on the show with me because she wasn't yet baptized in the Amish church and could do more English things while on her *rumspringa*. Her church elders weren't thrilled with the idea, but Charlotte's heart had been set on going with me to New York and being on the show. I couldn't bring myself to disappoint her.

"I—I've never seen anything like this!" Charlotte said in awe.

I glanced around and tried to take everything in through Charlotte's eyes. The thousands of people of every race, ethnicity, and national origin milling around, the bright lights and signs glittering on the towering buildings, the smell of bodies, car exhaust, and food trucks mingling together. It was sensory overload for anyone; for a girl who had lived most of her life in a very conservative Amish community, it must have been like the dark side of Mars.

I wrapped my arm around her shoulders. "Since you've been working so hard on the show, and since we haven't been able to get out much with the shooting schedule, I'm glad I can finally show you some of the city."

"Is all the city this loud and bright and . . ." She trailed off, searching for the right word.

"Maybe not this loud and bright," I said with a smile. "We are in the thick of it now, but every city has life to it, but that's not any different from Holmes County."

She looked at me with wonder in her large blue eyes. "How can you say that? This place is nothing like back home."

"Holmes County has as much life and color as New York does. It just shows up in a different way."

My best friend Cass Calbera ran up the sidewalk, maneuvering expertly through the crowd like someone who had lived in New York her entire life, which she had. "There you are! I've been circling the Square for the last ten minutes looking for you two." She glanced at Charlotte. "I thought it would be easy to spot Charlotte, but I got fooled by a nun in full habit walking down the street. I swore it was Charlotte."

I rolled my eyes. "Charlotte doesn't look like a Catholic nun."

"From the back she might. Anyway, why weren't you answering your phone? I tried to call too!"

I pulled my phone out of my pocket. I had put it on silent during our last shooting session and had forgotten to turn the sound back on. Whoops.

"Seriously, Bailey, you've lived in Holmes County too long. I think being away from electronics has addled your brain. You don't know how to behave in normal society."

"What is normal society?" I asked.

She shook her finger at me, and as she did, her purple bangs fell into her eyes. "Don't you go and get philosophical on me, King!"

Before I could make a comeback, she retorted, "Jean Pierre sent a car for us. I left it just up the street. It was the only place that the driver could find to park. We have to go. No one keeps Jean Pierre waiting if they know what's good for them."

That much was true.

The ride through the city to JP Chocolates was slow, but by the looks of it, Charlotte didn't mind a bit. She had her nose pressed up against the tinted glass, taking everything in. I could just imagine the stories she would tell my grandmother and Emily Keim, my other shop assistant, when we got back to Swissmen Sweets.

When we finally walked through the front door of JP Chocolates, a wave of nostalgia hit me. This was where I had spent six years of my life working eighty to one hundred hours a week. Unlike Swissmen Sweets, my grandmother's Amish candy shop back in Ohio with its hardwood floors and pine shelving, JP Chocolates was striking white and sleek, accented with chrome. It might have looked sterile or plain if it had not been for the chocolate itself. Elaborate chocolate creations sat under glass encasements. There was a replica of the Statue of Liberty that I had carved in white chocolate in one of the glass cases.

With Easter just a week away, JP Chocolates was dripping with Easter bunnies in every size and flavor of chocolate. I even saw Easter rabbits made out of molded peanut butter.

"I wish I could have spent more time with you in the last week, but you know what a nuthouse this place is around Easter," Cass said as she walked through the showroom to the back of the shop, where the chocolate happened. Cass was the head chocolatier at JP Chocolates, and it was obvious that she was the woman in charge as the under chocolatiers backed away from her, not making eye contact as she passed by. Cass didn't seem to notice the power that she had over them in the least.

I most certainly did. Before Cass got the position

as head chocolatier at JP Chocolates, I had been next in line to receive the promotion as Jean Pierre's protégé, but then my grandfather died and I found myself giving up the position to live with my grandmother in Holmes County, Ohio to help with the candy shop that had been in our family for generations. I left thinking that I would never be back in the city for more than a short visit, but then Linc offered me my own show on his network. I didn't think much would come of it, but to my surprise, the network love the pilot we shot in Harvest, and the next thing I knew I was in NYC shooting my own candy making show. Somehow fate was giving me the best of both worlds: Holmes County and New York, the two places on earth that had captured my heart. I called it fate, but my Amish grandmother would have called it providence.

"*Ma Cherie!*" Jean Pierre floated into the giant kitchen. "You have come back to me. Please say that you plan to stay!" Jean Pierre Ruge was a tall, thin man with a Parisian nose who carried himself as erect as any dancer. He moved his arms in such a way that it seemed he might have been just that once upon a time.

I gave Jean Pierre a hug. He always smelled of chocolate, which wasn't all that surprising considering what he did for a living. But the thing was that he wasn't supposed to be doing it for a living any longer. Months ago, he had retired from the candy shop when Cass took over. From what Cass said, he was there every day giving her advice. Cass said that she didn't mind it, because it made the day go faster.

"You know I can't stay, Jean Pierre. Charlotte and

I leave tomorrow morning. We just dropped by to say our goodbyes."

"Oh dear me, how are you getting home?"

"We have a flight going out of Newark."

"A commercial flight?" He shuddered. "You should take my plane. No protégé of mine should ever fly commercial."

I chuckled. "I appreciate the offer, Jean Pierre, but the network paid for the flight and Charlotte and I will be more than comfortable sticking with that plan."

He sniffed. "What kind of television network would fly their star commercial? It is a disgrace!"

"Not to worry, Jean Pierre," Cass chimed in. "Hot Cop is picking them up from the airport."

I rolled my eyes. "Hot Cop" was the name Cass had given my sheriff's deputy boyfriend Aiden back in Ohio. Her description was accurate on all counts, but it was also embarrassing. As of yet, Aiden hadn't heard the nickname, and I would do everything in my power to keep it that way.

Jean Pierre set a long finger against his cheek. "I do not know of this Hot Cop. How do I know if Hot Cop is trustworthy?"

Cass patted his arm. "I gave him the once over and she has my support on this one. We both know what a bulldog I can be."

Jean Pierre sniffed. "This is very true. You make a judgment on a person's character and stick with it. I like that decisiveness on your part. This is a good skill to have in chocolate and in life. In chocolate, there are no second chances."

"In life there might be," I mused.

Jean Pierre smiled. "This is my wish for you,

Ma Cherie." He clapped his hands. "Now if you want to help us carve some more chocolate Easter baskets, we won't turn you away."

I grinned, making chocolate Easter baskets and weaving with chocolate had been one of my favorite jobs at JP Chocolates. I planned to teach my grandmother the fine art when I got home. "I thought you would never ask."

I was just settling in to weave chocolate when my cell phone rang. The ringer went off since I had turned it back on after Cass's reprimand. I removed my gloves and pulled the phone from my pocket. When I checked the screen on my cell phone, I saw the name "Margot Rawlings" there. Margot was the village of Harvest instigator. Whatever she had to say to me, chances were high I wouldn't like it. Against my better judgement, I answered the call.

Without so much as a hello, she said, "I need to talk to you about a rabbit."

And a dark cloud of foreboding fell over me.

Connect with U\(s\)

Visit us online at
KensingtonBooks.com
to read more from your favorite authors, see books
by series, view reading group guides, and more.

Join us on social media

for sneak peeks, chances to win books and prize packs,
and to share your thoughts with other readers.

facebook.com/kensingtonpublishing
twitter.com/kensingtonbooks

Tell us what you think!

To share your thoughts, submit a review,
or sign up for our eNewsletters, please visit:
KensingtonBooks.com/TellUs.

Follow P.I. Savannah Reid
with
G.A. McKevett